Gillian Linscott's journalistic career has ranged from reporting chip-pan fires in Bootle to street riots in Belfast, and she has worked variously as a civil servant, playwright, market gardener and parliamentary radio reporter.

She lives in a cottage in Herefordshire with her husband – also a writer – and enjoys skiing, riding and hill-walking. Exotic locations and off-beat, first-hand research are characteristic of her books.

Dead Man's Music is her twelfth whodunnit, and the sixth to feature Nell Bray, the suffragette sleuth with wit, wisdom – and a wide range of fans.

DEAD MAN'S MUSIC

GILLIAN LINSCOTT

A *Virago* Book

First published in Great Britain in 1996
by Little, Brown and Company
This edition published in 1997 by Virago

A CIP catalogue record for this book
is available from the British Library

ISBN 1 86049 319 X

Typeset by Palimpsest Book Production Limited
Printed and bound in Great Britain by
Clays Ltd, St Ives plc

Virago
A Division of
Little, Brown and Company (UK)
Brettenham House
Lancaster Place
London WC2E 7EN

Dead Man's Music

ONE

'NELL, IF YOU'D BE SENSIBLE for just one moment . . .'

Stuart, my brother.

'Nobody else is sensible. Why should I be?'

Once, when Stuart was eight and I was five, he'd been sent up to bed supperless for hitting me over the head with his butterfly net during a political argument. Allegedly I'd said something rude about Mr Gladstone. He apologised the next day. He said he was sorry about the butterfly net – he should have hit me with his cricket bat instead. I sensed that he was feeling the same way now. I didn't care.

'I can't come to Whinmoor and that's that. There's too much to do here.'

'You've just been saying it's all useless in any case.'

'No, I haven't.'

'Yes, you have, you said . . .'

'Oh, be quiet, be quiet, be quiet.'

My voice, louder than I'd intended, echoed round the room, setting the dust flecks dizzing up and down in the early autumn sun, or as much of it as could fight a way through my neglected windows. Typical brother's trick, twisting the things you say and quoting them back at you. Or perhaps I really had said it. But I couldn't have meant it, could I?

'You admitted that you . . .'

'Admitted? So I'm on trial, am I?'

To be fair to Stuart, he'd supported me in every way possible. It isn't easy for a surgeon rising in his profession to admit to a sister who throws half bricks and argues from the dock with magistrates, but he'd never suggested that I should limit my activities. Until now.

'Nell, you know I'm on your side.'

'But?'

'But enough's enough. I'm not saying you should give up altogether . . .'

'I should hope not.'

'But it's time you took a rest. This place looks like an explosion in a paper mill. There's no food in the cupboard and as for you, you look like . . .'

'Well?'

'Well, to be honest I've seen healthier things on a dissecting slab. You're as thin as a besom broom and your complexion's like something out of the British Museum manuscript room.'

'Well, at least you didn't say the mummies' gallery.'

I started laughing, then couldn't stop. It had been like that over the last few days, either laughing or crying. I expected Stuart to laugh too, but he had on his professional face and was looking at me like something on his rounds. I stopped laughing.

It had been a bad year, 1913; the worst. The Vote, that until then had seemed so tantalisingly close, looked further away than ever. Two bills had failed in Parliament. Mrs Pankhurst had been sent to prison, convicted of being an accessory to the bombing of Lloyd George's house. Emily Wilding Davison had died under the hooves of the king's racehorse. The Cat and Mouse Act had done exactly what it was designed to do, sent us into a constant shuttling between prison and freedom more wearing to nerves and body than imprisonment alone would have been. Sometimes it seemed that the only reason for not giving up and waiting patiently through the next decade or so, as our opponents said we should, would be the nonsense that would make of all the sacrifices so far. I was normally glad to see my brother. Now his visit – since he happened to be in London for a conference

– and his well-meant, interfering invitation, were only part of the general aggravation.

He made a dive for my hand and, for a moment, I thought he was trying to make an uncharacteristically sentimental appeal to sisterly feeling. Then I realised he was taking my pulse.

'Stuart, for goodness sake . . .'

'Keep still.'

He used his professional voice and, to my own great surprise, I kept still. Looking over his bent head as he stared at his watch, our grandfather's watch, I saw a worried face gazing at me from the armchair in the corner. I'd almost forgotten Simon Frater was there. He'd come to consult one of my German dictionaries before Stuart arrived, and had simply stayed quietly there in the corner reading while all the arguing was going on. Silenced, I tried to signal with my eyes that he should save me from my brother. Stuart let go of my hand, looking grave. Another professional trick.

'Well?'

The question came from Simon. Not to me, to Stuart.

I stared from one to the other. 'What is this?'

Stuart said to Simon, 'It's up.'

Simon blinked and adjusted his glasses, sorrowful as if he'd just found a corruption in one of his classical texts.

'It's *my* pulse. If you insist on talking about it, talk about it to me, not Simon.' Then it dawned on me. I must have been feeling very run down indeed or I'd have got there half an hour before. 'It's a plot, isn't it?'

Stuart made a business of tucking away his watch. Simon's eyes went back to the dictionary.

'All the way from Manchester for a conference. And University College running out of German classical dictionaries all of a sudden. I suppose Simon wrote to you and arranged to meet you here.'

Simon said nothing, but his face gradually turned a slow and painful red.

Stuart managed to look me in the eye. 'We should have allowed for your detective talents.'

3

'You don't need detective talents to see what's going on here. What exactly did you tell him, Simon?'

Simon is probably the most honest man in London. He raised his head from the page, and if I hadn't been in such a bad mood I might have pitied his look of misery.

'I told him the truth, Nell. That you've made yourself ill and your friends think you should get away for a while.'

'So my dear brother comes out of the north on his white charger to carry me off.'

'Actually, Nell, it was the London and North Western Railway and I'm due back on it an hour from now.'

'Then you'll have to hurry. Give my love to Pauline and the children.'

'And can I tell them you'll be seeing them in a couple of days?'

'No, you cannot. I want to see them, but . . .'

'Young John worries about you, you know. He saw a photograph of the Home Secretary in *The Times* the other day and wanted to know if that was the wicked man who locked up Auntie Nell.'

'You shouldn't let an eight-year-old read low organs like *The Times*.'

'Nine, Nell. His birthday was in June.'

'I'm sorry, I'm sorry, I'm sorry. I really do want to see them all, and of course I'd like to be at Whinmoor again . . .'

'The heather's still out. We could have some strolls over the moors when you're a bit stronger. Remember the secret path behind the waterfall?'

I remembered. Even mentioning it was a low blow, though the consciousness of that was submerged by a surge of memory, the smell of warm peat in the sun, bees blundering in heather, a gritstone ledge with a sheet of water pouring over it, clear as a pane of glass, small rainbows in the spray at its edges. Whinmoor, on the Manchester side of the Pennine moors, was where Stuart and I spent long holidays in our childhood. We were

4

the guests of my father's elder brother, Uncle Marcus, who was sorry for us because he thought our parents made us lead lives that weren't good for children. He needn't have been. Our father's work as a doctor, and his political convictions, meant that we spent a lot of time in cities. His capacity for picking quarrels with authority also meant that we never stayed anywhere for more than a year or two. But Stuart and I enjoyed all that. We loved it when he was standing for election to parliament or local councils and took us canvassing with him, and if we grieved for his frequent defeats then it was a kind of grown-up political grief that did us no harm. But we loved the long holidays at Whinmoor too, the freedom of the moors and ponies to ride. Our cousin Fred was older than we were, supercilious but tolerant on the whole. We followed his horse over piles of birch logs on our fat ponies, usually fell off but sometimes didn't. We scrambled up the faces of long abandoned quarries and challenged him to follow us, which he did although his head for heights was poor. He taught us to fish where streams running off the moor made green pools under shelves of rock and we, ungrateful, pushed him in one day and were punished.

Uncle Marcus died while I was still at school and cousin Fred inherited Whinmoor. Then Fred died too, serving with his cavalry regiment in the Boer War and, to the consternation of Stuart, Whinmoor passed to him. He was newly qualified then, in no condition to take on a country estate, even a small one that was mostly heather, like Whinmoor. Sensibly, he put off the decision by letting it out to a tenant for seven years, and by the end of that time the problem had solved itself. By then he was a married man with two sons and a position in a Manchester hospital that made Whinmoor just possible. The family moved in, and now my nephews played around the same streams and quarries. Stuart loved the place and knew I did too, which was what had made the path behind the waterfall a low blow. I wanted to be there.

'After all, Christabel Pankhurst's gone off to live in Paris. I don't see why you shouldn't spend a few weeks with us.'

'That's different. She'll be arrested if she comes back.'

Another sore point. Christabel had fled to Paris to escape the police and was superintending the struggle from there, while her mother was in and out of prison. Only sensible, but some resentments about her more comfortable life abroad had added to the tensions and splits in our movement that terrible summer. Of course, none of us believed the calumnies our opponents tried to spread, like Christabel shopping for fashionable clothes or riding in the Bois de Boulogne. Still, it didn't help.

'I don't see how it's different. If I leave you here, you'll only go and do something and get arrested again. Another few months like the last ones will finish you, Nell.'

'I'm tougher than that and you know it. And how dare you talk about leaving me here, as if I were a parcel in a left-luggage office.'

Simon closed the dictionary and unfolded himself to his full, thin height. His face was still pink and his eyes behind his glasses were screwed up as he struggled for words. He could read aloud a passage of ancient Greek as clear and fluent as one of those moorland streams, but struggled pitifully when it was a matter of human emotions.

'I . . . I really think you should, Nell. Just for a week or two, until you're stronger. All of us think so. Anyway, it's not as if – and families and so on, it's only . . .' His voice trailed away and he stared at me miserably. It was his inarticulate anxiety, far more than a brother's bullying, that weakened me.

'But there's my report on women on local councils to finish.'

Both of them, Stuart in his medical-lordly way and Simon stuttering in his eagerness, told me I could take it with me.

'Then there's the cats. I don't want to leave them on their own again.'

Stuart said he'd stop at a pet shop on his way to the station and have them send up a travelling basket. I was slipping down the grey rock and into warm heather.

'You'll be entertaining other people and I'm bad company.'

Although Stuart and Pauline didn't play the squire and his lady, they had a wide circle of friends and a reputation for hospitality. Polite conversation over the marmalade was something I couldn't face.

'Pauline knew you'd say that. You can have the old keeper's cottage. It's primitive but you won't mind that, and you need only see us when you want to.'

In Uncle Marcus's time there was grouse shooting on the moors and a keeper, Old Ferris, to look after it. His cottage was a little stone hummock of a building, looking more like a fall of boulders than anything planned by humans, at the point where the estate's unambitious lawns gave way to gorse and heather. The part of all our minds that remains in childhood – turned traitor already at the first mention of Whinmoor – bounded at the idea of living there, if only for a while. I tried not to let Stuart see this, but from the tone of his voice, I failed.

'That's settled then. You'll come?'

'A week, no more.'

'It's not worth coming all that way for a week. Two at least.'

'I can't possibly . . .'

Simon said, falling over himself with eagerness, 'You could say t-t-ten days and s-s-see . . .'

I was already regretting giving in, seeing their plot to keep me there for weeks or months.

'Tomorrow, then. Send us a telegram to let us know what train you'll be on, and I'll see there's a cab for you at the station.'

'Not possibly tomorrow.'

'The day after, then. I'm sure Simon will see you to Euston.'

He nodded, blinking with relief and eagerness.

'And you c-c-could take this new German book on P-P-Plautus. Let me know what you think of it.'

I'd been on the point of saying something sarcastic about not needing an escort onto the train, but when I saw the thickness of the book he was holding out to me I couldn't help laughing again. Simon's idea of light holiday reading.

'Oh, dear. Oh, both of you.'

Stuart was already gathering up his hat, gloves and travelling bag.

'You're welcome to bring a friend with you, if you like. You know there are two upstairs rooms in the cottage.'

I thought for a moment of proposing Simon, which would have served him right, then decided it would be unfair to him. My reputation was past caring about, but the college authorities might take an austere view of unmarried lecturers living in moorland cottages with wild women – and only Plautus as chaperon.

Stuart left in a hurry, but still trying to extract promises from me as he went out of the door. Simon lingered for a while with nervous questionings about timetables and cabs and suitcases, then he went too, wandering towards Hampstead Heath where I guessed he'd restore his nerves by reciting passages from the Georgics to the trees which, being Hampstead trees, would have heard them all before. I sat there for a while, accusing myself of being weak and tractable and cowardly, and yet the idea of the tumbled cottage and the heather slope behind it kept coming into my mind with a feeling of warmth and rest.

I slept better that night than I had for weeks and, in the morning, dragged my suitcase out from under the bed and began packing. I put in only enough in the way of stockings, blouses and underthings to last a week, no more. One respectable dress and pair of shoes went in, since it would be rudeness to my sister-in-law not to dine with them at least once, but no more than one as I had no intention of being drawn into the social swim. The rest of the case was taken up with walking boots, tweed skirt and jacket, my notes on women on local councils and, of course, Simon's book on Plautus, plus German and Latin dictionaries.

My packing was interrupted several times. First was a telegram from Stuart, reply pre-paid, with recommended train times for the next day, just in case I'd become incapable, in my supposed weakness, of reading a railway timetable. After that, the midday post, most of it vexatious but including a joint letter from my nephews, in a mixture of painstaking joined-up writing and haphazard block capitals. 'Dear Auntie Nell, We are glad you are coming to see us. We have a starling with a broken leg which Daddy has set. Mummy says to send her love.' And a drawing of a jaunty bird with its leg in a splint. Pauline wasn't leaving anything to chance. When she made them write that letter, she couldn't even be sure that I'd accept.

While I was reading it the boy from the pet shop arrived with the cat basket, then another telegram, from Simon this time, wanting to know when he should come to collect me. He suggested that if I knew somebody with a telephone I should ring him at college, and he gave a number. I dislike telephones. It was a considerable surprise to me that Simon, less competent than I was in most practical matters, could bring himself to use one. I made the telegraph boy wait and scribbled a reply instead.

With all this, I wasn't in the best of moods when another knock came at the door when I was upstairs trying to entice one of the cats out from under the bed. (The first experiment at getting them used to the cat basket had not been a success.) I looked out, expecting the telegraph boy again, but instead found myself looking down at the crown of a navy straw hat. It was a neat hat, not new or fashionable, trimmed with a tight rose made of navy blue ribbon. As I looked out the person beneath it banged on the doorknocker again, but there was a hesitancy about the knock, as if she were just trying again for form then would walk away. I opened the bedroom window and leaned out. A pale, oval face, with brown eyes under decisive eyebrows, looked up at me.

'Well, Rose. Rose Mills. Wait there till I come down.'

In spite of the interruption, I felt pleased as I hurried down the stairs to the front door. Rose Mills was one of our success stories.

Four years ago she'd been a ten-shilling-a-week seam-stress in one of the sweat shops of the East End, then became a suffragette. Rose and I were involved in one notably wild case together, and after that I decided it was time somebody gave her the chance that life hadn't dealt her so far. I got together with a few friends, and by arm-twisting and a little fund-raising that Rose never knew about, we got her a place at a teachers' training college. She qualified, a model student, and got a position at an elementary school in Wimbledon. I saw her sometimes on marches and at meetings, but we older and wiser ones had impressed on her that she should keep away from any of our less legal activities. We were proud of her progress and didn't want it endangered.

'Hello, Nell.'

There was no gladness in her face when I opened the door to her. She looked as wary and resentful as in the old days when she was trapped. When the dark eyes met mine, they were full of misery.

'Rose, what's wrong?'

'Can I talk to you? Just for a minute.'

'As many minutes as you like. It's good to see you.'

But as she followed me silently through to the kitchen I knew, with the feeling of depression settling back round me, that this wasn't just a social call. She settled in the chair at the scrubbed wooden table, overflowing with papers as usual, and watched as I filled the kettle and put it on the gas stove. When I sat down opposite her she said flatly, 'I've been dismissed.'

'What!'

The last I'd heard, at the end of the summer term, both she and her employers had been happy. She had a gift with the young and shy ones, they said, a natural teacher.

'Was it for going on marches with us? That's quite unfair. We'll take it up with the governors and . . .'

But she was shaking her head, lips pressed tight together. Rose wasn't the sort to cry in company, but her eyes were stretched wide as if tears weren't far away.

'Why not?'

'It wasn't anything like that, Nell. It was a man.'

I felt boneless with weariness. I couldn't stop it showing in my face and Rose looked away from me, down at the hands clasped tightly round the strap of her bag. A bag in navy blue leather to match the hat, big enough to carry exercise books for a whole class. I imagined Rose buying it from her first salary.

'I've let you down, haven't I? I'm sorry.'

'What happened?'

Her eyes met mine again, direct as ever. 'His name's Philip. He teaches science to the senior boys. I . . . We liked each other. He invited me to a photograph exhibition and after that we went to the ABC for a cup of tea and . . . and he asked me if I'd go out with him again, and I'd enjoyed it, so I said yes. This was in July, just before the summer holidays.'

She stopped as if that was all that needed saying. I waited for her to go on.

'Well?'

'We went out together quite a lot, walking in Epping Forest, and to the Science Museum, and the Natural History Museum because I'm teaching my seven-year-olds about insects. I mean I was, until . . .'

I was unmoved by this idyll and thought I could see the end of it. I wished this Philip had been left there in

11

the Natural History Museum under a glass case: Man the Destroyer.

'And at what point did he tell you?'

'Tell me what?'

'That he was married.'

'Married!'

She stared.

'I'd assumed that was what we were leading up to.'

'Nell, you don't think I'd let a married man take me out, do you? Of course he isn't married.' The look she gave me was hurt, even scandalised.

'Rose, I'm sorry. Of course I'm not implying that you'd do anything wrong. But what I can't understand is why you've been dismissed.'

'Someone from the governors saw us together.'

'Where?'

'By the stick insects.'

I was on the point of making my blunder worse by asking what she and Philip were doing by the stick insects, but decided against it.

'If you and this young man decide to study natural history in your own time, what's that got to do with your employers?'

'They ... they said they don't encourage friendships between staff members of the opposite sex. They think it sets a bad example.'

'To seven-year-olds? This is ludicrous. Didn't you tell them so?'

'I couldn't say anything. It's the rules after all, and ...'

'Rules!'

I'd been so pleased with what we'd done for Rose and it had come to this. A wild girl who'd been prepared to defy the world now wore a hat with a navy blue rose, suffered injustice without protest and talked about rules. The kettle was hissing. I took it off the ring to warm the teapot and they clashed together, chipping a big piece out of the pot's spout.

'Damnation.'

'I'm sorry.'

'Don't be. It's their fault, not yours.' Or mine. Or the world's.

'So they dismissed you for going out with a male colleague.'

'Yes.'

'What about Philip? Did they dismiss him as well?'

'No, of course not. He's a senior teacher.'

'Did he speak up for you?'

She twisted the bag strap round her fingers. 'He tried. There wasn't a lot he could say.'

So her misery wasn't only about dismissal. He'd failed her and she knew it, even if she wouldn't criticise him to me.

'They paid me to the end of the month.'

'I should hope they did. Did they give you a reference?'

'Yes. They said I was a good and conscientious teacher. But . . .'

Faint praise, and even I could see that a teacher dismissed near the start of term would come to prospective employers trailing doubt and suspicion. In another mood I might have gone straight out to Wimbledon, demanded to see the governors, protested about the injustice. Now I couldn't see the use of it. They didn't deserve Rose.

'The question is, what we do now.'

'I don't expect you to do anything. I only came to tell you, that's all, because of what you've done for me.'

And might as well not have done.

'Have you any plans?'

'The rent on my room's paid up until the end of September.'

'After that?'

'Well, I suppose I could go to my sister, but . . .'

Tansy, once maid to a successful courtesan, now living in a cottage with duck-pond near Marlow. Tansy loved her sister, but disapproved of almost everything she did.

'. . . but I can't tell Tansy. She'd blame me. I might go back to the old job, sewing.'

'Oh, no, you don't.'

'Well, what then?'

I made the tea, taking time to think, but still didn't have the answer. 'We'll think of something, I promise. Just give me time.'

The tea brewed. I put cups on a tray and carried it through to the living room. Rose followed me and registered the suitcase open on the floor.

'Going away?'

I'd forgotten about it in worrying about her news.

'Up to my brother's, not far from Manchester.' An idea struck. 'Why don't you come with me? He said I could bring a friend.'

'You wouldn't want me along.'

'I would, though.' At least that was one decision I could still make for myself. 'It's only for a week and you might enjoy it. Even if you don't, it will give us a chance to discuss what to do next.'

She hesitated.

'Is it very grand, your brother's house?'

'Heavens, no. Dogs and cats all over the place and the boys running wild. And you'll like my sister-in-law.'

I guessed that she was worrying about the fare and let her know, as tactfully as I could, that I'd meet the expenses. As a loan, she said, until she started earning again. I didn't argue, as that meant she'd agreed. By the time we'd finished our tea it was arranged that she'd meet Simon and me by the ticket office at Euston half an hour before the train was due out. She left looking marginally less miserable.

I felt, if anything, worse. Not at the prospect of having Rose with me. She was easy company when not miserable and had a dry sense of humour that Whinmoor might, with luck, revive. What sickened me was the feeling that of all we'd tried to do, nothing was turning out as we'd hoped. I rampaged round the house, looking for things I'd forgotten to pack, until dust flew and the cats took refuge under the bed again. When I'd buckled the suitcase straps for a fifth and final time I remembered to go out to the post office to send another telegram, letting Stuart and Pauline know that there'd be two of us arriving.

TWO

SIMON SAW US OFF FROM Euston, hectically overactive as usual, signalling for porters like a man shipwrecked on a desert island, swinging the cat basket until protesting claws started poking through the wickerwork, loading us with fruit, magazines, and a bunch of chrysanthemums bought on an impulse from a flower-seller. He knew Rose, and it had been a glowing character reference from him that helped her to get the teaching post at Wimbledon. I'd told him about the latest disaster in the cab on the way from Hampstead. His sympathy for her, and anger at the injustice, made him even kinder and clumsier than usual. It was a relief when the whistle blew and we were on our way, with Simon running alongside as we gathered speed, then brought to a halt when the platform ran out, dimly waving through clouds of steam.

The scent of his chrysanthemums and the smell of ripe William pears grew as we were carried northwards. Rose and I read a little, talked a little. We were both wondering how we'd been persuaded into this journey.

Around Crewe she said, 'You know, I've never been this far north before. Isn't that silly?'

'Why silly?'

She didn't answer, but I noticed that she went very quiet and spent most of the time after that looking out of the window. At Manchester we found a porter and got ourselves, the cats and the suitcases up to the barrier. Pauline was waiting there, holding John and Duncan firmly by their wrists. When they saw me they started jumping up and down and waving, and her arms were jerked up and down with them.

'Nell. It's so good to see you again.' She stood on tiptoe to kiss my cheek, momentarily releasing the boys. 'And you must be Miss Mills. We're so glad you could come.'

Rose, burdened with chrysanthemums and cats, murmured thanks but looked ill at ease. I could see she thought Pauline 'grand', which was unfair but understandable.

It's hard to describe my sister-in-law without making her sound intolerable, but in fact she's one of the most likeable people I know. Even her appearance is calming, all curves. Curves of fair hair swirled up on the back of her head, topped on this occasion by a little green dab of a hat. Smooth curves of cheek and chin. Curves of a figure that's rounded without being plump. Her voice is quite low but usually with a laugh in it. She has a quick sense of humour but I'd never heard her say a bad word about anybody, which is possibly because she has about as much political sense as the birds of the air. Of course, she loyally supports Stuart and, by extension, me. She wants votes for women, naturally she does, but if she went to the end of her life without voting, it would probably cause her no more than a mild regret – and on my behalf, not her own. I should have found that infuriating, but nobody could be angry with Pauline.

'We've got a taxi waiting outside. Is that all your luggage? You're staying in the house with us tonight, but we've got the cottage ready for you. John, yes I know there's a cat in there, dear. Two cats? Well, don't annoy them. They're probably tired. Yes, I'm sure you and Duncan can carry them if you're very careful. I'm sorry it's such a walk to the taxi.'

It's a long journey by motor taxi from London Road station to Whinmoor. On the way Pauline and the boys chattered on, not needing much conversation from us. She apologised that Stuart hadn't been there to meet us. He was running one of his all-comers' clinics, but had promised to be back for tea. The baby was at home, being looked after.

'Becky. We've called her after you, Nell.'

Rose glanced at me.

'Rebecca's my middle name.'

I felt both touched and guilty. In the events of the year, the birth of my niece had made little impact. What was it, four months, six months?

'Stuart says she has to be Chancellor of the Exchequer at least, or perhaps you'd prefer Foreign Secretary. He says she has a voice loud enough for the hustings, poor little scrap.'

We were out of the city centre by then, going through the suburbs. I saw Rose looking out at the rows of back-to-back houses and cobbled streets.

Duncan asked if she liked stag-beetles. 'I've got one in a cigar box at home. Daddy's trying to find out what they eat.'

Shades of the Natural History Museum. Poor Rose. Yes, she said. She'd like to see it very much. She didn't know what they ate either. While this was going on I noticed Pauline looking at me out of the corner of her eye, serious for once. I supposed she and Stuart had been discussing me. Well, two could play at that game. Sitting close to her, I thought that Pauline looked tireder, a shade older, than when I'd last seen her about a year ago. Well, there'd been a baby since then, which might explain it. And if there was the slightest hint of strain about her, two guests could account for that.

The suburbs of Manchester fell away and after a while I saw the long curve of hills that was always there at the back of my mind, then the town with its forest of tall brick chimneys and the lines of back-to-back houses curling up to the moor, like the tentacles of a sea creature clamping itself to a rock. It was mid-afternoon with the cotton mills working at full stretch and columns of smoke from the chimneys rising into the pale blue sky. When the town was

18

busy making cotton there was a hum from the place that you felt as a vibration through the skin rather than heard through the ears. Inside the taxi cab I couldn't feel it, and yet the sight of the chimneys and the solid, handsome mills brought it back again. Few places in the world are as intensively industrious as the Lancashire cotton towns and yet they're not as oppressive as other manufacturing places because of the moors behind them.

The taxi went through the town, past the railway station, the Wesleyan chapel, the temperance hotel and the municipal bath-house that had been built in some spasm of community pride as a smaller version of the Doge's Palace in Venice. Up the High Street, past the Victoria Jubilee clock tower, with the cobbled streets rising up steeply on our left, front doors of the terraced houses opening directly onto the pavements. There were a few women talking in the streets and children too young for school playing on the cobbles, but at this hour most of the women as well as the men would be in the mills. We turned onto the road curving steeply out of the town, towards the Victorian gothic villas where the managers and professional classes lived, then there were only dry peat banks on either side with fringes of heather and the occasional sheep looking over.

When we arrived at Whinmoor we had tea on the lawn, and the nurse brought the baby out to join us, which makes Whinmoor sound starchier than the reality. There was no tea-table, so cups and saucers balanced alongside us on the two old wooden benches shaded by a trio of birch trees. The benches were faded from the sun, covered with bird droppings and the dark outlines of leaves that had clung to them all winter. The lawn never grew lush, like southern lawns, in the poor soil on the edge of the moors and was yellowed by drought. The nurse, a cheerful girl of around fifteen, with a Lancashire accent, sat down with us for a cup of tea while Becky crawled on a blanket on the grass. Rose was dragged off by John and Duncan to see the stag-beetle.

I leaned back on the bench and looked up at the moorland that was the boundary of Stuart's little estate. The heather was still well in flower, with edges of rock breaking through and the gold of gorse clustering round them like spray round the prow of a boat. The sky up here was as clear and blue as June, with a kestrel hovering. I could already feel tension slackening a little, then wondered what right I had to be relaxed anyway.

Pauline was watching me.

'It's nice of you to have us.'

'You're welcome as long as you like. And Rose Mills.'

'It can only be a week. Don't worry if she seems quiet. She's had a bad time.'

I told her about Rose and she was sympathetic, but it struck me again that there was a slightly distracted air about her. You had to know her well to notice it, but there were little lines between her eyes that hadn't been there before, and she seemed to be listening for something. It couldn't have been the baby that worried her. As far as I could see, my namesake was all that she should have been at six months. Or was it four?

We were still sitting there when there was a crunch of bicycle wheels on what was left of the gravel, and Stuart arrived. He turned his bike off the drive and over the lawn towards us, his doctor's bag strapped on the back. One of his economies that made Whinmoor just possible was having no pony-trap or motor car and cycling every day to and from the station to take the local branch line. He leaned the bike against a birch tree, kissed Pauline and me, picked up Becky and tossed her in the air.

'You're late,' Pauline said. 'We heard the train go past half an hour ago.'

I hadn't heard, or hadn't noticed. But I'd been right that Pauline was listening for something.

'I stopped in the town on the way up.'

'I see. Would you like some tea?'

All happy and domestic. Was I wrong to see a little ruckle

20

of annoyance on Stuart's face when she said he was late, or to hear a coldness in her offer of tea? Quite possibly. I was so strung up from the big events that I could now find trouble in the harmless little ones, over the teacups, heaven help me. He settled down with his tea.

'Another furniture lorry passed me on the way up. Nearly knocked me off my bicycle.'

'Another one. That's at least four since yesterday.'

'And the place was furnished anyway.'

'Perhaps they don't like his uncle's taste.'

'Whose uncle?'

'Nosy as ever, Nell. Our new neighbour. Do you and your friend want to see your cottage before dinner?'

The five of us walked the half-mile to it together: Stuart, Rose, the boys and I. It was much as I remembered it. The walls sloped inwards so that it was narrower at the top than the foundations. Much higher and it would have ended up as a small pyramid. Missing slates from the roof had been replaced long in the past by Old Ferris with thin rectangles of birch wood, now mellowed to much the same silver-grey colour as the slates. The dark green leaves of pennycress grew out of gaps in the stone.

'If it rains at all you'll just have to move back into the house. It's barely weatherproof, even in summer.'

The boys dragged us inside to admire the provision made for us. There was a primus stove on the wooden draining-board of the old stoneware sink, cups, plates and cutlery from the house. A new meat safe stood on a table, ready stocked with cheese and ham and a bar of nut milk chocolate with two squares already eaten, the boys' contribution. The living room had two wooden chairs, some cushions and a pile of freshly cut wood by the fireplace.

'Water's from the stream, and of course you'll come up to the house for your baths. Are you sure this is what you want?'

He knew it was what I wanted, but he looked uncertainly

21

at Rose. She was staring at the stone walls, almost as rough inside as outside.

'You're welcome to stay in a proper bedroom, Miss Mills. You don't have to be mad like my sister.'

No, she said, she'd like to stay here, thank you very much all the same. I'd have liked to move in right away, but Pauline had been insistent that we must spend at least one night in a civilised manner under their roof. We walked back to the house, were shown up to our bedrooms and changed out of our travelling things. There was hot water on tap now, instead of the washbasins and ewers of cold water in the bedrooms that I remembered from Uncle Marcus's time, but then Uncle Marcus had kept around a dozen inside and outside staff while Stuart and Pauline managed with the nurse, a cook-housekeeper who lived in and a girl who came up from the village every day to clean.

Dinner was early and informal, with the boys allowed to stay up for it. Both Rose and I were too tired to be very sociable but Stuart never had any inhibitions about talking shop at table and chattered on about his afternoon at the all-comers' clinic in Moss Side. In addition to his post at the Manchester Royal Infirmary he'd joined with a group of other young specialists to run free clinics in the poorer parts of the city. His speciality was ear, nose and throat conditions and the sooty air from the mills and factories gave him plenty of patients.

'For half of them, the best thing I could prescribe would be a couple of months of mountain air. But you might as well talk about giving them a suite in Buckingham Palace.'

Rose looked up from her pie. 'Perhaps that would be a good idea.'

He looked at her and I could see him reevaluating her. Up until then, she'd simply been my depressed friend. After that he managed to draw her out a little. Her childhood in the East End hadn't been so very different from the lives of his Moss Side patients. A little of the Wimbledon teacher began to peel away, and I saw traces of the old rebellious Rose underneath it.

After dinner the boys insisted on showing Rose their pet donkey before they'd consent to go to bed. Pauline went with them, and Stuart suggested that he and I should have a walk round the grounds to see what changes he'd made. As we'd dined early there was still plenty of light and the air was summer-warm. The changes were modest enough – a rose pergola, a place where he and the boys had widened the stream into a pond where frogs might, with luck, take up residence. We strolled slowly and came to a point where the path forked, one branch dropping towards the road leading to the town, the other climbing steeply towards the edge of the moor. Stuart wanted to go down towards the road. I thought he was suggesting it because I was in too feeble a state for the steeper climb and insisted on the high path, for a view of the moors before it got too dark.

I set off and Stuart followed, grumbling. Either the path was steeper than I remembered or I was more unfit than I thought, because I was near breathless by the time we got to the broken wooden fence that marked our boundary. It was some consolation that Stuart was panting too from keeping up with me. We stood looking westwards, watching the last of a golden sunset over the distant haze of Manchester, then turned to the east and the moors stretching away towards the long backbone of the Pennines.

'Where's The Toad?'

That had been the name Stuart and I gave as children to a particular rock formation on the moor.

'You can't see The Toad from down here. We had to climb up the top of Shelf Rock.'

That was a rock not far from where we were standing, about forty feet high and easy enough to climb, with the gritstone formed into ledges and large handholds. I walked over to it and started climbing.

'Don't be silly, Nell.'

Alarm in his voice, and I thought I sensed an elder

brother's irritation that his sister should be first at anything. I turned and put my tongue out at him and climbed on. Certainly more of a scramble than I remembered, arms gone weak as well and the shoes I'd worn at dinner weren't meant for climbing, but I pulled myself over the last ledge and stood there on the broad shelf of rock at the top. Stuart, still protesting, came up after me.

'The Toad's still there.'

'Of course. Did you think it wouldn't be? Now come down while there's still some light.'

But the peat and heather smell rising off the moor was unbelievably sweet after months of city stinks. It was a long time since we'd stood there together and memories came back.

'I suppose Brigadier Fish-Face is long gone.'

An ancient and probably gallant veteran, real name Brigadier Brent-Haddock. He and Uncle Marcus had been arch enemies over some old boundary dispute and as children we'd often trespassed in the unkempt grounds of his estate, Crowberry Hall. The house itself was much grander than Whinmoor, a kind of moorland château.

'Of course he has, years ago. I'm sure I told you. If we don't go down Pauline will be worrying.'

I strolled to the north side of the rock shelf. From there you could look down on part of the Crowberry Hall garden and there had been a long earth slide under brambles that was one of our illicit points of entry.

'Nell, will you please . . .'

'All right, I'm coming. I just wanted to see if . . . Oh, ye gods, what have they done to it?'

It was still light enough to see outlines of the garden next door. Where I'd remembered unkempt shrubberies and fallen tree-trunks slanting among thickets of bracken, everything was so orderly it was positively shocking. The overgrown shrubbery had become a paved terrace, with a colonnade of stone columns. A boggy pool where we'd fished was now a round formal pond with a rampant dolphin and stone summerhouse, classical in style. The birches and rowans had been replaced by disciplined ever-greens, box or juniper cut into conical shapes. The general effect was of a formal Italian garden, nice enough beside Lake Como, thoroughly out of place on the moor edge.

'They've spoiled it.'

'Don't be silly. There was nothing much to spoil. Anyway, it's been like that for a long time.'

'How long?'

'Since the Brigadier died and Osbert Newbiggin bought it. Ten years or so.'

'It must have cost thousands.'

'Plenty where that came from. Cotton mills.'

My instinctive dislike of the arrangement was confirmed. Lock-outs by the Lancashire cotton bosses had been among the worst of the bitter industrial disputes pulling the country apart over the past few years.

'So some of the people you treat at your clinics have been squeezed to produce that.'

'Don't make speeches at me, Nell. I know that better than you do. Anyway, Osbert Newbiggin's dead.'

'When?'

'Nearly a year ago. If we don't . . .'

I knew that he was regretting the political turn things had taken. I supposed he was trying to keep me away from all that for a while, which presumably explained his uneasiness. I knew my brother well enough to detect the tension in him, more than could be accounted for by a worry that we might slip in the dark.

'So who's living there now?'

'His nephew inherited it. He's just moved in, as a matter of fact.'

'Hence all those furniture vans?'

'Yes.'

'Did the nephew inherit the cotton mills as well?'

'Yes, I suppose so. There were no sons or daughters. Now, if I go down first you can . . .'

'Why has he only just moved in now if his uncle died a year ago?'

'I think there was some trouble over probate of the will or something like that. Now will you please come down.'

Only his head was visible, looking at me over the top of the rock shelf, the rest of him already on the way down. I'd have followed because the idea of the cotton boss had taken away most of the pleasure from the moors and anyway it was nearly dark by then. But at that point something happened. There was a flickering of light round the pool and the colonnade, so quick that at first I thought it was lightning out of a clear sky. Then more flickerings, red, yellow and green, growing stronger until they became steady points of colour, lighting up the columns and the little trees and a fountain of water spurting from the stone dolphin. No lightning and no magic, simply coloured electric light bulbs slung along the colonnade and round the summer house, but in that time and place it felt for a moment as if Merlin had come out of the moor. Not a pleasant Merlin either, but one trading in pantomime effects. I glanced down at Stuart's face, expecting to see the same dislike that I felt. It was there, but alarm too, and for a level-headed man like Stuart, far more than seemed appropriate. He was gaping towards the lights and his apparently disembodied head resting on the rock ledge increased the pantomime effect.

'Is that the nephew's idea of a house-warming?'

But before I'd finished saying it, the next thing hit us. A trumpet call. It brayed out over the dark moor from the direction of the house and went on and on. Military trumpet. Was it a protest from the ghost of Brigadier Fish-Face? I could almost have thought so, because there was a quality about it that seemed not quite of this world.

Then a voice singing, male, baritone, also from the direction of the house.

> 'Trumpeter, what are you sounding now?
> Is it the call I'm seeking?
> "You'll know the call," said the Trumpeter tall,
> "When my trumpet goes a-speakin"'

26

It had the same echoing quality as the trumpet. I listened, then started laughing, the sort of quivering laughter that comes from having been scared without reason.

'Oh no, the man's got a gramophone too. How horrible.'

I had friends who were enthusiastic for the things, but I couldn't take them seriously. To me the sounds that came out of a gramophone horn had the same relation to real music as pallid bottled cherries have to those warm off the tree. It seemed all of a piece with the dead cotton boss and his nephew that they should drain the life out of their workers and spend it on deadening toys like gramophones. The song too – patriotic ballad, full of easy sentiment. I moved over to Stuart, still laughing. He didn't seem to find it as funny as I did.

'It's all right. I surrender. I'm coming down.'

'About time too.'

I followed him down, having to feel for hand- and footholds. When my feet touched ground at the bottom we could still hear the recorded voice, now at the climax of his song:

> 'But they'll hear it again in a grand refrain,
> When Gabriel sounds the last "Rally".'

It was dark by then, getting cold, and the song didn't seem funny any more. As a final trumpet call sounded faintly over the moor above us, I thought of cousin Fred who really had died in a battle, with or without trumpets.

'Confounded machines.'

'I quite agree.' From the seriousness in Stuart's voice, the same idea might have occurred to him.

We hurried back to the house to find the boys gone to bed and Pauline and Rose drinking coffee in the drawing room.

'You've been a long time.'

'They've got the garden lit up next door and they're playing the gramophone.'

Pauline looked at him, the long wordless look that

couples exchange when there's bad news. Then, unmistakably, she looked at me and glanced him a question. He gave a little 'no' movement of the head, so little that I shouldn't have noticed it if I hadn't been watching them closely. Then Pauline saw me looking and made a great business of pouring me coffee, blaming him gently for dragging me round and letting me get cold. I did feel cold, but I didn't know why.

THREE

FOR THE NEXT THREE DAYS Rose and I went for walks over the moors, read books in the evening by the light of a paraffin lamp in Old Ferris's cottage, picked mushrooms and fried them over the primus stove. Rose turned out to be a good walker. At first she went at it as if it were another task – so many miles of moor to be crossed off before evening – but the weather was still as warm as summer and it's hard to hurry over heather. We sauntered along sheep tracks, not caring much where we went, talking a little but not about anything that mattered such as how we'd find work for her. She began to look less strained and I daresay I did too, but there were no mirrors in the cottage. Rose left the choice of our walks to me, and I realised that I was avoiding anything that would bring us a view of Crowberry Hall and its grounds. No particular reason. It was more a case of unreason, the uneasy memory of the trumpet call blown out of a gramophone horn. I'd said nothing about it to Rose, but I couldn't get it out of my mind, which was a sign to me my nerves weren't in as much control as I'd wanted. Also, if we saw the house from the moor, Rose would quite reasonably ask who lived there, I'd have to tell her about the cotton boss and his nephew and that would have for her the same associations it had for me – exploitation, lock-outs, bitterness. Rose and I were here for only a few days, couldn't pretend to be any use.

The boys were at our door every day as soon as they were let out of school, dragging us by the hand to show us secret haunts of their own. They'd taken to Rose and, from her polite interest in the stag-beetle, had got it into their heads that nothing could please her more than presents of insects. Black beetles, rampant earwigs, even a hornet were presented in a variety of boxes with the kindest of intentions. She'd close the boxes hastily, express amazed thanks and we'd set the creatures free once the boys had gone. We saw very little of Stuart. He'd go down the road on his bike to catch the early morning train and sometimes wouldn't return until it was getting dark in the evenings.

One day Pauline brought the baby over for a picnic outside the cottage and delivered an invitation. They were having a few friends in to dinner on the following evening and would like us to meet them. Nothing formal, of course.

Rose turned it down, polite but immovable. 'I'm no good at that kind of thing. If you'll excuse me, I'd rather stay here and read by the fire.'

Although I'd have been glad to get out of it as well I had to accept. On the evening I changed into my respectable blue dress, saw Rose settled with the oil lamp, bread and cheese and *David Copperfield* and crossed the dry lawn to the house.

The others were drinking sherry in the living room, with its french windows open onto the terrace. There were seven of us altogether: Stuart and Pauline, a doctor friend and his wife who'd driven over from Rochdale, and two men I didn't know. Stuart poured me a sherry and performed introductions. The two men were Ted somebody, a square-shouldered and blue-eyed man in his mid-forties, the other was Bill Musgrave, about the same age. He was tall, with dark eyes set deep into their sockets and a quiff of dark hair falling over his forehead. Ted was one of those men who make you feel calm just to look at them. Although he was wearing a dark suit like the other men, you could tell he'd be more comfortable in an old tweed jacket and was longing to ask permission to light his pipe. I wasn't surprised to discover that he was a veterinary scientist from Manchester University, specialising in lung diseases of cattle. If I'd been a cow with a cough I'd have had no hesitation in taking my problem to him. Bill Musgrave was quite another matter. I once heard somebody described as being like 'an ill-sitting hen on a nest of fleas'. Although too long and thin to be a hen, he was so restless that the whole room crackled with it, like static electricity. Even when we sat down after the introductions he was on the edge of his chair, glancing from one person to the other as if a moment's inattention would make him miss something vital, although we were only talking about trains versus motor cars.

I was concentrating on the two men on their own because I'd met the doctor and his wife once before. Also, it was a matter of self-preservation for the next two or three hours. Pauline, I'm afraid, is a confirmed matchmaker, especially where I'm concerned. She wouldn't actually use the phrase – at least not in my hearing – but she thinks I should settle down. I knew I had to identify the hapless man she'd selected as the latest candidate and, for his sake as well as mine, make it clear that I had other things to do with my life. In justice, I have to admit that her taste on my behalf wasn't entirely bad. None of her candidates had been a fool and most had been instructive or entertaining – for an evening though not for a lifetime. The question was, was it supposed to be Ted or Bill this time? Even with Pauline, I acquitted her of parading two at once for my choice. Seven was an odd number for a dinner table. Perhaps one of them was meant for Rose. If I found out which, was I supposed to wrap him up in a table napkin and take him home to her?

Through the soup course, I was almost sure it was meant to be Ted. He was sitting on my right with the doctor on my left and Bill opposite. Ted was interested in what I'd been doing, but not too interested. Politically he was irreproachable and knew the Pankhursts, said the right things about the government, though without heat. By the time we got to the halibut he was suggesting new walks over

31

the moors, offering himself as guide at the weekend. I said, feeling a little regretful, that we'd be gone in a few days. This produced an unexpected reaction from across the table. Bill Musgrave sat bolt upright and stared at me.

'What do you mean, gone in a few days?'

Annoyed, I explained none too politely that we were only here for a week.

'That's no time.'

'It's quite enough time to be away from my work.'

If Stuart had recruited him to get me to stay longer, he'd have to do better than that. From the annoyed look Stuart was giving him, he thought so too. Bill forked his fish moodily and the conversation became general again. But there was one more sticky moment during the main course as Stuart got up to pour the wine. The doctor asked him, 'Seen anything of your new neighbour yet?'

'No, and I don't suppose we shall.'

This time the annoyed look came from Pauline to her guest. Crowberry Hall was evidently not a fit subject for conversation. I had to admit that this wasn't one of their more successful dinner parties. Perhaps it was just because I was feeling jaded, but I didn't think so. There were too many undercurrents, quite apart from Pauline's matchmaking designs. For one thing, I had the feeling that Pauline and Stuart were not quite as much in harmony as on past occasions. Then there was the inexplicable tension of Bill. I noticed that he was drinking a lot, emptying his glass twice as quickly as the other men, but it didn't seem to relax him.

When we went into the sitting room for coffee I found myself next to him. At least with Stuart and Pauline, there was no nonsense about leaving the gentlemen to their port. I asked if he were a doctor too.

'No, a lawyer. Barrister.'

'Civil?'

'No, mainly criminal.'

I'd have liked to talk to him about that. Once I wanted

to be a lawyer myself and I have several barrister friends. But Pauline, unusually clumsy, cut in.

'Bill went walking in the Andes last year, all among the Incas.'

At least he recognised his social duty and talked about a trip he'd made the summer before. He began almost angrily, but then couldn't help getting enthusiastic about the mountain people and the Inca ruins. The restlessness fell away as he talked. His dark eyes were alert and he kept pushing the quiff of hair away from his forehead. We were all listening to him and Pauline was lying back in her armchair, relief in every line of her body. But relief about what?

After that everybody started talking about travelling and the party relaxed, probably because we'd drunk quite a lot of wine by then. It was nearly midnight when the doctor and his wife got up to go. Ted lived not far away from them and they were giving him a lift in their motor car. I went out with Stuart and Pauline to wave them off and we returned to the sitting room to another minor social crisis. Bill Musgrave was still sitting there as if he intended to stay all night. It turned out that he did.

'I'm afraid I've missed the last train by now.'

Stuart was annoyed. 'Why didn't you ask the others? They could have dropped you off at the junction.'

'Too late for that, I'm afraid.'

In his place anybody else would have been embarrassed. He wasn't in the least. I liked him more for that.

'Then I suppose you'd better stay here.' Pauline got up wearily.

'Don't bother to make up a bed for me. I'll take off my boots and stretch out on the sofa.'

Pauline looked at Stuart. 'If that's what Bill wants . . .'

'It is, thank you very much. Don't lock the french windows. I'll be away as soon as it's light to catch the early train. And thank you for a very pleasant evening.'

He was more relaxed now, as if a decision had been taken. Or perhaps he just enjoyed being difficult. Pauline gave up on him, said goodnight to us all and went up to bed. I opened the french windows and stepped out to the terrace.

Stuart called, 'Wait, Nell, I'm walking you back.'

'Isn't Nell staying with you?' Bill sounded alarmed again.

Stuart, in no very good temper, explained about the keeper's cottage.

'I'll walk with you too.'

'Oh, no, you won't. It doesn't take two of us to see Nell back. If you're catching the early train, you'd better get to sleep.'

We stepped out into the darkness together. This late, there was a bite of autumn in the air. As we went, Stuart moaned about Bill Musgrave.

'First he invites himself to dinner, and then goes and misses his train.'

'Invites himself?'

'Yes, I've known him quite a long time, but he wasn't supposed to be coming tonight. I met him in Manchester, happened to mention we were having a few friends in to meet you, and that was it.'

So Ted had been Pauline's chosen victim.

'Cool.'

'Oh, Bill's got enough cheek when he wants something. Odd bloke in some ways. Clever. Goes his own way.'

'Interesting.'

'Yes. Still, he'll be gone by the time you're up and about tomorrow.'

I wondered why he seemed quite so pleased about that, but didn't ask. We parted at the door of the cottage.

Rose was waiting up for me, yawning over Dickens with the fire burning low.

'Good evening?'

'I don't think you missed a lot, but the food was good and you'd have enjoyed the Incas.'

I imagined Bill Musgrave stretched out on the sofa,

34

taking a bed where he found it, without fuss, like a proper traveller. We talked for a while, then went up the rickety, ladder-like stairs to our bedrooms. I fell asleep almost at once and woke in the pitch dark to hear Rose's whisper from somewhere near the foot of the bed.

'Nell, there's somebody outside.'

'What time is it?'

I groped for matches and my watch. Quarter-past two.

'How do you know?'

'Something hit my window.'

'Probably a slate falling off the roof.'

'No. It happened twice, so I opened the window and looked out. There's somebody down there, Nell. I could hear breathing.'

She's not the nervous type any more than I am, but she wasn't used to the country and I thought the something down there was probably a sheep come off the moor for easier pickings.

'I'll have a look.'

I found and lit the candle, revealing Rose in a nightdress with her hair down. My bed was right up against the window, so I had to kneel on it to push open the window and look out. Dazzled by the candle, I couldn't see anything at first.

'Miss Bray?'

A voice from right underneath the window. I almost fell out of it in surprise.

'Who's there?'

'Bill Musgrave. We met at dinner.'

A giggle from Rose, and I couldn't blame her. It was the contrast between the formality of the words and the daftness of the situation.

'I remember. What are you doing here?'

'I'd like to talk to you.'

No please, thank you or apology. Rose whispered, 'Sounds as if you've made a conquest.'

'I'm happy to talk to anybody, but not at a quarter-past two in the morning. Won't it keep?'

'No.'

If he'd tried explanations or excuses I'd probably have shut the window and told him to wait till morning. It was the blank confidence of that one syllable that decided me.

'Wait there, then. I'll be down in a minute.'

I unhooked my coat from the back of the door and buttoned it over my nightdress. Rose was wide-eyed in the candle-light.

'What does he want?'

'Goodness knows.'

'Shall I come down with you?'

'No, you get back to bed. I'll get rid of him as soon as I can.'

I couldn't be bothered to look for shoes so went barefoot down the stairs and across the stone floor. Ashes were still glowing in the grate. When I unlatched the door he was waiting for me on the step.

'Come in.'

He bent so as not to hit his head and closed the door behind him. I lit the paraffin lamp and its glow spread round the room.

'You probably guessed that I missed that train deliberately. I wanted to speak to you.'

'We were in the same room for about four hours this evening. I was under the impression you'd spoken to me then.'

'Not what I wanted to say. I think your brother would have thrown me out if I'd tried it.'

I sat in the chair by the hearth. Without invitation, he sat opposite.

'He didn't want to invite me tonight in the first place. He only did it on the understanding that there was a particular subject that mustn't be mentioned to you.'

'An understanding you're now breaking?'

'Not at all. That covered dinner last night. Now it's this morning.'

'An ingenious sophistry.'

'I am a lawyer, after all. You haven't asked me what the subject was. Or perhaps you've guessed already.'

There were curls of birch bark in an old basket beside the hearth. I dropped a handful on the red embers to make them flare up. His eyes followed me.

'It's not my best time of the day for guessing games. No, I haven't.'

'I have a problem, Miss Bray.'

'Haven't we all?'

'Not this kind. There's a client of mine in the condemned cell. They're going to hang him in two weeks for a murder he didn't commit.'

He looked at me and waited.

FOUR

'WHO?'

'Davie Kendal.'

'Who's Davie Kendal?'

'It doesn't mean anything to you?'

'No. I don't normally read crime reports.'

'He's the man who's supposed to have shot Osbert Newbiggin.'

I was on the point of saying that didn't mean anything to me either, when it connected.

'Osbert Newbiggin owns the place next door – Crowberry Hall.'

'Owned. He was shot last November. Didn't your brother tell you about it?'

Stuart's behaviour became explicable. No wonder he hadn't wanted me to see the house next door, or that he and Pauline were nervy about the furniture vans. Here he was, trying to drag me away for a rest in the bosom of the family, embarrassed by a murder case on the doorstep. With my record, I could hardly blame him for being concerned. I shivered under my coat, remembering the lights flickering on in the dusk, the ghostly trumpet call, and saw Bill looking at me.

'Stuart and I were looking down on it the night I arrived. The new man – the nephew, is it – started playing a gramophone.'

'Gramophone!' He sounded, for some reason, as startled as I'd felt. 'In the circumstances, that's odd.'

'Why?'

'Since if they hang Davie Kendal it will be because of a gramophone. Possibly that very machine you heard.'

We stared at each other and I was aware of two things. One was that Bill Musgrave was a clever man. The other was that he knew more about me than I'd thought. He knew something about the detective reputation that had attached itself to me unsought, like a stray cat. He also knew, probably from Stuart, about my vice of curiosity – or nosiness as my brother would put it. He wanted very much for me to listen to him, badly enough to spend an uncomfortable night and walk half a mile through the dark to find me, and yet he sat there with the deceptive quiet of a fisherman, waiting to see if the bait would be taken.

'Your brother said nothing to you?'

'Not a word.'

The curls of birch bark were flaring. I leaned forward and threw a log on the fire, conscious of his eyes on me all the time. Every fish ever caught must have thought it could take a taste of the bait and swim away.

'Was he killed at Crowberry Hall?'

'Yes. In his study.'

He waited for the next question. I waited too and the silence drew out. He gave in first.

'I'll try to tell you about it the way you might have heard if you'd been here. The first sign that something was wrong was when people in the town heard a bell ringing from the hall, ringing quite wildly, at about half-past ten at night.'

'I know that bell. Brigadier Fish-Face rang it for Queen Victoria's Jubilee.'

It hung in a tower on the roof and made a noise like the foundries of hell, echoing back from the moors and out over the town.

'It was the cook ringing it that night, to fetch help. People heard it down in the town but they weren't sure where it was coming from. I gather it was a long time since it had been used. Some people thought it was a fire at one of the mills. The first to realise it was coming from the hall seem to have been the men drinking at the Cross Keys.

39

That's the public house nearest the end of the drive from Crowberry Hall. Do you remember it?'

I tried to picture it and remembered vaguely that Crowberry Hall did possess a drive in the grand manner, running through banks of rhododendrons all the way down the hill and coming out onto the High Street, a relic of the days when Crowberry Hall had been the squire's house and the town no more than a village.

'Some of the men from the pub went rushing up the drive. They hadn't gone far before they met a young woman running down it. She was in her indoor clothes and started screaming as soon as she saw them. That young woman was Laura Newbiggin, the dead man's cousin. They managed to calm her down a little and she told them that Mr Newbiggin was dead. By then a couple of police had arrived. They went on up the drive and found the maid hysterical as well, hardly able to open the door to them.

'The cook had stopped ringing the bell by then and she and the old lady, Osbert Newbiggin's aunt, were waiting outside the door of his study. He was on the floor of an alcove inside, shot through the head. He must have put up quite a struggle because there were chairs overturned, blood and feathers from a cushion all over the place and some of his beloved collection of gramophone records scattered and broken. In fact, he wasn't technically dead at the time, but deeply unconscious. There's no doubt from the post-mortem that he'd have lost consciousness as soon as the bullet hit his brain. He died in hospital in the early hours of the morning.'

'Who else was in the house?'

'Just the four women, the aunt, the cook, the maid and the cousin who'd come running down the drive. Osbert Newbiggin had been a widower for some time and had no children. The aunt acted as his housekeeper. The only other servant was an old chap who worked as odd-job man and gardener, but he lives in the lodge half-way down the drive.'

'So where does your client – what was his name – come into it?'

'Davie Kendal. He used to work for Osbert Newbiggin. He had an appointment to see him at the hall at six o'clock that evening. We know he kept the appointment because the maid let him in. We don't know when he left the house, but there are several witnesses that he was in the Cross Keys at about half-past seven. When that bell started ringing around three hours later he was in there again.'

'When was Osbert Newbiggin killed?'

'We don't know.'

'But if he was shot with four people in the house . . .'

'There are special circumstances. You remember that I told you if Davie Kendal hangs it will probably be because of a gramophone? Well, that's true twice over, but to get to that I need to tell you something about Osbert Newbiggin. Do you know anything about him at all?'

'Only that he was a mill owner and involved in the lock-outs.'

'Yes, second generation. He inherited two mills from his father and added another of his own. It's true enough that they've had trouble with their workforce in the last few years, but I don't want to give you the idea that Newbiggin was any worse than the rest. Even the unions wouldn't claim that. There was one thing that made him stick out from the rest, and that was, he was a moderniser. Any new process he heard about, he'd want a good look at it and if it worked, he'd have it. It might have been disastrous for the business, but anyone will tell you that Newbiggin had good judgement. He left three times as much as he inherited from his father . . .'

'To the nephew?'

'Yes, to the nephew. Anyway, as I was saying, Newbiggin was usually the first to try out something new. He was one of the first round here to sell his carriage and buy a motor car, first to have a telephone installed. He wanted it and he could afford it. It was even more so with the gramophone. I gather it was quite a passion with him, personal and

41

commercial. He bought a large block of shares in the first gramophone company to be set up in this country and took a very close interest in the technicalities. Like most of his commercial ventures it paid dividends, but he wanted more than that. He was genuinely a music lover – I gather he had quite a good bass voice – and was the main benefactor of the choral society in town here. I'm told they're more than usually good.'

'Stuart says they're probably the best choir of their size in Lancashire, which is quite a tribute.'

I wouldn't trust Stuart's judgement on everything, but his musical ear is good.

Bill nodded. 'You know it's almost impossible to make a good recording of a choir. Soloists yes, brass bands possibly, choirs, no.'

My opinion was that it was impossible to make a good recording of anything, but I said nothing. Bill was relaxing back in his chair now, becoming absorbed in his story.

'Osbert Newbiggin wouldn't accept that. He had an ambition to make the first complete recording of Handel's *Messiah* – solos, choruses, trumpets, the lot.'

'All those discs – you'd have to carry it around in a suitcase.'

'He bought himself a disc recording machine and had his study rebuilt so that part of it could be made into a kind of studio. It was soundproofed.'

'I see, and he was shot in there?'

'The studio part wasn't completely closed off, but there seems very little doubt that he was forced up against one of the soundproofing panels and shot. There's also clear evidence that his killer fired a shot through a cushion. There were feathers in the wound, and one of the cushions from his sofa was on the floor with a hole through it and scorch marks.'

'That suggests whoever shot him knew about the recording place and counted on it to muffle the shot.'

'Yes.'

'Was that the case with your Davie Kendal?'

42

I hadn't bothered to light the lamp and with the fire burning low again I could only see the reflection of its light in his eyes when he looked at me, not their expression.

'Yes. Nobody in this town, or anywhere else as far as I know, knew more about Newbiggin's recording work than Davie Kendal. He was Newbiggin's chief assistant.'

'He employed him just for that?'

'No. Also until a few months before the killing, Davie was an engineer in Newbiggin's mills. Newbiggin had taken him on straight from school and paid for his training. He had a reputation for spotting useful talent and encouraging it. I suppose if he wanted his new machinery he had to train the men to run it. The recording thing was a sideline – but by most accounts Davie was as interested in it as Newbiggin himself. He had a bit of a reputation as an amateur inventor. That didn't help either.'

'So Davie Kendal went to see Osbert Newbiggin on the evening he died and nobody knows when he left. He was seen in the pub at the end of his drive. He knew about the soundproofed part of the study. Anything else against him?'

'I'm afraid so, in fact I haven't even got to the most damaging thing yet.'

'Which was?'

'The gramophone alibi – or rather, the attempt at it. Just after eight o'clock on the night of the murder, the telephone rings in the house of one of Newbiggin's friends. This friend is a reliable man, well-known locally as a pillar of the methodist church, chairman of magistrates, the lot. He picks up the telephone. The operator says there's a call for him. Silence at first, and he's about to put the telephone back on its hook when he hears Newbiggin's voice. "Hello, this is Osbert Newbiggin. I hope you can hear this all right. Osbert Newbiggin at Crowberry Hall." Then the call's cut off at the other end. I don't suppose I need to tell you what that was.'

'A gramophone recording.'

'Yes. The first time the soloists got together in his

study to record some arias for the great *Messiah* project, Newbiggin said a few words to test the apparatus. He decided to have copies of that disc made as souvenirs of the occasion. That was what was played down the telephone to his friend.'

'It can't have sounded very natural.'

'It didn't. Right from the start the friend guessed exactly what it was, except he thought it must be Newbiggin himself playing it down the telephone as some kind of scientific experiment. He said he could even hear the needle hissing over the disc. He expected another call from Newbiggin to tell him what the experiment was. When it didn't come, he just thought Newbiggin would explain next time they met. Next day he heard that Newbiggin was dead.'

'It should have been easy to find out where the telephone call came from. After all, there can't be many people round here with telephones and gramophones.'

'No, but it was easier than that. When the police searched Crowberry Hall and its grounds the day after the murder, they found Newbiggin's own gramophone in the gate lodge, on a table beside the telephone.'

'Do we know how it got there?'

'It had been taken from Newbiggin's study in a wheelbarrow. The wheelbarrow had been left outside the lodge. There were tracks of its wheels in the flower-bed outside his study window, along with some indistinct boot-marks. It was a sash window, not locked. The window had been pulled shut, but there was mud on the sill, as if somebody had scrambled over it.'

'So the inference is that on the evening Newbiggin was killed, a person unknown loaded his gramophone into a wheelbarrow, pushed it down to the lodge and set it up there, then played Newbiggin's voice over the telephone to his old friend. Wasn't there anybody in the lodge?'

'No. The odd-job man goes out most evenings, playing billiards at the working men's club. He didn't know what was going on until he heard the bell like the rest.'

'An odd-job man with a telephone?'

'Put in by Newbiggin. He liked the idea that he could summon him at a moment's notice if he wanted something done.'

'How long would it take to get from the lodge to the Cross Keys?'

'We tried it and so did the police. Four minutes walking.'

'So if Davie Kendal was at the bar around half-past seven he could easily . . . ?'

'Yes.'

'What about the gun?'

'Newbiggin kept a revolver in a drawer of his study after a scare about burglars some years ago. It was missing and the assumption is that the murderer used it. It's never been found. The police spent days looking for it. They even dragged the flooded quarry at the back of the house.'

I remembered the quarry. Stuart and I once sailed across it on a raft.

'So his murderer must have known about the revolver in the drawer?'

'Yes.'

'I suppose the police searched Davie Kendal's home.'

'His home and his lodgings.'

'And didn't find the gun?'

'No. But they found something else in the ash-bin in the yard behind the house where his family live.'

'The record with Osbert Newbiggin's voice, I suppose.'

'How did you know that?'

I'd known from his voice that there was even worse to come, so it had been an easy guess.

'Anyway, you're right. It was in several pieces and burnt from the hot ash dumped on it, but they were able to identify it from a number in the middle.'

'What did your client say about that at the time?'

'He couldn't say anything. He'd gone missing by then.'

'I thought you told me he was back at the Cross Keys when the bell started ringing.'

'He was, but he disappeared in the confusion. Nobody

saw anything of him for more than two months, then he was arrested in a churchyard in Liverpool.'

It was the coldest and darkest time of the night. The log had burned to a cylinder of ash. To get more I'd have had to go to the woodpile outside.

'Aren't your feet cold?'

I looked at them, narrow on the flagstones in what was left of the firelight. A few feet away, Bill Musgrave was no more than a dark shape.

'So the jury convicted.'

'In less than an hour.'

'On the grounds that your client was probably the last person to see the murdered man alive, knew about the mechanics of gramophones, disposed of a recording of his voice, then fled as soon as the murder was discovered.'

'Yes.'

'I'm sorry, but I have to tell you that if I'd been on that jury, I'd have come to exactly the same conclusion.'

'Yes, I thought you'd say that.'

'In that case, why are we both sitting here catching our deaths of cold?'

I was annoyed. I couldn't have been surprised if he'd been annoyed back at me because I sensed he wasn't a man who sat down easily under rudeness. If he was resentful, he hid it well.

'Three reasons, none of which may make sense to you. The first one comes closest to being rational, and it's this – to expect that telephone trick to work as an alibi, the murderer would have to be a very stupid person in some ways. I'll grant that he would have to be ingenious to think of it and technically skilful enough to operate it. But you see, it just doesn't work. I tried it. I borrowed an office with telephones and got my clerk to stand in one room with the telephone held close to the horn of a gramophone playing another copy of that disc, while I listened at a telephone in the next room. My clerk got very good at it, and we achieved a result much like what the friend must have heard that night. But – and here's the crunch – even at our very best I could never have mistaken it for a live human voice. And of course, the friend didn't either. To expect otherwise, a man would have to be very stupid – and I don't think my client is that kind of man.'

I refrained from saying that, in running off, Davie would have behaved very stupidly indeed for an innocent man.

'The second thing?'

'Here I can only offer you my impression, for what it's worth, because you haven't met them. It's simply that I have the strongest impression that some of Davie Kendal's own family know something that even now they won't tell me.'

'If so, perhaps it's because it would be even more damaging to him. After all, I take it that they don't want to see him hanged.'

'No. In fact his sister's getting up this petition to the Home Secretary. She seems to be putting the most pathetic trust in it. I've tried to disillusion her but . . .'

'And your third thing?'

'Simply this. In my profession, I'm used to being lied to, almost as a matter of course. I've known men three times as guilty as Cain look me in the eye and declare their innocence. Part of my job, like septic tonsils are part of your brother's. Only this time, in that cell under the dock when he'd just seen the judge putting the black cap on and heard him saying those words, he looked at me and said, "I didn't kill him, Mr Musgrave." And, heaven help me, I believed him. I still do.' His voice had gone quiet and his shoulders hunched.

'Hasn't it happened to you before, a client hanged?'

'Just once. It was the worst night of my life, even though I was quite certain that that one had done it. With this one . . . Can you imagine talking to somebody, hearing him talk, and knowing that in fourteen days he'll be dead because of something you've failed to do? Like standing on the bank of a stream, seeing a waterfall pouring down on somebody, and his face looking up at you, eyes open, knowing what's going on, and you not being able to save him. I . . .'

47

'Perhaps you're in the wrong job.'

I was bone tired and weary of demands on me, but I shouldn't have said that. He had every right to resent it and yet he answered quite seriously.

'Yes, perhaps I am, although I didn't think so until this case. But that doesn't matter. I swear to you that I'd give up the law tomorrow and take to shovelling coal for a living if I thought it would help. But it wouldn't, would it? So I have to try to do the best for him with what I am. I'm sorry to have got you out of bed.'

Then he lifted the latch and was gone before I could think of anything to say.

FIVE

I SLEPT LATE. WHEN I got up, Rose had the coffee brewed. The smell of it filled the cottage, with an undertone of woodsmoke from the night before.

'He went, then?'

'He went.'

She poured coffee. I couldn't tell from her face whether she was amused or disapproving.

'He's a barrister. He wants me to prove that one of his clients didn't commit a murder.'

I told her about it.

'Can you do anything?'

'What? It happened nearly a year ago. I don't know any of the people involved. In any case, he's probably guilty.'

'So they'll hang him?'

'Almost certainly.'

She'd finished pouring coffee but was still sitting there with her hand frozen round the handle of the pot, staring at me.

'Has he got a family?'

'Brothers and sisters at any rate. One of them's getting up a petition – though it probably won't do any good.'

I could see from her eyes that she thought I was being callous. I was trying to stamp out of my mind the memory of Bill's voice when he said, 'And heaven help me, I believed him.'

'That would be something, I suppose. You'd go mad otherwise. Can you imagine waking up every morning and knowing . . . ?' She went quiet.

We both sensed it was one of those days when we'd prefer our own company and after breakfast she said she thought she'd go down to the town to find a cobbler to put some nails in her boot-soles. All this gritstone was tearing away at the leather. Once she'd gone I decided I needed a long walk and went for most of the day, out past The Toad rocks to the point where you couldn't even see the town and there was nothing to the east but miles of empty moorland rolling out of Lancashire into Yorkshire. It looked from there as if you could walk on for ever with nothing in the world but heather and blue sky. I turned back reluctantly as the sun started to dip down. By the time I'd got back to the boundaries of Whinmoor the air was getting cold and bats were flying around the face of the quarry. As I came down the path alongside it a figure stood up beside the rowan tree.

'You've taken your time, Nell.'

Stuart.

'Is there something wrong?'

'Why, should there be?'

But I doubted whether he'd been sitting there simply from brotherly affection. There was no light on in the cottage, so Rose wasn't back yet.

'Did you enjoy the dinner last night?'

'Very much, thank you.'

'Sleep well?'

'Why not? Shall we stroll?'

I guessed that a little gentle bullying was on the agenda, for my own good, of course, and hoped the cooling air might cut it short. He definitely suspected something, so I decided to go onto the attack.

'You might have told me about next door.'

'Told you about what . . . ? Oh, I see.'

'Were you here when it happened?'

'So that's what the man wanted. Never trust a lawyer. When did he tell you?'

'Never mind about that. I don't know why you and

Pauline were trying so hard to protect me. I don't go running after every passing murder case, you know.'

'Then why are you asking me about it now?'

'Normal curiosity. After all, most people would mention it if there'd been a murder next door to them.'

'In your case, it's abnormal curiosity. You're here for a rest and Bill Musgrave had no business trying to unload his professional worries on you. I assume that was what he was doing.'

'He thinks the man is innocent.'

Stuart heaved an exasperated sigh. 'Sheer arrogance. He's too used to succeeding, that man. Now he's come across a jury with the bad taste not to be swayed by his eloquence, he can't let it rest.'

The Bill Musgrave talking beside the fire hadn't struck me as an arrogant man. Desperate, perhaps.

'Who says Davie Kendal is innocent, apart from Bill? Twelve good men and true didn't think so. Suppose I carried on like this every time I lost a patient.'

'I told him he might be in the wrong profession.'

'That's my dear sister, tactful as ever. What did he say to that?'

'He said he was thinking of giving up the law.'

He whistled. 'All this over the coffee cups? He really must be in a bad way.'

I didn't correct him. If he knew about Bill Musgrave's visit in the early hours he'd be even more annoyed with him.

'Anyway, what did he expect you to do about it?'

'If he expected anything, he'll have been disappointed.'

'So you're not getting involved?'

'No.'

That made him happier. We strolled towards the quarry and sat down on a couple of slabs of rock.

'Did you hear the bell ringing that night?'

'Nell!'

'If I'm not getting involved, surely I'm allowed to be normally curious. You must have heard it.'

'I was on night duty at the infirmary. Pauline did. It woke the boys up.'

'When did you know what had happened?'

'Pauline heard all about it next morning from the girl who comes up to do the cleaning. Her brother was one of the men in the Cross Keys when Laura came running down the drive for help.'

'You know, it's an odd thing about that . . .'

'Nell, for goodness sake don't start.'

His face was screwed up with anger and tension. He must be more worried about me than I'd realised.

'I'm not starting anything. Did you know Osbert Newbiggin?'

'Hardly at all. Pauline and I aren't on visiting terms with the local mill owners. I think the only times I've been in the same room with him were choral society occasions.'

'Bill Musgrave mentioned the society.'

'Newbiggin darned near owned it. Paid for the rebuilding of their rehearsal room, subsidised the concerts. Even poached singers.'

'Poached?'

'From other choral societies. If there was a voice he fancied in another town, he'd offer the man a better job at one of his mills to move here, especially good tenors because they're scarce. That caused a bit of ill feeling.'

'Perhaps he was murdered by a consortium of rival choir-masters.'

'Still, I have to admit that the results were good. I don't suppose you'd hear a better choir this side of Huddersfield.'

'Did you know about this grand scheme to make gramophone recordings of *The Messiah*?'

'The whole town knew about that. After they'd recorded some of the solos he organised a concert entirely from discs – just Newbiggin on the platform and one of those confounded machines. I'm told the hall was packed.'

'Would you say he was well-thought-of locally?'

He hesitated. 'Not by the unions, but you know how

things have been in that direction. For the rest – I suppose a man who provides jobs and spends his money locally is usually popular enough. His funeral procession was half a mile long. The obituaries called him a universally respected local benefactor, and so on.'

'That can cover a multitude of sins. Was he an old man?'

'Oh no, early fifties I'd say. Perfectly hale and hearty.'

'What about the aunt and the cousin?'

'The aunt's a widowed lady called Mrs Bolter. I met her just once. Arthritic, but as tough as gritstone. According to our cleaning girl she was the sort who'd sniff out dust under a rug from fifty yards away.'

'Is she still at the hall?'

'No. Newbiggin left her two thousand pounds in his will, and she took herself off to live at Southport.'

'And Laura, the cousin?'

'Her parents died in an accident two or three years ago so he gave her a roof over her head.'

'Kind of him.'

'It was her voice he wanted. If she didn't happen to have one of the best young soprano voices for miles around, he might have paid somebody to take her in, but I don't suppose he'd have given her house-room at the hall.'

'That good?'

'Untrained, or at least not properly trained, but when she was younger it had a quality about it and freshness. She could sing something you might have heard a hundred times and make it sound as if it had just come into her head on a May morning.'

From Stuart, that was poetry.

'When she was younger? She can't be very old now.'

'No, early twenties. But all this has been a bad blow for her.'

'Does she still live at the hall, with the nephew?'

'No. She's got a room down in the town. She teaches voice and piano.'

'Newbiggin didn't provide for her, then?'

'Two hundred pounds. Enough for the rent and a piano.' He was silent for a while, then suddenly: 'Look, I'd rather you didn't talk to Pauline about this.'

'About the murder?' Pauline had never seemed to me the squeamish sort.

'Oh, she doesn't mind about that. I mean about Laura. The fact is, I look in on her sometimes, try to keep an eye on her. Pauline doesn't like that very much.'

'Why not?'

'You know Pauline – soul of generosity most of the time, but she can take dislikes to people.'

'So I don't raise the subject of Laura. But it's all right to talk to Pauline about Newbiggin and the rest?'

'Why do you want to, if you're not getting involved?'

'Just curious, that's all.'

'I hope it is all.'

He walked with me back to the cottage where we parted company. I went inside and lit the lamp. No sign of life apart from a couple of hungry cats. I fed the cats, filled the kettle from the clean-water bucket, warmed the teapot. Still no sign of Rose and I was worried, wondering if she'd gone for her own walk on the moor and got lost. I was about to change back into my walking shoes when I heard steps outside and the latch lifting.

'Hello, Nell.'

Something odd about her voice, tiredness perhaps.

'I've got the kettle on. Did you have a good day?'

'Nell, I've brought somebody to see you.'

She said it like bad news. When I looked at her I got that level, defiant stare of hers.

'Who?'

'His sister.'

'Whose sister? Oh.'

'Yes.'

'Davie Kendal's sister? How did you find her?'

'Asked at a shop. Everybody knows her.'

'Where is she?'

'Waiting outside. I'm sorry, Nell. Only, I couldn't not

do anything. I thought if I could find out who was helping with the petition I could spend a day going round with it, just to do something. So I met Janet. I . . . I told her about you. I'm sorry, but she wants to talk to you.'

I looked at her face and the dark sky through the uncurtained window.

'Then I suppose you'd better tell her to come in.'

SIX

THE FIRST THING THAT STRUCK me about Janet Kendal was a likeness to Rose. That was when I had a chance to sit and look at her. The first few minutes after Rose sprang the surprise on me were taken up with fetching her in and getting her to sit down. As there were only two chairs in the room, that left none for Rose so she stayed on her feet and attended to the kettle and teapot. There weren't obvious physical similarities. Janet was fairer in colouring, taller and sturdier. Probably in her late twenties, but it wasn't easy to tell because she had the air of a woman who'd never been childish. Oldest girl in the family, most likely, wiping noses and darning socks for the others. Her shoulders and forehead were broad, her light brown hair scraped back from her face into an untidy bundle at the back and topped with a red and green headscarf. She was gloveless, her hands red and raw, her boots scuffed. The likeness was in the eyes, direct and challenging under prominent eyebrows. The eyes of somebody who expected to have to fight. She was fighting the world, including me.

'Well, are your friends in London going to help?'

It was the first thing she'd said since striding in. She hadn't wasted breath in introductions or apologies. From behind her back Rose, teaspoon in hand, gave me a look that was a little shamefaced.

'I told you, it's not so much a matter of Nell's friends . . .'

'Well, it's got to be, or I'm just wasting my time coming here.'

It was a Lancashire voice, strong but not harsh.

'I didn't promise anything, Nell. I just told her about some of the other things you'd done and . . .'

Janet ignored her. 'It's all very well us collecting signatures up here, but it's London where it'll be decided and I don't know anybody down there.'

Her eyes were grey. They hadn't wavered from my face since she sat down.

I explained, as best I could, that Rose and I had many friends in London who'd sympathise and sign her petition but we were not well placed to influence the Home Secretary. I didn't add, since it would have been pointlessly cruel, that support from the likes of me would probably make the situation worse and that a government which had ordered troops to fire on strikers in Wales was unlikely to reprieve a man convicted of killing a mill boss. She listened.

'I see.'

She stood up.

'Where are you going?'

'I can see I'm wasting your time and you're wasting mine.'

She moved towards the door. Rose intercepted her.

'Janet, don't go. Nell, don't let her go.'

I was standing up as well.

'Since you've come all this way, you might at least let us talk.'

'Can you help him?'

'I don't know until we've discussed it.'

'What is there to discuss?'

'For a start, do you think your brother killed Osbert Newbiggin?'

That stopped her in her tracks. She looked at me over her shoulder and the near brutality of my question seemed to work in a way that kindness or politeness wouldn't have achieved.

'Davie didn't kill him.'

'How do you know?'

She was still half-way to the door and it seemed to me

57

that the kindest thing might be to let her go as she'd intended, rather than raising more false hopes.

Rose said, 'You'll stay for a cup of tea at least. The kettle's boiling.'

She looked at Rose, at the kettle, at me, then grudgingly came back and sat down.

'Your petition, I assume it's asking the Home Secretary to commute the sentence to . . .'

'To exercise his prerogative of mercy.'

'On what grounds?'

'On the grounds that he's innocent.'

'Yes, but are you offering any new evidence, anything that didn't come out at his trial?'

A forlorn hope. If there had been anything, his lawyers would have seized on it.

'They slanted things at the trial.'

'What things?'

'Trying to make out that he'd threatened the old bugger.'

'Threatened?'

'This business about him being seen round the house. And the argument he was supposed to have had with him.'

The kettle boiled. Rose made tea.

'Argument?'

It sounded as if the case against Davie Kendal might be even stronger than Bill Musgrave had admitted.

'They twisted it. Whatever he did, they'd make it sound bad for him. Then that business about the machine.'

'What business?'

'Making out he'd damaged the machine at the mill. They had no proof of that.'

Arguments, threats, sabotage. She thought that I knew all the details of the case already. Every word she spoke was making it look more hopeless.

Rose poured tea. Janet drank hers in big gulps, as if she grudged the time it took to get down her throat.

'Is Davie younger than you?'

58

'Four years younger.'

'How many in the family?'

'Four children. Jimmy, Davie, they're younger than me. Then there's Tom, the oldest one, but he's married and gone to live over Wigan way.'

'Are your parents still alive?'

'Dad is, but I don't know for how much longer. He's fair wrecked with it all. Mum died of TB when Davie was five.'

'So you brought him up?'

She nodded. Then the angry, defensive look came back into her eyes in full force.

'Anyway, what's that got to do with anything?'

She thought I was prying, and unless I intended to try to help, that was exactly what I was doing.

'Rose brought you here because I've been involved with things like this a few times in the past . . .'

'With murders, you mean?'

'With murders, yes. The only way I could possibly help your brother is by turning up some new evidence which would cast enough doubt on the verdict of murder to justify a reprieve. It's very unlikely that I could do it, but even trying would mean going round asking questions that people would rather I didn't ask. And I'd start with you because you probably know better than anybody else what kind of man he is.'

For once she didn't stare at me. She looked at the fire and adjusted round her shoulders the big knitted shawl she was wearing.

'What do you want to know about him?'

'What was he like as a child? Was he clever? Friendly? Quarrelsome?'

'Quarrelsome! There you go, like all the others, trying to make out . . .'

She was raising her voice, so I raised mine louder.

'I'm not trying to make out anything, only I don't suppose your brother is a saint and it won't help anybody trying to pretend he is. Either we talk without you firing up

59

at me all the time or you might as well go as you wanted to. After you've finished your tea, that is.'

'I've finished it.'

Ungraciously, and yet she didn't get up. Rose was giving me a shocked, hurt look. I was sorry for her, but it was her fault after all. There was silence for a while, then Janet said, more quietly, 'What do you want to know?'

Once we'd got that over she talked more calmly, some of her combativeness draining away. She even seemed to get some pleasure in talking about the better times before the skies fell in on them. The family had been working in the cotton trade since there were mills in Lancashire. Her father had been a spinner, one of the most skilled and highly paid classes of mill worker, then he'd had his arm broken pulling somebody out of the way of a machine and had to give it up. Her mother worked at the same mill before her lungs went from tuberculosis and the cotton dust and it was an accepted thing that the children should follow as soon as they left school at fourteen.

'There wasn't a lot of money around, especially after Dad's accident, but enough to keep a roof over our heads and meat on the table most days. After Mum died the neighbours were very good.'

She'd been just nine years old when her mother died, only female in the household and keeper of the family, whether she liked it or not. With the neighbours' help she got to school most days, and a week after her fourteenth birthday she took a job at one of the Newbiggin mills. This in addition to cooking, cleaning and washing for her father and three brothers. All this emerged without a trace of self-pity.

'Did Davie work at the same mill?'

'Yes, before he went to study at Manchester. Mr Newbiggin had picked him out, you see. He wanted him to get his qualifications as an engineer.'

'Osbert Newbiggin paid for Davie's training?'

'Only because it suited him. Davie had brains, you see.'

I noticed that she was putting it in the past tense. Also, that the idea that she might have brains too didn't seem to occur to her.

'So how did he know about Davie?'

'He won a prize for arithmetic at school. It was in the paper, so when he went up for his interview for a job at the mill, the foreman had a note about it and said the owner wanted to see him.'

'How long ago would that be?'

'He's twenty-four now and he was fourteen then, so that's ten years.'

'Can you remember what happened?'

'Well, he came home from the interview a bit nervous, as if he'd done something wrong, and said the owner wanted to see him and my dad up at the big house.'

'Crowberry Hall, that is?'

'Yes. Anyway, we got him up in his Sunday clothes and Dad went up with him. And Mr Newbiggin offered that if he did well in the mill for two years and went to night school to keep up his arithmetic he'd send him to Manchester when he was sixteen to train as an engineer.'

'Was Davie pleased?'

'Of course he was, and our dad was as proud as a dog with two tails, his lad being picked out by the owner.'

'Did he interview them in his study?'

'Yes, I remember Dad kept going on about all the books and pictures, and a harmonium. You'd have thought it was the Albert Hall itself, the way our dad kept on.'

When she talked about her father there was affection as well as annoyance in her voice. I imagined the father and the boy just out of school sitting there very upright in their best suits and starched collars, the owner dispensing patronage across his polished desk. Ten years later, if the jury were right, the boy had shot his benefactor in that very room.

'What about Davie? What did he think about Osbert Newbiggin at the time?'

'He didn't say much, but he was impressed. Like the fairy coming down off the Christmas tree it were, for him. He'd always wanted to go to college, but of course there'd been no question of that until Mr Newbiggin came up with the idea.'

There was a twist to her mouth every time she mentioned his name.

'Did you dislike Osbert Newbiggin at the time, when he was doing this for your brother?'

'No. I won't say I'd have kissed his shadow on the wall but I didn't dislike him. I was pleased enough for Davie, but I knew Newbiggin wouldn't be bothering with him unless he thought he was going to get more than his money's-worth out of him later. No, *I* wasn't bothered about him one way or the other. It was . . .'

'What?'

'Jimmy didn't like it. He was already in the union then and he didn't like his brother licking the boss's boots.'

'Jimmy being Davie's elder brother.'

'Two years older. I wouldn't want you to think he was jealous of Davie getting his chance – he's not like that – but he always says that favours from the bosses turn out expensive for the workers. He was right too.'

'Jimmy's a strong union man?'

'He's convenor for the whole mill.'

'The same mill, Newbiggin's mill?'

'Yes. He'd gone there from school, like the rest of us.'

'So Davie and Jimmy argued?'

'It wasn't so bad for the first two years, when Davie was just working at the mill like everybody else. Then he went away to Manchester for his training, and of course he came back with his head full of machines and how they'd soon be doing everything for themselves, with not even men to mind them. Of course, that was poison to Jimmy.'

'You had to try to keep the peace, I suppose.'

'God knows I tried to, though if the truth be known I was more on Jimmy's side of things than Davie's. I was in the union too by then. To be honest, it was a relief when Davie decided to move out into lodgings of his own.'

'He could afford that?'

'He was making more money than Jimmy. That was another thing.'

'Did he keep in touch after he moved out?'

'Oh, yes. He was only living two streets away and there was his washing for one thing. He'd drop it off every Sunday evening for me to do before I went in to work on Monday and he'd come to collect it after the ironing on Wednesday night. He'd sit in the kitchen and have a cup of tea and a chat. And Christmas, birthdays and funerals and so on, he'd be there. I mean, we hadn't quarrelled, not in that sense.'

'So Davie and Jimmy were still on speaking terms?'

'When they were in the same room, yes. But Jimmy was usually out at meetings and so on. Then it came to the lock-out eighteen months ago, when the bosses wouldn't let us work even if we wanted to, but Davie was still kept on to look after the machines.'

'Jimmy was angry about that?'

'As I said, Davie went on working in a lock-out. There's a word for that and I don't like using it about my own brother, but that's what he did. After that, Jimmy wouldn't have him in the house.'

'So you didn't see him?'

She looked uneasy. 'I still did his washing, only he'd have to bring it and collect it when Jimmy wasn't there. I'd put an old boot on top of the dustbin at the back to let him know it was safe.'

Rose, sitting on the floor on the other side of Janet, caught my eye and let her jaw drop, but then she wasn't used to the formidable family ties of these mill towns.

'Were things still as bad between them by the time Mr Newbiggin was killed last November?'

'No, because by then Davie wasn't working for him any more.'

'Why not?'

'First any of us knew of it was when he came in as we were sitting down to our tea, one Thursday in August, it was. As soon as he walked in the door, Jimmy grabbed his cap to walk out, but Davie told him it was all right, he wasn't a scab anymore.'

'Was that how he put it?'

'He said he'd given in his notice to Newbiggin, so Jimmy could stop looking at him like something the cat had sicked up.'

'Was Jimmy pleased?'

'He didn't let on he was at first. I suppose he was a bit suspicious and I couldn't blame him. But when he realised that Davie really had left, yes, he was pleased.'

'But Davie didn't move back in with you?'

'He said he was well suited where he was. He got a job in Manchester and went in on the train every day. We saw more of him though. He'd be in for his tea every Sunday.'

'And he and his brother got on well again?'

'They did. They'd go off to the pub together when he was home early enough, not that they were great drinkers but Jimmy meets his trade-union friends there.'

'Did Davie ever tell him or you why he'd left Newbiggin's?'

This was the first question I'd asked her that touched directly on the murder. I saw her go tense, but she answered calmly.

'He just said he was fed up with him.'

'Did you ask why?'

'That was his business. Jimmy and I thought they'd maybe had a quarrel over something to do with the machinery. He could be a bad tempered old bugger when someone crossed him.'

'But you didn't know that for sure?'

'We didn't pry into it very much. If Davie had taken a bit of a blow to his pride, we weren't going to make things worse. We were just glad to have him back in the family.'

Rose knelt to light the fire. We were near the dangerous

64

territory now and I shouldn't be surprised if Janet walked out after all.

'You say there was sabotage of a machine at Newbiggin's. Was this after Davie left the mill?'

'Yes.'

'Was Davie accused of it?'

She yanked on the ends of her shawl until it went tight round her shoulders.

'I'm that sick of the way everybody goes on about that bloody machine. No, nobody accused him in so many words. But it was a machine he'd been working on, a drawing frame. He'd invented a way of putting a new cylinder of slivers on automatically when the other one was empty. It was only the bit of it he'd invented that got damaged so . . .'

She shrugged. I had my answer. She thought Davie probably had damaged his own invention and was both too loyal to say it and too honest to deny it.

'Anyway, up to November last year Davie was still living two streets away from you and working in Manchester, and he and Jimmy were meeting for a drink when they could.'

'He got laid off the Manchester job in October. It was only seasonal.'

'So he had no job. What did he live on?'

'He had a bit of money put by from when he earned good wages.'

'Did you see more of him?'

'Not a lot. The lock-out had finished by then, and I was back working.'

'When was the last time you saw him before the murder?'

'Three days before. The Monday. He came in for some extra collars he'd wanted me to starch and had a cup of tea, then he and Jimmy went out to the pub.'

'The Cross Keys?'

'Yes. That was their usual.'

'Did he say anything about Newbiggin wanting to see him?'

'He hadn't heard from him by then. He didn't get the note from him until the day it happened.'

'The day Mr Newbiggin was murdered?'

She nodded.

'And this was the note asking Davie to go up to Crowberry Hall and see him?'

'Yes.'

'Did it come here or to his lodgings?'

'Here. I found it on the doormat when I was going out to work in the morning and dropped it off at his lodgings on my way.'

'Did you know who it was from?'

'I recognised the handwriting. Mr Newbiggin had written to Dad a couple of times when he took Davie on.'

'Was Davie in when you delivered it to his lodgings?'

'I just put it through the door. I don't think he was up. It was before six o'clock because I was on the early shift.'

'So you didn't know what was in the note?'

'No.'

'Didn't you think it was odd, Mr Newbiggin writing to Davie when there'd apparently been some sort of quarrel between them?'

'I thought he might be trying to make up to him, asking him to come back. Davie was a good engineer.'

That past tense again.

'If it had been that, how would you have felt about it?'

'Mixed. I'd have been glad for Davie, but things had been better between him and Jimmy and I didn't like the thought of them going back to what they had been.'

'Were you going to ask Davie about it?'

'Yes. I thought he'd be round as usual when I was doing his ironing and he'd tell me about it then.'

'And did he come round as usual?'

'No. I got tea for Dad and me – Jimmy was out at a union meeting – then I put up my ironing board in the kitchen and got on with it, expecting him to come in at any minute.'

'Were you worried when he didn't?'

'Not really. I thought maybe he'd met some friends or gone into Manchester on the train.'

'What was the first you knew about it?'

'The bell ringing. I'd gone out to the yard to call Dad in from his canaries and we both heard it tolling away up there.' Unconsciously, she drew the shawl closer round her.

'Did you know it was from Crowberry Hall?'

'We knew it was from one of the big houses up there. We thought it might be a fire practice. Then Jimmy came home and told us.'

'Told you what exactly?'

She stared at me. 'That he'd been shot.'

'How had Jimmy heard about it?'

'He was in the Cross Keys when it started and went running up the drive with some of the others. This girl, Newbiggin's cousin, came running down it, yelling blue murder. Then the police arrived and were trying to organise everybody into search parties in case someone was hiding in the shrubbery. Jimmy doesn't take kindly to being given orders from the police, so he came home. He'd seen Davie there in the bar and thought he'd most likely gone off with some of the others, then gone back to his lodgings.'

'You weren't worried about him?'

'Why should we be? We didn't know he was supposed to have been up at the Hall. The three of us sat up for a bit and had a cup of tea, talking about what had happened, then we went to bed. The next we knew it was still pitch dark, and there were the police pounding on the front door. Four o'clock in the morning, it was. We had to let them in because there were people hanging out of their windows all the way down the street. They wanted to know where Davie was, so of course we told them he was at his lodgings. They said no he wasn't, because they'd been waiting there for him all night. That was how it started.'

'Did they search the house there and then?'

'Yes. They'd come ready with a warrant. I suppose they expected to find him hiding under one of the beds.

Then when they didn't find him they were going through everything, the cupboards in the kitchen, the canary sheds, the pigswill bin, the lot. They were civil enough, I suppose, but they wouldn't tell us what they were looking for. I know now, of course.'

'What?'

'The gun.'

'Did they find anything?'

'One of them was out the back going through my ash-bin by lantern light. He came in with those bits of black stuff, all melted and twisted with bits of cinders sticking to them, to show the sergeant. Did we know what they were? Jimmy said it looked like bits of a gramophone record. Did we have a gramophone? No, of course we didn't, we couldn't afford one. Anyway, they took them away on the off-chance.'

And a few hours later the police would hear, from Newbiggin's old friend, about the recorded voice on the telephone.

'Do you know how the bits of gramophone record got in your ash-bin?'

'No more than the man in the moon.'

She gave me a look that said 'take it or leave it'. She'd done what I'd asked and told me about it, now she thought it was my turn.

'Why did Davie run away?'

The question came quietly from Rose, still kneeling on the floor and looking up at her.

'Because he thought he'd get blamed, and he were right.'

I asked if she'd seen him at all in the months from the murder until the police had found him in a Liverpool churchyard. She shook her head.

'Never a sight or a word, not to any of us. I thought maybe . . .'

'That he was dead?'

'Yes.'

'Have you seen him since?'

'They let him have visits. Dad and I went to see him last week. We're allowed once a week now that they're going to . . .' Even she had to fight to say it. '. . . now that they're going to hang him.'

Silence for several breaths, apart from the fire crackling.

'When you see him, do you talk about what happened?'

'Sometimes.'

'And he's told you he didn't kill him?'

'Yes.'

'Has he said anything to you about who he thinks might have killed him?'

'How would he know?'

She muttered it, head down. Since she'd said that they were going to hang him, all the energy had gone out of her. She must be deathly tired, tramping the streets with her petition all day, not sleeping properly at night, still with the washing, cooking and cleaning to do for her father and remaining brother.

'Have you eaten this evening?'

She had to think about it.

'I had a bite of tea.'

Rose looked at me, then put the kettle on again and got bread and cheese out of the meat safe. While this was going on Janet sat staring at the fire and when it was ready accepted food and drink, but I doubt if she even knew what she was eating. Then she stood up.

'Well, are you going to help?'

'In all honesty, I don't see how I can . . .'

Her eyes on me, also Rose's eyes. I was caught between grey and brown stares like a hare between two greyhounds.

'. . . but if there's anything I can think of, I'll do it.'

She adjusted her shawl and would have walked out into the dark without a light, except Rose and I insisted on taking her as far as the road with the oil lamp. We wanted her to take the lamp with her but she wouldn't. 'I can see the way from here.'

The road was a pale streak, running down to the slate roofs of the town, silver in the starlight. As we stood there, the town clock chimed nine, a loud chime that you'd hear far over the moor.

I thought of '*When he will hear the stroke of eight/And not the stroke of nine*', and hoped Janet had never read Housman. But what did it matter, because you couldn't hear a clock chime without thinking. We said goodnight and watched her as she walked down the hill, striding fast. When we couldn't hear her footsteps any more we turned and made our way back across the dry grass towards the firelit window of Old Ferris's cottage.

'Oh, Rose, what have you gone and got us into?'

She didn't answer.

SEVEN

I COULDN'T SETTLE TO SUPPER, reading or anything else. It might not have been much of a promise I'd given Janet Kendal, but it was enough to wreck any peace of mind. Rose said little, but there was a mixture of apology and expectation in the way she moved round the small space. What did she expect me to do, for goodness sake?

About half an hour after Janet had left I went out too, telling Rose not to wait up for me. She didn't ask questions, which was just as well because I didn't know where I was heading or what I intended to do. I just wanted to get out.

There wasn't much moon, but my feet took me by force of habit up the path Stuart and I had followed on the first evening. Since then I'd been avoiding the sight of Crowberry Hall, but now an itch to see it took me scrambling up Shelf Rock, the gritstone ledges of it so familiar to my hands and feet from a long way back that I could find them in the dark. I stood on the flat top, looking down. No lights or music in the garden tonight, but several lighted windows in the house itself. I was looking onto the back of it, so the lights in the downstairs windows probably belonged to the kitchen area.

Ten o'clock. The maid would be washing up the dinner things. Was it the same maid who'd been there on the night Newbiggin was shot, the one who'd let in Davie Kendal? Probably not. The house had been unoccupied for a while so the servants were probably paid off. The trail had gone colder than the night air rolling down from the high moors. In any case, there was no reason to hope it would lead anywhere but back to Davie Kendal.

I walked to the edge of the rock. In the old days there'd been what Stuart and I called the bramble slide. You sat on the edge of the rock then pushed yourself down a steep bank to one side of the rocks, keeping hands tucked on chest and head curled down over them to protect exposed skin from the tunnel of brambles as you plunged through it. At the bottom of the slide you were in Crowberry Hall territory and on hostile land. I found myself sitting on the rock with my legs over the edge, curious to know if the earth slide were still there. Probably not, after all these years. I probed with one boot toe and it slid easily on dry, hard earth. Then memory took over and I heard in my mind Stuart's voice at twelve years old or so, daring me, telling me to get on with it. I pushed off, curled and plunged.

A few seconds later, covered with bits of bramble and leaf mould, I was picking myself up in a thicket of scrub willow and juniper at the far edge of the Newbiggins' lawn. Climbing back up the bramble slide would have been a pricklier business than coming down it, so I went on across the lawn, through a gap in the stone balustrade and onto the terrace. As all that had been built since my time I had to step carefully round benches, under the lines of unlit light bulbs, round the stone dolphin in his pond. I'd been right about the kitchen area. That was off to my left, with the clashing of pans coming from it. If anybody had come out I couldn't have told them what I was doing as I didn't know myself. But nobody came and I went on round the side of the house. My foot crunched on a gravel path and I took a hasty sideways step onto lawn. On the other side of the path was a flower-bed, full of chrysanthemums, from the smell of them. Last November there'd been marks in the flower-bed, so Bill Musgrave had said, where somebody had taken a wheelbarrow up to the study window to wheel away Osbert Newbiggin's gramophone. The windows on my left might be Newbiggin's study itself, where it had all happened. I stopped and looked but there were no lights on in the room and the blinds were pulled right down. But there was a patch of light further ahead of me along the path, falling dimly on chrysanths, gravel path and lawn. The sitting room, probably, with Newbiggin's nephew in residence. I edged up to it cautiously, saw the heavy cream lining of curtains drawn over the window and tiptoed past, still on the lawn. At some point, if I was going on with this, I'd need to talk to Osbert Newbiggin's family, but not now.

At the front of the house was a wide apron of gravel for motor cars and carriages to turn. Standing at the edge of it with a shrubbery behind me, I could look down on the town, the line of gas lamps that marked the High Street, the long ridges of slate-roofed terraces climbing the hill at right angles to it and further off the huge rectangular cotton mills, windows glowing even at this hour. Immediately below me there were no roofs, just more shrubbery with an occasional taller tree heaving out of it and a space between rhododendron bushes that was the opening of the drive. I stood for a few minutes in the dark under the rhododendrons, looking up at the front door. There was a light showing from the glass panel above it. An imposing door between Ionic columns with three steps up to it and then a wide, tiled porch. Ten years ago a clever boy and his father had walked up those steps at the boss's summons. Ten months ago the clever boy had walked up them again, intending murder. That elaborate, although unsuccessful, attempt with the gramophone record certainly proved premeditation.

Before I started down the drive I struck a match and checked my watch. Five minutes past ten. It was a steep drive and although it must have been wide enough for cars and carriages it seemed narrow in the dark, with the rhododendrons pushing in from both sides. It was slippery too, the gravel sparse and probably mossy in places. A nasty place to run down on a dark night. The cousin Laura was wearing her indoor clothes when the men from the public house met her; indoor shoes as well, probably. Half-past ten on a November night, so darker and colder than this. Terrified, slipping, probably falling, 'yelling blue murder'. That's what Janet had said and she'd had it from her brother Jimmy, who'd been there. The drive turned a bend, then widened, and there was a building just below me on my right. Bill Musgrave had talked about a gate lodge from which the recording of Newbiggin's voice had been played.

I checked my watch again. Twenty-past ten, so it had taken a quarter of an hour to get here from the house in the dark, not hurrying. Somebody pushing a gramophone in a wheelbarrow would probably have taken longer, as I presumed they were sensitive machines, intolerant of jolting. In the dark, too, as this was supposed to have happened between six and eight o'clock. Twenty minutes, say, from the house to the lodge by wheelbarrow. It was a squat little stone building. There were no lights on, but a dog round the back started barking when it heard my footsteps and a chain rattled. I hurried on in case anyone came out to see why the dog was barking.

Once past the lodge the drive made another bend and delivered you to the centre of the town. I walked between stone pillars into a narrow cobbled street with a blank wall on one side and an open shed on the other that looked like a repair place for beer barrels. On the corner where it joined the High Street, about a hundred yards away, was a public house with the sign of two crossed keys on a velvet cushion. It was large and respectable-looking, with windows patterned in frosted glass and a gas lamp over the door. I went closer to check my watch again and found it had taken me no more than four minutes to walk from the lodge to that point. While I was standing there the door opened, wafting a warm smell of beer and a buzz of conversation, and four men came out.

They were calling goodnight to the men inside, absorbed in that and their conversation. They wore dark jackets and cloth caps and were quite sober, as if they'd been at a meeting rather than a sociable event. I hadn't intended to say anything to them – although it had crossed my mind that they might have been some of the men who ran out when they heard the bell tolling – but as they came out one of them turned and saw me. I could see his face clearly in the light from the door and for the moment there was something like shock in it. He stood there and stared at me without saying anything. I realised that a woman coming on them suddenly, late at night, from the direction of the Crowberry Hall drive, might bring back a memory the town would rather forget. One of the men with him, not seeing me, went on talking to him.

'Jimmy, did you hear what I've been saying about . . .?'

Then he followed the direction of the man's eyes and saw me too. He looked surprised and instantly took off his cap.

'Goodnight, miss.'

The three others did the same, but Jimmy's cap came off last. The one who'd spoken first asked me kindly if I needed directions anywhere. When I said no thank you, they walked away along the High Street, carrying on their conversation. The man called Jimmy was tall, probably in his late twenties and a little older than the others. There might be half a dozen men named Jimmy among the customers of the Cross Keys, but that look he'd given me, a very direct look from under dark bars of eyebrows, reminded me of Janet Kendal. I was almost certain that I'd just met Davie's elder brother.

It was a long walk back to the cottage by road and Rose was asleep when I got there. When I got up the next morning she'd left breakfast ready for me and a note to say she'd gone down to the town. I could guess why. It was a fine day outside. Through the open doorway I could see the rowan tree, berries scarlet already although the leaves were still green against the blue sky. A robin was singing from it, practising for winter. A wasp buzzed round the dish of pears next to me on the table, settled on a bruised and squashy place and speared it with its black tongue. I was just finishing my second cup of coffee when there were footsteps outside.

'Nell, are you in there?'

Pauline's voice. I called to her and she came in, carrying baskets.

'It's such a lovely morning, I wondered if you'd like to come out blackberrying.'

She was wearing a black skirt and an old jacket of mulberry-coloured wool, so that the stains from black-berries wouldn't show, and had a walking stick for hooking the brambles. After Janet's visit the picnic air of Pauline's invitation seemed a cruel contrast and I had to remind myself that she didn't know anything about it. Or did she? Pauline was far from a fool. Even if Stuart had said nothing to her she might have drawn her own conclusions about Bill Musgrave's arrival at her dinner party. Was it a blackberrying or a fishing expedition she had in mind? She waited while I got my hat and jacket. No lock on old Ferris's cottage, just a wooden latch to drop. Both cats were under the mountain ash, looking up, tense with desire, at the robin. We strolled to the road, swinging a basket apiece.

'There's a little dingle on the other side of the road where they ripen late. We were there with the boys last weekend, but they weren't quite ready.'

'The Pass of Glencoe, we called it. Stuart and I used to ambush each other.' With terrible arguments about who was to play the traitorous Campbells.

When we got there it was more overgrown than I remembered it, with clusters of huge shining blackberries untouched. Typically thoughtful, Pauline had brought old leather gloves for both of us, with a third pair in the bottom of the basket.

'I thought Rose might be with us. Is she any happier? I do wish we could do something to help.'

'Not unless you've got a school in your pocket. I feel guilty about Rose.'

'Why? You've done a lot for her.'

'Not enough. I've helped to take her out of one world, but there isn't another one ready for her yet.'

I explained that she'd gone down to the town and added experimentally that I thought she was helping Janet Kendal with her petition. Pauline picked away, her back to me.

'You know Stuart and I have signed it?'

'Stuart thinks he's guilty.'

'Yes, but he doesn't want him to hang.'

'What about you, do you think he's guilty?'

She turned away to drop a handful of blackberries into the basket.

'Nell, I just don't know.'

'The evidence against him sounds almost conclusive.'

'I suppose so. Can you reach that big cluster if I hook it down a bit?'

For some time we picked in silence with the sun warming our backs. The blackberries were warm to the tongue and sweet as mountain honey. I'd abandoned the gloves and soon my fingers were stained purple like the feet of wine treaders. I might have left it there, except I sensed that Pauline wanted to be persuaded to speak.

'And yet you have your doubts?'

'I know nothing about it, really.'

'You must have known something about Osbert New-biggin, even if you weren't on visiting terms.'

'Only what everybody knew.'

'The mills, the music and so on?'

'Yes.'

'What about the rest of the family? Did you know the old lady or the cousin?'

'I'd seen both of them across a room, that was all.'

She'd been holding a bramble down precariously by the edge of the leaf. The leaf tore and the bramble sprang away from her, whisking across her face. It hardly touched her, but she cried out in alarm as if it had drawn blood.

'I'm sorry. I understand if you don't want to talk about it.'

'No. I'm glad you're looking into it. You are, aren't you?'

'How did you know?'

'Bill Musgrave is very persuasive.'

I was nettled. 'As a matter of fact, I sent Bill Musgrave away with a flea in his ear. It was Janet Kendal who persuaded me.'

She gave a little smile, as if she didn't quite believe that.

'Stuart was annoyed with Bill. I told him we couldn't have kept it from you in any case.'

'You're glad I'm taking an interest. Why?' I watched her pouring blackberries carefully from her basket to mine. 'You must have a reason.'

She hesitated. 'Nothing you could call a reason. Only . . .'

'An instinct then. Only what?'

'Only . . . oh, I don't know. Just odd little things people have said, or probably not said. Or the way they've looked, or looked as if they wanted to look . . . I'm not making sense.'

'About the Kendal family?'

'No, about him, Osbert Newbiggin.'

'Did you get the impression that he was the kind of man somebody might have wanted to kill?'

She peeled off one of her gloves, looked down at it as if trying to work out where it had come from and spoke hesitantly at first, then faster.

'I didn't know him well enough. But . . . but I do remember something odd the week after the funeral. Our local paper had two pages on it, of course – who was there, who sent wreaths and so on – and everybody saying what a loss and what a great benefactor he'd been. You know the kind of thing. Anyway, I'd gone out to the kitchen to talk to Jeannie about making the Christmas puddings and . . .'

'Jeannie being the cook?'

'Yes. Anyway, as I came along the passage, I could hear her reading the report from the local paper out to Sarah, all about what a good man he'd been. Sarah's the girl who comes up from the town to clean. She can't really read. I mean, she pretends she can, but once Jeannie asked her to bring the redcurrant jelly out of the larder and I found her in tears with all the jars round her and . . . anyway, the point is that Jeannie was reading to Sarah, so I hesitated before going in. I was afraid they might think I'd be annoyed with them for reading instead of getting on with their work, which I wouldn't be. So I thought I'd wait there until Jeannie had finished. Only she didn't. She read out the bit about how he was a pillar of the community, then she made a rude noise, a really surprisingly rude noise for Jeannie. Then she said, "Well, I'm not going to waste any more of my breath reading this nonsense. He was a wicked old hypocrite and I hope St Peter's not waiting up for him, because he'll be going to the other place for certain." Then she told Sarah to get on with brushing out the range and I coughed to let them know I was there and went in.'

'Did you ask her about it?'

'Of course not. It would have sounded as if I'd been spying on them.'

'Does Jeannie come from a strong trade-union family?' I thought her resentment might come from the strikes and lock-outs.

'No, that's the funny thing. She's Tory through and through. Stuart tries to tease her about it sometimes, only I won't let him. She's convinced trade unions are ruining the country.'

'So it wasn't anything to do with his record as an employer?'

'I shouldn't think so. Nell, you aren't going to question Jeannie, are you? I'd hate her to think . . .'

'Not if you don't want me to. If there's anything, I should be able to find out from elsewhere.'

'There's one good thing about it in any rate. You'll be staying here longer.'

'A couple of days, if you'll have us.'

Long enough to keep my promise to Janet, such as it was. Long enough, probably, to convince myself that Davie

Kendal had been guilty as charged. If that was the case, I'd go back to London and add my voice to those trying to persuade the Home Secretary to commute his sentence to life imprisonment. But that would be only a nod to my conscience, with no hope of success. One morning I'd open my *Manchester Guardian*, read that sentence had been duly carried out and that would be the end of it.

We picked a few more blackberries, but the enthusiasm had gone out of it and Pauline said we should be getting back. I helped her carry the blackberries to the kitchen, refused an invitation to lunch and went down into the town to send some telegrams.

When I got back, Stuart was sitting under the rowan tree looking as black as a peat bog.

'Pauline says you've decided to stay.'

'You might try to look pleased about it.'

'I might be pleased, if I didn't know the reason. I should have kicked Bill Musgrave from here to Huddersfield.'

'It's really not his fault. But I'm going to see him tomorrow, so if you want me to give him a message . . .'

'So he's summoned you to Manchester, has he?'

'Not at all. I've sent him a telegram and told him I'm coming.'

'You'll be raising false hopes. Stirring it up again will only make things worse for the family.'

'But it was his sister who asked me . . .'

'It's not just the sister to consider.'

'Who then?'

I was looking at his face when I asked the question and recognised, from the stubborn set of the jaw, that Stuart was embarrassed by it. If I'd known him less well I might have misinterpreted it, but it was exactly the look he'd had on his face at nine years old when the adults wanted to know who'd put a ferret in the sideboard.

'Well, there's the nephew and so on.'

'Nephew! How long have you been holding a brief for

the heirs of mill owners? The nephew seems to be the only one who's come out of it better off.'

'Is that what you're trying to do? Prove the nephew killed the old man for his money? I'm afraid it won't work because he happened to be away in Hamburg at the time, buying machinery.'

'I'm not trying to do anything so stupid!'

'Well, then, what are you trying to do?'

Stuart and I bickered about it for a while, then Rose came back, hungry and footsore, and he left us to our supper. Rose asked what I'd been doing all day.

'Blackberrying,' I said.

She looked reproachful, but was pleased when I told her I was going to discuss things with Bill Musgrave. Too pleased. I wished Stuart would give me credit for a little more practical intelligence, and Rose for much less.

EIGHT

THEY DIDN'T LOOK LIKE THE most prosperous chambers on the northern circuit, either inside or out. The brass plate needed polishing and the names on it were already blurred by the sooty air. The door opened directly onto a steep wooden staircase with thin carpeting. At the top of the staircase, behind a door with an opaque glass panel with 'Knock and Enter' painted on it, was the clerks' room. Mr Musgrave was expecting me. He came striding across the room to shake hands, dodging files piled several feet deep on the floor. The sash window was open onto the street, but the smell of pipe tobacco lingered.

I said, 'I was abominably rude to you. I'm sorry.'

'Were you?'

There was a carved oak chair with a cracked leather seat in front of his desk. He dusted it off with a handkerchief before inviting me to sit down and called through to his clerk to bring coffee.

'I still think it's a desperate case.'

'Of course it's desperate. Why else would I come to you? What's funny?'

I was smiling at meeting a person even more tactless than I am, but didn't tell him so.

'I've met his sister Janet since we spoke.'

'Ah. I suppose she told you about my shortcomings.'

'She didn't mention you.'

'She believes I could have done more for him. If he'd had Solon and Solomon representing him in chorus, she'd still be convinced his lawyers let him down.'

'He can't have been the easiest of clients.'

'He certainly was not. So Miss Kendal persuaded you to take up the case, did she?'

Was there a hint of hurt pride, that she'd succeeded where he failed? For all his confidence, he was clearly not a successful lawyer if you measured success in terms of prosperity. His dark suit was decent but a little shiny round the cuffs, and his eyes were tired.

'If anything, what she told me makes things sound even worse.'

The coffee arrived, good Mocha from the smell of it, and a plate of biscuits. He poured, then settled down at his desk. The files on it were arranged in heaps of varying heights tied up with pink tape, so that he looked out at clients like a defender from beribboned castle ramparts.

'Even worse than I told you?'

'Yes. What's this business about an argument with Osbert Newbiggin, and threatening him?'

'Davie Kendal never threatened him. Unfortunately there's some evidence that he was seen outside Crowberry Hall at night about a month before the shooting. The prosecution chose to present that as a threat, and the judge didn't stop them.'

'What happened?'

'Newbiggin, his old aunt and Laura, the cousin, were sitting at dinner, with the curtains undrawn, and this face appeared at the window. The old lady jumped up and screamed, and whoever it was ran away. Newbiggin himself had his back to the window, so he didn't see anything. Laura only had the impression of somebody out of the corner of her eye. The old lady is convinced it was Davie.'

'Did they call the police?'

'Yes. They looked round the grounds but didn't find anybody, then left it at that because no harm had been done after all. But Newbiggin made a great business of getting all the locks reinforced and let it be known that he had a gun and wouldn't hesitate to use it.'

'Extreme in the circumstances, wasn't it?'

'There were the lock-outs, remember. There'd been a lot of bad feeling.'

'Did the police question Davie?'

'No, because he hadn't been mentioned at the time. It was only after the murder that old Mrs Bolter let it be known that she thought it was Davie Kendal outside the window.'

'Does Davie deny it?'

'He did at first, then some evidence came out in the course of the trial that made it very likely he was there. I tried to have it ruled out, but the judge thought otherwise. When the prosecution cross-questioned Davie he admitted that he was there but wouldn't say what he was doing.'

'That must have been a bad moment for you.'

'It was. I could have strang . . .' He looked down at his hands, twisting as if at a dish-cloth, and stopped what he was saying. 'Well, let's say it didn't make my job any easier.'

'Then there was this question of sabotage at one of the Newbiggin mills.'

'Yes. The prosecution would have liked to bring that up too, if they could, but at least I managed to stop that. There was no evidence against Davie.'

'But I gather it was sabotage of a specialised kind, and on a piece of machinery that Davie had invented.'

'Who told you that?'

'Janet. I think she assumed I'd heard something about it already.'

There was a lump of rock on his blotter with a vein of white quartz slicing through it. He took it in his hands and turned it over and over as he looked at me.

'She also assumed that I knew there'd been some kind of falling out between her brother and Osbert Newbiggin months before the murder. I suppose that's common knowledge too.'

He sighed. 'Very much so. Until sometime last summer, Davie was not only one of Newbiggin's favoured workers, he was practically a collaborator on one of his favourite projects.'

'The recording of *The Messiah*?'

'As far as I can gather, Davie wasn't too concerned with what they were recording but he was fascinated with the mechanical business of it. Newbiggin was buying all this equipment, and for a young man of Davie's mechanical turn of mind it was like catnip to a cat. He was up there at the hall at all hours working on it.'

'In Newbiggin's study?'

'Yes.'

'So he knew the place well?'

'Better than almost anybody. Newbiggin wasn't paying him extra. He'd be up there after his work, just for the interest of it.'

'But last summer Davie gave in his notice at work and this all stopped. Why?'

'I wish I knew.'

'You must have asked him?'

'Time after time. All he'd tell me was that he'd had a disagreement with Mr Newbiggin and given in his notice.'

'A disagreement over work?'

'What else would it be?'

'I gather his brother is an important man in the union.'

A shadow came over his face. He had a very expressive face for a man.

'Yes, the ambitious Jimmy.'

'I think I may have seen him. Dark, quite tall. Walks like a man who's used to people stepping aside for him.'

'Yes, that sounds like Jimmy.'

'According to Janet, he was pleased when Davie had the quarrel with Mr Newbiggin. Does he know what it was about?'

'He said he was glad his brother had left. He claims not to know why.'

'Claims?'

'Oh, I got some rhetoric about Davie having realised that his place was with the working class, but no more than that. I don't believe him.'

'Does he dislike Davie?'

'I didn't get the feeling of much warmth there, but I don't think he wants to see him hanged. He put a lot of work in trying to support Davie's alibi.'

'Which I assume isn't good.'

'It's hardly an alibi at all. Even if that business with the recorded voice had worked, it was shaky. When that didn't work it was worse than useless. More coffee?'

He poured, then picked up one of the biscuits without offering any to me. 'Roswal.'

A grey muzzle came out from under the desk, grabbed the biscuit and disappeared. It was so fast that I'd have thought I'd imagined it, apart from the sound of crunching.

'A wolfhound?'

'Deerhound. Good dog, but hates being left on his own. We were talking about an alibi, or the lack of it. You know Davie had an appointment to see Newbiggin at Crowberry Hall at six o'clock.'

'Yes. A note came to his sister's house and she delivered it to his lodgings.'

'That's right. I've seen that note and it was exactly what Davie claims, two lines in Newbiggin's indisputable handwriting on Crowberry Hall notepaper, asking him to call at six o'clock that evening.'

'It doesn't give a reason?'

'No, and neither does Davie. When I pressed him very hard he said he supposed Newbiggin might be hoping to persuade him to come back and work for him, but it wasn't convincing. Anyway, Davie kept that appointment to the minute and was taken to Newbiggin's study by the maid. We don't know what happened at that meeting and we don't know when he left. Neither the maid, nor the cook nor the two ladies heard or saw him go.'

'What does he say?'

'According to Davie, Newbiggin and he talked for some time about something to do with the recordings, then Newbiggin let him out the back way so as not to bother the maid again.'

'Odd, wasn't it?'

'Yes. That's another of the little things that made my job difficult. We only have Davie's word that things happened that way. There's no witness for how and when he left the house.'

'If he really was let out of the back door, wouldn't the cook and maid have heard him go?'

'Not necessarily. The kitchen is up a side corridor and they were clashing plates about, getting ready for dinner.'

'And I suppose your client's version is that he left Newbiggin living and breathing?'

'Very much so. He says the first thing he knew about anything being wrong was when the bell started ringing sometime after ten o'clock that night.'

'And in his story he doesn't know what time he left Newbiggin?'

'Not precisely. We know it must have been before seven-thirty, because he was seen in the Cross Keys about then. It's a long drive to walk down . . .'

'About twenty minutes in the dark, from the front of the house to the Cross Keys. So if his version of events is true, he would have left Newbiggin by around ten-past seven.'

'Yes. Any number of witnesses saw him at the bar, including his brother Jimmy. A few of them remembered that he seemed a bit upset or excited about something. Others, including Jimmy, say he seemed quite normal.'

'What time did he leave the pub?'

'Nobody's sure. It was a busy night.'

'So he could have gone back up the drive to the lodge and played that recording over the telephone at eight o'clock?'

'Yes. It's about five minutes from the pub to the lodge.

He could have gone up there, played the recording and been back before anyone missed him.'

'And the assumption must be that Newbiggin was unconscious and as good as dead by then, otherwise there'd have been no point in pretending he was making the call?'

'Exactly.'

'So what does Davie say he did between leaving the bar and being back there in time to hear the bell ringing at about half-past ten?'

Abstractedly, Bill bent down with another biscuit. The muzzle appeared from under his desk, engulfed, disappeared.

'He says he went up on the edge of the moor, about a mile out of town, to see Rolling Toby.'

'Who or what is Rolling Toby?'

'Just about the least convincing alibi witness you could think of – even if we could find him, which we can't. Rolling Toby is an itinerant tinker. He's got a rackety old pony and trap and in summer he goes off in it and might be anywhere from the west country to the Scottish border. Every winter he comes back here to hibernate in a hovel up on the moors. All the local lads know him because he breeds lurchers and takes them out hare coursing. He's done several terms in prison for poaching and petty theft and would have done a lot more if the landowners had their way.'

'He doesn't sound a likely friend for an ambitious young man like Davie Kendal.'

'He isn't. But the fact is that at about seven-thirty on the night Newbiggin died, Davie was in the bar of the Cross Keys asking if anybody had seen Rolling Toby. Davie says so, and several witnesses confirm it.'

'Rolling Toby was known at the Cross Keys?'

'He was known everywhere, mainly as a man to throw out. Anyway, Davie was told he hadn't been seen there that night, so he went off to look for him. According to his story, he found him and talked to him in his place up on the moor.'

'Why did he want to see him?'

'He says he was thinking of buying a dog off him.'

'A mile out of town on a November night.'

'I know. It doesn't stand up for a moment.'

'And what does Rolling Toby say about it?'

'He doesn't, because we haven't been able to ask him. Newbiggin was killed in November. The police didn't catch up with Davie until February and he was tried and sentenced at the assizes at the start of April. The only reason he's still alive now is that there were a couple of points in the judge's summing up that made a not particularly hopeful basis for an appeal. By the time Davie came up for trial Rolling Toby was on the road again and nobody knew where he was. We've been looking for him all summer, but quite without success.'

'You say he comes back here for the winter?'

'Yes, but by then . . .'

We looked at each other, over his ramparts of files.

'Even then, he'd be a forlorn hope. The only safe assumption is that Newbiggin had been shot before that telephone call at eight o'clock. Therefore whether Davie was or was not with Rolling Toby later in the evening doesn't matter a damn – excuse me.'

'Except as part of a fake alibi. If Davie had managed to make out that Newbiggin were alive at eight o'clock, he'd have to try to account for his movements after that.'

'Yes. So why throw away the whole elaborate plot by choosing the least reliable witness in the whole of Lancashire?'

'It's a mixture of ingenuity and stupidity.'

'Yes, and I don't believe that Davie is stupid.'

'So what's the explanation? Or are there things you can't tell me?'

'Of course I can't tell you anything that's confidential to the client – although there's nothing of that nature that would help in any case. All I'm telling you either came out at the trial or is a matter of public knowledge. But there's nothing that says I can't give you my impressions.'

'And one of those impressions is that the man's own family know something they won't tell you?'

'Yes, Janet and Jimmy at any rate.'

'I think you must have at least a suspicion of what that something might be.'

'Oh?'

'That brother Jimmy was an accomplice.'

He nearly upset his coffee cup. 'Did Janet give you that impression?'

'No, not from anything she said. But as a union man Jimmy had more reason to dislike Newbiggin than Davie had. After all, the man had treated Davie quite well so far as we know. And Jimmy was in the Cross Keys that evening.'

'I assume we're talking in confidence here and I'll admit that it did occur to me. But there's one very strong objection. Jimmy has a solid series of alibis from five o'clock that evening until the time when the murder was discovered. He was in the Cross Keys because that's where the branch committee of his union meet. The landlord's a sympathiser and he lets them have an upstairs room for nothing, and Jimmy was in that room, with ten people as witnesses, until about seven when they all went down to the bar. From there he and most of the rest of them went on to another meeting, coming back into the pub just before ten.'

'Why are they so sure about Jimmy's movements?'

'Because Jimmy's an important man. He practically runs the union branch and there are always people wanting to talk to him.'

'He's not enthusiastic about new machinery. He might have encouraged Davie to commit sabotage.'

'Nobody can prove that. The sabotage didn't come up at the trial because the prosecution knew I'd be down on them like a ton of bricks if they tried it. Anyway, it seems to me that there's one very strong objection to your theory of a conspiracy.'

'What?'

'It would be such a poor one. Just look at it – Davie takes all the risks and Jimmy can't even provide him with a proper alibi. This business of happening to see him ordering a drink at about half-past seven is as good as useless. You're asking me to believe that he agrees to murder the man – mainly to suit his brother's purposes – and doesn't even insist on that in return.'

'And yet you still think Davie's family know something they won't tell you. If so, it must be even more damaging to any hope of a reprieve.'

He hesitated again, turning the rock with its quartz stripe round and round. 'Yes, I'd thought of that.'

'And yet you still have this hunch that Davie is innocent?'

I thought for a while he wasn't going to answer, then he burst out: 'Yes. I know when I have to talk about it to somebody from outside, it sounds crazy. The man's guilty and an arrogant fool into the bargain. And yet, don't you see, it's the very foolishness of it that makes me certain there's something I've not been told?' He stared at me, like the dog beseeching a biscuit.

'And if that something proved he were guilty . . . ?'

'Well, at least I'd know, wouldn't I, and I wouldn't have to go on blaming myself. Or waking up women I hardly know at two o'clock in the morning to talk about it.'

'So you make a habit of it?'

'No. That's not what I meant. Only you. You see, your brother had been boasting a bit about you . . .'

'Good heavens.'

'. . . so when I heard you were visiting I suppose I was ready to grasp at any straw.'

He looked startled when he saw I was laughing.

'I'm sorry, was that tactless?'

'Don't worry. Tell me, do you know much about the other side, the Newbiggins?' I was thinking, although I didn't tell him, about what Pauline had said.

'Only from hearing the evidence and seeing his aunt in the witness box.'

'Didn't the cousin give evidence too?'

'No. The prosecution didn't need her. It was the old aunt, Mrs Bolter, who found the body, and in the prowler incident it was Mrs Bolter who seems to have got the best view of the man's face. They called the aunt, and the maid who let Davie in at the front door, but not Laura. Judging by her statement to the police, she was too shaken to be much use as a witness in any case.'

'All the same, there's one question it would have been interesting to ask her.'

'What's that?'

'Why she went rushing down the drive.'

He stared at me. 'To get help, of course.'

'But they had a telephone in the house. They could have been talking to the police station in a matter of seconds. Instead of that, somebody rushes off to ring the bell and Laura goes shrieking down a long dark drive in her indoor things.'

'Shock, I suppose. I gather she's the hysterical type. We did think of calling her as a defence witness but if she'd broken down when I questioned her it might have prejudiced the jury against us even more. I don't like weeping women, professionally speaking.' He gave his piece of rock a few more spins. 'Or any other way, come to that.'

'Why were you thinking of calling her as a witness for the defence?'

'In her first statement to the police, Laura Newbiggin said she saw a gun there on the floor among the feathers and the broken records and so on. The aunt and the cook didn't see it and the police didn't find one. So the police concluded she imagined it, which is probably right. Where it mattered was in this question of identifying the man prowling round the house a few weeks before the murder. Laura didn't get a clear view of him in any case so we only had the aunt's word that it was Davie Kendal.

It did occur to me when we were preparing the case that I might try to play one witness against the other, to shake the aunt's story. But we decided she'd be a bad witness for us, and as it happened the aunt was a very good one for the other side.'

'Was Newbiggin's gun ever found?'

'No. The police spent days searching the shrubbery and everywhere else. The prosecution's assumption was that Davie disposed of it somewhere on his travels.'

'And Davie?'

'He says he never even knew where Newbiggin kept his gun.'

'If they'd found the gun, they'd have tested it for fingerprints, I suppose.'

'Of course.'

Going through the hopeless case again seemed to have depressed him. He sighed and I followed his eyes to the wall behind me. A blanket boldly patterned in red, indigo and sand colour was hanging there, the brightest thing in the cluttered, dusty office.

'From the Andes?'

'Yes. I keep it there to remind me there is another world. Do you ever feel you simply want to head away from it all and keep walking?'

'Sometimes.' I'd had it very strongly up on the moors the other day.

'Ah well. Is there anything else you'd like to know?'

'You told me nobody had heard the shot and that it might have been fired through a cushion to muffle it.'

'Yes.'

'So presumably whoever shot Osbert Newbiggin would have to hold the cushion to his head with one hand and fire through it with the other?'

'Yes.'

'But I gather he wasn't a weak old man. He was a powerful man in middle age. Why didn't he put up a struggle?'

'Judging by the condition of the room, he put up quite a considerable struggle.'

'But didn't shout for help?'

'If the cushion were being held over his mouth, he couldn't.'

'So the person who shot him comes up behind him, holds a cushion over his mouth, keeps it there while he struggles enough to knock over some of the furniture and break records, then shoots him through it?'

He was giving me a curious, narrow-eyed look.

'So what do you deduce from that?'

'I don't know. Did the police look for tooth-marks?'

'Tooth-marks?'

'On the cushion. If somebody were holding a cushion against your mouth, wouldn't you bite it?'

'You know, I didn't think of that. I don't think anybody else did.'

The look was even more curious, as if trying to work out what kind of world I came from, where people went around leaving tooth-marks on cushions. He started making a note, then threw his pen down.

'Before the trial there might have been some point to this. We need more than hypothetical tooth-marks on a cushion that's probably been destroyed by now. In any case, how would that help Davie?'

'I don't know. But anything, murder included, is made up of details. If you can only find the right details, you know what happened.'

'Like building up a dinosaur from a piece of bone? But that takes time, and we haven't got time.'

'I'm sorry, I haven't helped.'

I stood up and he started saying he was sorry he'd taken my time.

'May I borrow your transcript of the trial?'

He darted an arm into the ramparts and pulled out a thick wodge of paper, tied with pink tape and furred at the edges through much handling. 'Wait a moment, there's something else.' He opened a cupboard and brought out a dusty box file. 'Some of the things the newspapers printed at the time. They may fill in a detail or two.'

He called his clerk to have file and transcript wrapped up for me.

Suddenly: 'I suppose you don't happen to like Richard Strauss.'

'As a matter of fact, I do.'

'They're doing *Rosenkavalier* at the Theatre Royal tonight. First time in Manchester. I wondered if . . .'

'You're inviting me?'

'Yes. I could hand these over to you there if you like and put you on the late train back.'

I'd usually have said that I wasn't a parcel, to need putting on trains, but I was still regretting having been sharp with him that first night. Anyway, I'd only heard *Rosenkavalier* once and wanted to know if it would seem as good a second time.

'Thank you. I'd love to.'

We arranged to meet outside the theatre. He and the dog preceded me down the narrow stairs and watched as I walked back up the street to Albert Square.

NINE

MY SECOND TELEGRAM HAD BEEN to a man I'd known for a long time who was active in trade union circles in Manchester, asking him to arrange an urgent meeting for me with the secretary of Jimmy Kendal's union. I knew I couldn't expect much, which was just as well.

When I got to my friend's office it turned out that he'd been able to secure a few valuable minutes of the secretary's time at his headquarters, a bus-ride away on the northern outskirts of the city. I rushed there, just in time to keep the appointment and found my man in a disobliging mood. He said he could give me ten minutes and looked pointedly at the big school-room clock ticking away opposite his desk. He was a strong man in late middle-age, with an imposing career behind him as a union pioneer, but now run to bullying and fat.

As my friend didn't know why I'd wanted to see him, he'd assumed I'd come to beg him to use his union's money or influence in the suffragette cause. That hadn't made him happy. When he found out what I really wanted he was even less so and fired off question after question. Why was I sticking my nose into something that was no concern of mine? Why come to him? Didn't I know that Davie Kendal had never been a member of his union?

'His brother is, though.'

'I'm sick to the stomach with people trying to blacken Jimmy's name, and the union's, because of something his brother's done. Jimmy's worth a hundred of murdering little scabs like Davie Kendal. Men like Jimmy are the future for the working man and don't you forget it.'

Since he was in such a bad mood anyway, I used up one of my seven remaining minutes by asking about the sabotage of machinery at Newbiggin's mill the summer before last. That annoyed him so much that for thirty-three seconds by the big clock he was coughing into his handkerchief.

'I hope you're not implying that was anything to do with the union, because if you are I'd remind you that there's such a thing as the law of slander.'

'I'm not implying anything. I'm only asking if you have any idea who was responsible.'

'Whoever it was, it was nothing to do with this union or with Jimmy Kendal.'

'Were you pleased when you heard Osbert Newbiggin was dead?'

I got seventeen seconds of glare for that, then:

'I wasn't glad and I wasn't sorry, because whether Osbert Newbiggin was dead or alive made not one ha'p'orth of difference to us one way or the other. There's always another one of him, and there's always another thousand of us. Why Jimmy's brother shot him I don't know and I don't need to know, but one thing I'll tell you – it had no more to do with the union than the man in the moon. Now if you'll excuse me, I've got work to do.'

'You're very sure that Davie Kendal shot him.'

'Aren't you, then?' But he wasn't even interested enough to wait for an answer. 'I'm sick of hearing about him. I'm sorry for his sister and brothers, but they're better off without him.'

'In other words, you think the sooner he's hanged and out of the way, the better?'

He was an honest man at least. He paused for no more than a couple of seconds before replying, 'Since you're asking me, yes, that's what I do think. Now good afternoon.'

It left me depressed, all the more because I felt I'd

deserved it. All I'd done in taking up his time was to confirm something I'd already guessed – that Newbiggin's death had nothing to do with the dispute at his mills. If men were killed for that, there'd hardly be a mill owner left alive in Lancashire. If I'd gained any crumb from it at all it was that the union thought highly of Jimmy Kendal, which meant he could look forward to a promising career as an organiser, possibly even in politics if he were ambitious for that. It suggested too that he must be a level-headed young man, unlikely to be involved in acts of murder or sabotage. Unless he was so ambitious and level-headed that he'd let his brother take the blame. I was on the verge of disliking him without even speaking to him.

I said nothing about my meeting with the union secretary to Bill Musgrave when I met him outside the Theatre Royal. He was carrying a brown paper parcel.

'What have you done with the dog?'

'Left him at home. His taste in Strauss is Johann, not Richard.'

'Where's home?'

'I've got three rooms over the office, one for me, one for Roswal, one for books and maps.'

Like the state of his chambers and his suit this suggested that he was not prosperous and yet he'd bought the best seats for us. The excitement of the music was like drunkenness, especially as he was hearing it for the first time. We were still dazed by it when he insisted on walking me to the station afterwards, but had to stride out fast because I was cutting it fine for the train. Not a word about Davie Kendal had been said all evening. It wasn't until I was settled in the corner of a carriage that he gave me the parcel.

'The press cuttings are mostly from the local paper, plus a few from the *Daily Mail*.'

I thanked him and waited for him to go. The train had steam up. Under the gaslight at the top of the platform the guard was unfurling his green flag.

'You'll let me know if anything occurs to you?'

'Of course. But don't be too hopeful.'

The guard's whistle and the noise of the train drawing out drowned whatever he was saying. I waved to him, undid the parcel and settled down to read as best I could by the dim light.

The *Daily Mail* had gone to town on it for a few days. It became 'The Mystery of Crowberry Hall', complete with sketch plan of the hall, drive and gate lodge. The hall was promoted to 'cotton millionaire's opulent mansion' and the town itself, quite a comfortable place in reality, was 'overshadowed by dark moorland and trackless peat bog'. The same magic wand had been waved over the characters in the drama, with the dead man's local philanthropy and probably modest musical talents elevated into a blend of Croesus and Caruso. Laura's screaming flight down the dark drive to the Cross Keys was much as it had been told to me, with the added information that she was 'herself a talented singer and professionally trained pianist'. But for the newspaper reporter the biggest attraction of all was the attempted alibi with the recording of the dead man's voice. If the police had tried to keep that aspect of things secret, they'd been totally unsuccessful. 'A Friend's Voice from the Dead in Alibi Attempt' headed the account of the telephone call and the discovery of the machine at the gate lodge. There was speculation about whether this was the first murder in history involving a gramophone and even a feature piece on 'The Gramophone – Is it the Murderer's Accomplice?' The only point not made was the one seized on by Bill – that as an alibi attempt the recording had been a total failure, convincing nobody. But then, that would have damaged a good story.

The local newspaper cuttings were more sober and predictable but they had one thing in common with the *Daily Mail*. With one voice they reported that police wanted to question Davie Kendal, a former employee, who had vanished from his lodgings on the night of the murder. If they'd come straight out and named him as the killer it couldn't have been more obvious.

The *Daily Mail* had even printed a photograph of Davie. It was the conventional, posed studio portrait, with him standing there in best clothes and stiff collar against a painted backdrop of columns. The face that stared out at me was pale and serious with rounded cheeks, a high forehead, dark hair coaxed over it in two symmetrical waves, a neat moustache. A pleasant enough face, although perhaps without his sister's strength of mind. He carried a bowler hat in his hand. The fact that he'd bothered to have the photograph taken at all suggested a degree of self-confidence. I guessed it had been done at a studio in Manchester after he'd completed his engineering course. Perhaps he'd seen it as the first in a career of increasing prosperity, with a photograph every five years or so showing him a little plumper, a little more prosperous, eventually with wife and children ranged alongside. The next things in the press cuttings box were about the arrest: 'Wanted man apprehended in Liverpool' and 'Gramophone Killing – Man charged'. Then the trial, sentence and appeal. I had no time to read those before we came into the station and I had to bundle everything together for the dark walk up the moorland road to the cottage.

Next morning, when we'd cleared away the breakfast things, I showed some of them to Rose. We didn't have much time because it was a Saturday and a family picnic had been organised, attendance obligatory. She looked at the photograph.

'Fancies himself a bit, wouldn't you say?'

'But not bad-looking. You've been around the town a lot. Have you heard any talk of a girlfriend?'

'No.'

'Surprising, don't you think? After all, he's twenty-four years old and he was earning quite good money. You'd expect him to be courting somebody.'

Through the day we had to pretend to put the problem aside for the boys' sake. Along with donkey and baby we got ourselves up as far as the waterfall to picnic and then played the Glencoe game in the heather. Rose and Pauline had to be Campbells. In spite of the fine day and the laughter, none of the four adults in the party relaxed. Now and again I'd notice Rose looking down towards the town, twitching to be pounding the cobbled streets with the petition for mercy, even though she knew as well as I did that it would be useless. Stuart was as noisy and boisterous as the boys, full of ideas and activity. Too much so, as if trying to drive out something. From the way Pauline looked at him, she thought so too. As the sun was going down we walked back with them and left them at the back door of the house, with nothing said all day about Newbiggins or Kendals.

Rose and I made up for that on Saturday evening and through most of Sunday, going through the rest of the cuttings and the transcript of the trial. We learned three things of interest. One, Bill Musgave was a very competent barrister. Faced with an unhelpful judge, a strong prosecution case and a jury that had probably filed into court convinced of the man's guilt, he'd done all that could be done. When Davie Kendal was being cross-examined by the prosecution, Bill had stepped in so many times to try to protect him that the judge's impatience crackled even through the dry pages of the transcript. He'd done his best, too, in cross-questioning the witnesses for the prosecution, especially the maid who'd admitted Davie on the night of the murder, and the cook. It seemed to be one of the best points for the defence that neither they nor anybody else had heard the shot that killed Newbiggin. Later the prosecution produced an expert witness to give evidence that a shot fired through a cushion inside the alcove where Newbiggin kept his recording apparatus might be muffled to the sound of a door slamming in the distance. The fact that neither maid nor cook reported a slamming door seemed a good point to me, but clearly hadn't impressed the jury.

The second point was confirmation that Davie Kendal had been something of a nightmare client. I already knew that, under cross-examination, he'd admitted to looking in at the windows of the dining room in October, when the family were at dinner. The prosecution barrister described it as 'prowling'. Bill had immediately objected to it as a loaded word, objection for once upheld by the judge. But that didn't help much in view of his client's refusal to give any clear reason for being at the hall. He had eventually admitted that he was just taking a walk around but although the question was put to him several ways, with the judge growing more and more impatient, he refused to say any more than that. The prosecution made a lot of this morsel in his final speech to the jury. '. . . And although we may not say that the accused was prowling around the house –' I could imagine the sidelong look at the judge, the legal titter '– we have established from the accused's own admission, as well as the evidence of Mrs Bolter, that a month before the crime was committed the accused was seen ambulating around Crowberry Hall in the dark, when he had no business to be there, observing Mr Newbiggin at his dinner.' You could almost feel the shiver going through the jury – the decent unsuspecting man at his dinner, his small household around him in the gaslight then suddenly, looking in from the darkness, the twisted, envious face of the prowler (the word had been used and would stick, whatever the judge had ruled), plotting to snatch him away from his food, light and security like a demon come down from the moor. They'd already heard from Bill Musgrave that the admitted presence of Davie Kendal outside the window on that night in October could not in reason prove that he shot Newbiggin a month later. The damage was done.

Not that it was the only damage. Under questioning, even friendly questioning from his own counsel, Davie Kendal had been a liability to his own side. He admitted to leaving Newbiggin's employment after an argument, but refused to go into any details. He said he thought

Newbiggin might have invited him to the hall that evening to offer him his job back, althought the court had heard evidence from Newbiggin's manager that he'd never expressed any such intention. He admitted proudly to knowing a lot about gramophones and recording and seemed quite ready to accept the prosecution's poisoned tribute that he was 'something of an amateur expert'. He denied having touched, let alone moved in a wheelbarrow, Newbiggin's gramophone on the night of the murder and volunteered, for once, that when he left the study it had been in its usual place on a table in an alcove beside Newbiggin's collection of discs. He knew of the existence of a recording of Newbiggin's voice because he had helped to make it. Asked how broken pieces of it came to be in the ash-bin at his family home, he could offer no idea. He hadn't put them there and didn't know how they might have got there. And yet, time after time and at every opportunity, he denied that he had plotted to kill Newbiggin or murdered him. Reading the transcript, it seemed as if he'd offered his denial as a magic charm against all that was happening to him and would go to the gallows still waiting for it to work.

The third impression was unexpected because it concerned somebody I'd neglected so far, the murdered man's widowed aunt, Mrs Cissie Bolter. She might be elderly but judging by her evidence in court she had a mind as sharp as a knife and, as far as Davie Kendal was concerned, more deadly. Had she a good view of the man who looked in at the dining room on that October night? Yes, indeed she had. Was he present in court? Indeed he was. Would the witness indicate? Witness pointed to the accused. Had she seen him before that night? Yes, of course she had, used to work for Mr Newbiggin and was in and out of the house all the time helping with his recording machines. What had been the relations between them at that point? Were they friendly? Osbert had always been generous to him and he used to be polite enough, like the little snake in the grass ... Objection from Bill Musgrave. Judge warns witness to stick to matters of fact. Did the accused subsequently leave her nephew's employment? He did, yes. Had Mr Newbiggin ever said anything to her about the reason for that? She understood it was something to do with what happened at work. She didn't make it her business to ask any more about it. Good riddance. Was she aware that her nephew had an appointment with the accused on the night of the murder? Yes, he said he'd asked Kendal up to the house. He didn't say why and she didn't ask. Returning to the night in October when she'd told the court she'd seen the accused staring into the dining room, had she observed the expression on his face? Indeed she had. Would she describe it to the court? Sneering. Sneering at poor Osbert like a demon out of hell. Objection from Mr Musgrave. Further warning from judge to witness.

After that the prosecution counsel took her through the story of finding her nephew with many regrets for having to do it. She seemed, as far as you could tell from the transcript, unmoved, giving the account of finding him unconscious in a pool of blood, with feathers and fragments of his broken records round him. She'd run to the door and shouted, and Laura, the maid and the cook had come running. She'd told Laura and the cook to fetch help and sent the maid for bandages but there was nothing they could do, he was bleeding too fast. Her nephew had never recovered consciousness or spoken at all. (I suspected that, if she could, she'd have had him sitting up and denouncing Davie Kendal with his dying breath.)

When it came to Bill Musgrave's turn to cross-examine he treated her with kid gloves, aware that anything else would have a bad effect on the jury. She didn't return the compliment and seemed to regard him as fair game. A necessary question on whether her nephew had any enemies produced a firm denial. 'He was respected by everybody who knew him – apart from the one.' I could imagine her glare at the man in the dock as she said it.

*   *   *

I read until the terrible end of the transcript and pushed it across the table, eyes tired. Rose was staring at me.

'Anything useful?'

'If useful means hopeful, no. I wish we knew what that argument had been about. You've spent a lot of time with his sister. Did she give you any idea?'

She hesitated a long time, then, slowly, 'I think there is something. Not Janet herself so much, but she and Jimmy, when they're together. It's not anything they say, but sometimes they look at each other, almost as if they're keeping watch.'

'Watch on each other?'

'Yes.'

'I'd almost bet that the aunt knew something. It would help if we had any way of scraping acquaintance with Newbiggin's family.'

I wished for once that my brother and sister-in-law had been pillars of the community.

'There is the choral society. Did you know they have public rehearsals every Sunday evening? I saw a notice about it in one of the shops.'

I hadn't known, and in our present trackless state it was better than nothing. The choral society and Osbert Newbiggin's recording experiments had been what brought Davie Kendal and Osbert Newbiggin closer together than they would have been simply as mill boss and worker. There'd be people there who'd known both of them.

Rose put on her respectable hat with the navy blue rose, I found my green felt under the mass of paper on the table and we walked in the soft evening light down the long road to the town. It looked and sounded different and it took us some time to realise why. On a Sunday the thrumming from the cotton mills that was always there as a ground base through the week dropped away to silence and only thin wisps of smoke were coming from the chimneys because the boilers were only just kept alight. A few hours more and the men would be stoking them up again, ready for the morning shift to come on duty at six o'clock. Another week and the second-to-last Monday of Davie Kendal's life. I don't know if the same thought had occurred to Rose as well, but we were both walking faster and faster – as if that would do any good.

TEN

THE HEADQUARTERS OF THE CHORAL society were just off the High Street, opposite the red-brick Venetian of the municipal slipper baths. The place looked as if it might once have been a baptist chapel, but even from the outside you could see how the late Osbert Newbiggin had cared for his pet. The paintwork was new, hardly touched by the overlay of soot that settled on everything in the town, the paved front courtyard free of weeds. A notice-board announced forthcoming concerts and offered anybody interested in joining the chance to apply for an audition. Under the printed information somebody had added, in handwriting, the eternal heart-cry of the choir-master: 'Tenors especially welcome.'

As Rose and I arrived the last of the choir members were just hurrying in. Most of them looked as if they probably worked at the mills, but today they were in Sunday best. The men snatched off their caps as they went in and stuffed them into their pockets. The girls were in shoes rather than clogs, with hair caught up loosely in combs as a holiday from the scraped-back style that made for safety among the machines on working days, and most of them had woollen shawls draped round their shoulders. There was a sprinkling of the more prosperous sort; the clerks and managing staff from the villas on the outskirts of the town, the women in tweeds, the men in dark suits and bowler hats.

Soon after that they let the audience in to the two rows of chairs at the back of the high, white-painted room.

Listening to the choir rehearsing was obviously one of the respectable things to do on a Sunday and there were about twenty people besides ourselves. The inside of the hall also showed signs of generous funding, with a coal-burning stove and electric lighting, a platform at one end where the choir were standing and a podium for the choir-master. He was a small, thin, bald man in a black suit. Most of the strapping young men among the baritones and basses could have picked him up and hardly noticed the weight and yet when he raised his baton there was instant silence and respect. As soon as they started singing it was clear that Osbert Newbiggin had got something worthwhile for his money. They were good, even by the high standards of the cotton towns where every self-respecting community had its choir. That evening they were rehearsing Haydn's *Creation*, with a lack of fuss, and devotion to detail, that were almost professional.

For a while I just enjoyed the music, then reminded myself that we were there to work. Not that I had to look far for it. A portrait was hanging on the wall at the back of the platform. It was partly obscured by the basses but there was enough of it visible to see that it was an oil painting, recently done, the colours new to the point of rawness, with a wreath of faded laurel leaves hitched to the top of the gilded frame and black crêpe ribbons hanging down the sides. When some of the singers put their heads together to sort out markings in their scores I got a better look at it. It showed a burly man in his early fifties, hair touched with just enough grey for gravity, standing in full evening dress with his hand on the edge of a grand piano. Behind him on a small table was something that looked absurdly like a half-opened umbrella. When the choir-master was having some terse words with the tenors about a late entry, Rose caught my eye and looked towards the portrait. I nodded. The late Osbert Newbiggin had done well by his choral society and they were returning the compliment.

The tenors, chastened, did the entry again and again, till they landed on it as squarely as rugby players on a ball. That sort of thing makes its demands on a rehearsal pianist. Either attention wanders from the boredom or the playing becomes sarcastic, over-emphatic. This one was a paragon, there every time with exactly the same limpid, unobtrusively helpful playing. The choir-master never needed to look at her. She kept her eyes on him or, when not playing, down at her folded hands. She was a young woman, very thin and pale, dressed entirely in black. Her tailored jacket and small felt hat, severe and plain, marked her out from most of the other women. Her long white hands didn't look as if they were used for threading cotton bobbins. At one point the choir-master thanked her. He called her Miss Newbiggin.

I watched her through the rest of the rehearsal until, after two hours of hard work, the choir-master gave the choir their reward by letting them loose on the final chorus, 'Sing the Lord, ye voices all', the way an equestrian gives his horse a canter after tedious schooling. They surged away with it and afterwards as they rolled up their music they were chattering and laughing, pleased with themselves. Not the pianist, though. As soon as the choir-master put down his baton she tucked the score into her music case, put on her black gloves and was away without speaking to anybody. The others took longer to go, first the older and more serious, then the basses, *en masse* and purposefully beerwards. The hall cleared slowly until all that remained were an old caretaker, waiting to switch out the lights, a dozen or so of the girls chattering together, half a dozen lads watching them wistfully. Although the girls seemed absorbed in their own talk, they'd glance now and again at the hovering lads, playing who-walks-me-home?

We walked past them onto the platform, now empty apart from chairs, for a better look at the picture. On top of the grand piano the artist had painted a musical score, obligingly tilted so that you could see it was *The Messiah*. On Osbert Newbiggin's right, a little in the background, was a bust of Handel on a plinth. The artist could do hands well, the big capable hands of a man who'd worked for what he had, with a heavy gold seal ring on the little finger of the left hand, carefully rendered. The subject had expected his money's-worth and the artist had given it. Close to, the thing that had looked like an umbrella was the horn of a gramophone. There were shelves of books in the background and a window with heavy red curtains. It looked like a study, probably the study where he'd died.

'Mr Newbiggin, that is, the one who was murdered.'

Two of the girls had come back onto the platform to join us. One was tall and powerful, with a thick plait of brown hair, the other small and dark with bright eyes.

'Did you know him?'

They were inclined to giggle. They couldn't have been more than sixteen or so, probably not used to strangers.

'Everybody knew Mr Newbiggin.'

They sounded excited rather than regretful about what had happened. They knew him, they told us, because of his singing with the choir, the recordings and the parties he gave at the hall, after *The Messiah* every Christmas and again in the summer. They regretted losing the parties because the nephew was regarded as a mean b . . . (giggle) well, you know, pockets sewn up, and nowhere near as devoted to the choral society as his uncle had been, even though he still sang with it.

'Was he here tonight?'

'Yes, with the baritones. Doesn't look like a baritone though, more like a string bean.'

'Thinks he's too good for us.'

We got down off the platform and went out, still talking. It was dark already, the air cold and the gas-lamps lit along the High Street. I noticed that two of the lads fell into step some way behind us as we walked and the girls were carefully ignoring them. If they were using us for their purpose, fair enough, since I was using them for mine. I complimented them on the singing of the choir.

'That's nothing to what we can sound like,' the one with the plait said. 'You should hear us at a concert.'

'You need to hear us with an orchestra,' said the dark one. 'It's not the same with just a piano.'

'A good pianist, though.'

I'd said it quite casually and was surprised by the quality of the silence that followed. We'd taken several steps before the dark one broke it.

'Well, Laura Newbiggin should be all right, shouldn't she? She's had training.'

'She gets paid too, seven and six a night. None of us gets paid.'

'Laura. Is that Osbert Newbiggin's cousin?'

'That's right. She was there when it happened.'

'Came screaming all the way down the drive in the dark. They say her head hasn't been quite right ever since.'

I said that wouldn't be surprising. They weren't sympathetic.

'My mum says it wasn't the shock of him being murdered that did it, it was not leaving her any of his money.'

'He did though, he left her two hundred pounds.'

'She'd have been expecting more than that. He was going to send her to Italy to get her voice trained.'

Thinking of my brother, I asked if her voice was exceptional. The one with the plait thought it was but her friend disagreed. Several at least as good among the sopranos in the choir, only they didn't have the luck.

'But then, nor did she as it turned out.' A shade of satisfaction in that.

'Where does she live now?'

'She's got rooms by the railway station, teaches voice and piano.'

That seemed to be all they had to say about Laura, so I asked them if they'd taken part in any of Mr Newbiggin's recording sessions.

'Oh yes. They'd bring all the equipment down from the hall in his motor car. We'd all have to stand a lot closer together than usual, round this big horn and keep stopping while they put the new discs on.'

111

'You don't get the same feeling from it, not like from a concert.'

'The piano has to be up high on a stand and the basses a long way back so as not to shake the needle off the disc.'

'And when we tried the "Hallelujah Chorus" he said it was too loud and the needle would break through the groove, or something like that. What's the point of singing the "Hallelujah Chorus" if you can't sing it loudly?'

'It was good fun, though. Later on, he gave a party up at the hall so we could hear ourselves on the records.'

'It didn't sound like us, though.'

'How do you know what we sound like? You don't, not if you're singing.'

'It didn't sound like anybody. It was like any old choir at the end of a tunnel.'

They were chattering happily as we walked along the High Street, almost certainly mindful of the lads still trailing faithfully behind us, but giving no sign of it.

I said, 'Was Davie Kendal helping with the recordings?'

A silence, then both said 'Yes' in subdued voices.

'What did you think of him? Then, I mean, before the murder?'

More silence, then the one with the plait said, 'He was all right. Some people said he had his nose in the air, because of going to college at Manchester, but I thought he was all right.'

'I liked him,' the dark one said, a touch defiantly. 'I work at the same frame as his sister. I'm that sorry for her.'

Both had signed the petition. There was no horror or moral indignation in the way they talked about Davie, just hushed voices as if he were in hospital dying of TB.

'What about Mr Newbiggin? Did you like him?'

I'd expected the conventional platitudes and was surprised by the silence that followed.

Rose said, 'You don't have to like the boss, do you?'

'Oh, it's not that. Only Betty and I didn't have much to do with him, did we, Betty?' Then she added, almost under her breath, 'Not like some we could name.'

Betty, the dark one, giggled. 'Just as well.'

'Why?'

'Well, you shouldn't speak ill of people when they're dead . . .'

'Go on with you, we said it when he was alive as well.'

I could sense that they wanted to be coaxed to tell the story. They were young enough to enjoy the unusual experience of talking to strangers and our presence gave the game of pretending to ignore the boys more spice than usual. The dark one giggled a bit, then plunged into the story.

'There's this girl called Teresa. She's older than we are, eighteen, but she'd be about our age when it happened. She's really beautiful looking . . .'

'I wouldn't say Teresa's beautiful. A bit on the pale side.'

'. . . anyway, she works at the mill with us and she used to be in the choir. She had a nice voice and took some of the solos . . .'

'Not the really important ones.'

'. . . and Mr Newbiggin started taking an interest in her, the way he did sometimes. I told you he gave these parties at the hall. Anyway, we all went to this party . . .'

'When was this?'

'Two years ago. It was the summer we started work and joined the choir. We were all having our tea out on the lawn and we noticed Teresa wasn't there, only we didn't think much of it. Then she came back later all shaken and you could see something had happened.'

Beside me, I felt Rose go tense.

'What had happened, or can we guess?'

'She says Mr Newbiggin invited her to his study to look at his record collection. So she went, not thinking any harm, and he's got this big, white marble bust of Handel in his study, next to the piano it was. Teresa was turned away from him, looking at it, then she feels his hands coming round her from behind.'

113

'He was touching her . . . you know.' The friend with the plait put her hands fleetingly over her breasts.

'And she said he was making a panting noise. It reminded her of her grandad, with his weak lungs, walking back uphill from the public house. It was the panting that scared her most. Then he put his face against her cheek and tried to kiss her.'

'What did she do?'

'What any girl with a bit of gumption would do, pulls herself away and tells him he should be ashamed of himself. She was really angry, she says, especially because of Handel.'

'Handel?'

'*The Messiah.* Creeping up on her while she was looking at his bust, all innocent, was like trying it in church. So she told him he should be ashamed of himself. And what do you think happened then?'

'I suppose the end of the story is that she worked at one of his mills and he sacked her.'

'No, odder than that. She says he just stood there staring at her for a moment like a puppy that's done something dirty on the kitchen floor, then his face went red and he started crying.'

'Crying!'

'Yes. Didn't say or do anything, just stood there crying. Of course, that scared her worse than anything so far because she'd never seen a man crying before, and she just dashed out and left him and came back to us outside.'

'Did he come out too?'

'No, the party went on but he never appeared. People were looking for him, asking where he was, and couldn't find him. In the end the old woman up there, the aunt, said he was indisposed and they all went home and that was it.'

'Did anything happen to Teresa after that?'

'Not to her, no. She stopped going to the choir for nearly a year because she was scared of meeting him. She's engaged now to a chap from Bolton, so that's all right.'

114

'Did you hear of Mr Newbiggin trying it with anybody else?'

They hesitated, then the one with the plait said, 'You'd hear talk sometimes.'

Soon after that we came to the clock tower and our ways parted. They said goodnight and turned up a steep cobbled street to the left, walking slowly enough for the lads to catch them up at last.. Rose and I walked on past the cotton mills and took the moorland road out of town. Below us the lines of gas-lamps picked out the pattern of the main streets and a train whistled from the station.

'So the late Mr Newbiggin was a bit of an old satyr.'

'Dirty old goat, you mean.'

I was surprised by the anger in Rose's voice.

'It squares with what Pauline overheard from her cook. I think we can take it that Teresa wasn't the only girl he tried it on.'

'I suppose he thought he owned them because he paid their wages.'

'To do him justice, he doesn't seem to have taken any revenge against Teresa. It sounds pathetic as much as anything.'

Rose's toe sent a stone skittering across the road and into the bank. I wasn't sure if it was deliberate or accidental.

'But since it's unlikely that he was murdered by a posse of outraged mill girls, I'm not sure that it gets us any further.'

'What will?'

'I don't know. It's a matter of finding out all the facts that you can and if you're lucky there's one that strikes you as out of place. Like that choir-master tonight, sixty people singing and he could pick up one false note.'

'An ear for murder, like an ear for music?'

'Perhaps. It's a pity Laura disappeared so quickly.'

'And Rodney, the baritone string-bean.'

The scents of the moorland were round us now we were clear of the town and the peat banks were rising on either side. Rose seemed very thoughtful and said nothing for the last uphill mile, except that she thought she'd go to see Janet Kendal again in the morning.

'She and her father are going in to see him at Strangeways sometime this week.'

'I'll come down with you.'

The Newbiggin family had at least one little secret. If Bill's suspicions were right, the Kendals had a bigger one. Whether it would help Davie Kendal to find out what it was I doubted, but could see no other way to go.

When we were walking across the grass to the cottage Rose said, 'The idea of hanging any man for murdering a slobbering hypocrite like that.'

I thought of pointing out that the moral shortcomings of the victim were not a defence against a murder charge, but from the tone of her voice decided against it.

ELEVEN

IN THE MORNING I GOT OVER to the house in time to catch Stuart and Pauline at breakfast.

'Morning, Nell. Watch out, Pauline, my dear sister's got an ulterior motive. I know the symptoms.'

The boys had finished breakfast and were packing their bags for school. Pauline was holding an invitation card in an accusing way and it was obvious that I'd interrupted one of those minor domestic arguments that make you realise that even happy marriages have their drawbacks.

'When did it arrive, then? It must have been days ago.'

'I don't know. It crawled into one of my journals and went into hiding.'

'It's tomorrow. They'll think we're so rude for not replying.'

'Well, let them. Do we really care what the likes of Rodney Newbiggin think of us?'

I began to take an interest. Pauline showed me the invitation. Mr and Mrs Rodney Newbiggin would be at home to friends and neighbours at Crowberry Hall from four o'clock till six-thirty. RSVP.

'I suppose it's to let the neighbourhood know they've arrived. We're their nearest neighbours, after all. They'll think we're being deliberately stand-offish.'

'I've got a clinic tomorrow afternoon, in any case. Of course, if you want to go . . .'

'You know I don't want to go, only it looks so discourteous to wait until the day before to say we're not going.'

'I've got to hurry. I'll leave it to you, darling. See you this evening. 'Bye, Nell.'

He grabbed his bag and practically ran out. Pauline stared after him, exasperated.

'Typical. Now what am I supposed to do?'

I wondered whether to admit that I'd come over with the single purpose of asking them if they could contrive to get us invited next door. Since I'd read the transcript and press cuttings the wish to have a look inside Osbert Newbiggin's study had grown beyond all reason. Logically I couldn't see that it would tell me anything. The murder had happened ten months ago and the police must have combed it several times over. But everything came back there – his first and last meetings with Davie Kendal, the shooting, the loading of the gramophone onto the wheelbarrow. And since last night I had to add that incident with the mill girl and the bust of Handel.

'If you want to go, I'll come with you.'

'Oh, Nell, would you? I don't want to go in the least, but I'd hate them to think we're being snobbish. Perhaps if we just looked in for half an hour that would be enough. Do you think Rose would like to come too? I'm sure they won't mind.'

She wrote the note there and then at the breakfast table and gave it to John to post on his way down to school. As I left she said, 'Anyway, what was the ulterior motive?'

I think she'd guessed.

Rose and I walked down to the town together. The streets were quiet, with the men and many of the women long at work. In yards behind the terraced houses lines of washing were flapping in a stiff breeze off the moors and the clean, steamy whiff of scullery coppers boiled up for washing day cut through the smell of soot from the chimneys.

'Won't Janet be at work?'

'She's taking time off, until . . .'

We turned into the High Street, then Rose led the way confidently up one of the cobbled streets to the Kendals' house. There were already people who recognised her and said good morning. Their house was just like the rest in a steeply rising terrace, red brick walls and slate roof, front door opening direct onto the pavement. The Kendals' doorstep was scrubbed as fiercely white as any other in the row. The windows glinted in the sun and the net curtains were like frosted icing. Janet opened the door to us at the first knock, wearing an apron with a scarf wrapped round her head.

'I'm just finishing off the range. Come through to the kitchen.' That was to Rose, then to me, 'Have a seat in the parlour, Miss Bray.'

She opened a door to the right, ushering me into a cold little room with red velour curtains and an arrangement of seashells glued to plywood in the grate. An aspidistra on a bamboo stand stood in one corner, an upright piano against the wall, lid closed. I envied Rose because her labours on the petition had earned her a place as family, in the kitchen. I was still visitor and the coldness of the parlour shouldn't be taken for lack of hospitality. It wasn't used for every day and the seashells would only make way for fire at Christmas, weddings or christenings. Or funerals. Decisive steps came downstairs and past the parlour door, then there was a murmur of voices from the kitchen: one man, one woman. Then steps again in the hallway and the door opened.

'Miss Bray. I'm Jimmy, his brother.'

It was the man I'd seen briefly outside the Cross Keys. The air of force and energy I'd noticed about him then came close to physical threat in the small room. He wore a dark jacket with a stiff collar and red tie. His hair was dark, eyes almost black and very direct. They weren't pleased.

'So you've been talking to the union secretary about me?'

I hadn't disturbed the plumped glacial chair cushions by sitting down, so our eyes were on a level. If he expected to take me by surprise, he was wrong. Of course a union would have good communications.

'Yes, I have. He told me that people shooting mill bosses belonged in the nineteenth century. Also that you'd have nothing to do with sabotage.'

'Right on both counts.'

'But the machines were damaged and Osbert Newbiggin was shot.'

'So my brother did both of them?'

'It was in my mind that you might both have done both of them.'

Up to that point, he'd kept his anger carefully controlled. Now I could see not just his fists but his whole body clenching.

'Is this supposed to be helping us?'

'I don't know what will help. If there is anything, I'm trying to find it. Did Janet tell you she was coming to see me?'

'Yes, she did.'

'Did you disapprove?'

'My sister's a grown-up woman. She does what she likes.'

'Let's take it that you don't approve. I don't blame you. She's heard something about cases I've been involved with in the past, when I have been able to help. But I don't know anything about you or your brother, or Newbiggin either for that matter. As far as you're concerned, I'm only raising false hopes and you're probably right. I wish you weren't, but you probably are.'

He looked at me, then looked away at last and sighed. 'I suppose that's straight, at any rate.'

I sat down on the edge of an armchair upholstered in shiny cloth. I still couldn't bring myself to inflict a dent on the cushion. He sat down opposite me, throwing himself back in the chair regardless.

'You say you thought we might both have done it.'

'Yes, but I didn't think it very likely. You'd have let him down badly if that were the case.'

120

'The alibi, you mean?'

'Or lack of it. Seeing him ordering a drink around seven-thirty was as good as useless.'

'I don't need you to tell me that. For goodness sake, woman, do you think I'd see my own brother where he is and not get him out of it if I could? I'll tell you, if lying would have done him any good I'd have lied for him cheerfully, sworn on our mother's grave I'd been standing next to him every minute of the evening. Only it wouldn't have done any good because half the town would know it wasn't true.' He didn't raise his voice and didn't need to.

'He was asking in the Cross Keys for Rolling Toby. Do you know why?'

'I do not.'

'Was Rolling Toby a friend of his?'

'We all knew him as lads. That was all.'

'So you can't think of any reason why Davie should have wanted to see him that night?'

'He must have had his reasons. I don't know them.'

'Have you asked him since?'

'Have you ever visited a man in prison?'

'Yes, I have.'

'A grille in between you, and a couple of warders listening to every breath he takes – is that any place for cross-questioning your brother?'

'You haven't always seen eye to eye with Davie, have you?'

'That's a different thing from wanting to see him where he is now.'

'I know that. But as far as you're concerned, he was a blackleg once.'

'Yes, he was, and I called him that to his face and worse, so he left home.'

'What do you think made him a boss's man?'

He relaxed deeper into the chair.

'I can see it now, though I couldn't see it then. It wasn't so much that he was a boss's man, he just fell in love with

121

anything that was new: machines, electricity. Even as a lad he'd be building little things from wires and old bits of tin, then when Newbiggin gave him this chance to do it for a living, he was like a kid let loose in a sweetshop. I won't say he didn't enjoy the money he was getting, but it wasn't the main thing for him.'

'So he really was grateful to Osbert Newbiggin?'

'Oh, the sun shone out of his rear end. Excuse me.'

'And yet last summer they quarrelled. Do you know why?'

I watched him carefully and thought a guarded look came into his eyes.

'Something to do with work, I suppose.'

'You don't know for sure?'

'No.'

'What did Davie say to you about it?'

'Not much. I said something like "Had enough of being on the bosses' side, then?" and he said I'd been right all along.'

'That was all?'

'Yes. If he'd had a blow to his pride, I wasn't going to make it worse. As long as he was back in the family, that was the main thing.'

Which was much what Janet had said. I didn't believe her either.

'Did Davie have a girlfriend?'

He looked startled at the change of tack. 'He wasn't much of a one for the girls. First he was too busy with his studying, then later when he came back from Manchester . . . It was one of the things we argued about, to be honest with you. I told him I supposed he thought girls from the mill weren't good enough for him.'

'Do you think that was true?'

'I don't know. I said a lot of things to him at the time. Some of them were true, some of them maybe not.' He looked away from me, staring at the seashells stranded in the cold grate beyond reach of tides.

'Do you think your brother killed Osbert Newbiggin?'

122

His eyes came back to me, hard and angry. 'What kind of question is that? What would you answer me, if your brother is where mine is now?'

'I'd probably tell you he didn't do it.'

'Well, then. The question is, can you do anything for us, or can't you?'

'I don't know. The one thing I'm sure of is that I can't do anything if you're not being straight with me.'

He stood up. 'Thank you very much, miss, for coming all this way to accuse us of being liars. You'll excuse me, I've got work to do.' At the door he turned. 'Dad wanted to speak to you. But don't you go asking him questions. It's bad enough as it is.'

I found my own way to the kitchen. Janet was working at the sink, Rose sitting at the kitchen table that was scrubbed to silvery whiteness. The range by the wall was already radiating heat even this early in the day, with a saucepan simmering on top of it that smelt like meat stock. Janet turned to look at me, apprehensively. I could tell she was wondering what her brother had been saying.

'I gather your father wants to see me.'

'He's out the back with his birds. I'll show you.' She dried her hands on her apron and opened the back door.

The yard was no more than a strip between brick walls. Part of it was taken up with a stone-flagged path and a line of washing. All the rest was flying and hopping and singing, as bright as if a field of dandelions had decided to take to the air. The aviary was built against a whitewashed wall, divided into four high and roomy cages, with dead tree branches for the birds to perch. Each cage held half a dozen or so canaries. After the first impression of brightness you could see that the colours ranged from pale to vibrant yellow. I was so fascinated with them at first that I didn't notice the small, dark-suited man by the dustbins inside the gate at the far end until Janet called 'Dad' and he turned round. I think he'd been absorbed in his birds, because as he turned there was a smile on his face that slowly faded as he looked at his daughter. I thought it wasn't Janet herself that made the smile fade, but being recalled to what was happening to the family. His hair was thick but entirely white. He had a lined face and wiry wariness of body, like a retired jockey. When Janet introduced me he gave me his hand and tried his best at a welcoming smile, but it was nothing like the one summoned up by his birds and when it had gone there was a sadness there that hurt to look at it.

'Hello, lass. Janet says you're trying to help. We're all very obliged to you.'

That was what his voice said, but his eyes were saying that it didn't matter, that he knew I couldn't do anything, that nobody could do anything. Janet had walked in on me and demanded help as a right because she was desperate. Her father didn't believe in help any more, but was too kind to hurt anyone's feelings by saying so. I guessed from the way Janet was looking at him, part protective and part exasperated, that she knew this and could hardly bear to be with him in case failure of hope might be infectious. She turned and went back to the kitchen. Her father tried to say something else, failed, gestured towards the aviary.

'Canaries. I keep them.'

'Yes.'

We stood side by side for a long time, staring into one of the cages. A bird perched near the wire, looking at us, and he whistled two or three low, soft notes to it. It put its head on one side but didn't answer him. The sleeve of his jacket brushed against me and the arm inside it felt as thin as the legs of the birds. He held the other arm in an odd way, stiff and permanently bent at the elbow.

'You've come a long way.'

'My brother lives here.'

It didn't matter what we said. He was signalling all the time, through the tense arm, the eyes fixed on the birds: *Help us. I'm sorry, I know you can't, but help us. I'm sorry.* He opened a small flap and picked the nearest canary off its perch, so gently that it didn't even seem alarmed. His hand, square and thin, with the top of the index finger missing, enclosed the bird with only head and claws showing.

'Harz Rollers. Nothing like them for singing.'

When he thought I'd had enough of looking at it he popped it back on its perch, so expertly that it didn't even need to shift its claws to get in balance.

'You can get very interested in Rollers.'

But his voice was only a ghost from a world where things had once had some interest. I was a guest in his house and a memory of hospitality survived, but he had no idea what to do with me or anything else. I wished they hadn't put him through this.

'He used to like them.' The way he said it left no doubt that he meant Davie.

'Did he help you look after them?'

He nodded, still apparently intent on the birds. 'He was a kind boy, you know that? That was just his problem, he was too kind.'

And he looked at me, as if he'd needed to see me to tell me just that. He wanted an answer. I suppose I said 'I'm sure he was' or something equally inadequate, but it didn't matter. After a silence I said, for want of anything more useful, that the birds must take a lot of looking after.

'Oh yes, I come and see they're all right last thing at night and in the morning before I go to work.'

'Work?' I thought Janet had told me that he'd retired from the mill after an accident.

He pointed to a long bamboo pole, propped against the back wall of the house alongside the galvanised tin bath on its hook. It had several long loops of wire wound round the top of it.

'Knocker-up, I am, the one who gets all the others up for work. When I couldn't work at the mill any more the old chap who'd been knocker-up round here for donkeys' years was retiring, so I bought his round off him.'

He took a few steps away from his aviary, picked up the bamboo pole and rattled the wires against an upstairs window, producing a sound like a lot of little pebbles hitting the glass. 'You keep that up until you see the light going on inside, or they shout to tell you they've woken up. Otherwise most of them wouldn't be up in time for the early shift.'

'You must have to start work very early yourself.'

'Out by five o'clock every morning. I get up at four, rake out the range and stoke it up so it's going nicely for Janet when she comes down, then see to the birds.'

Up at four. That was the time the police had arrived to search the house the morning after Osbert Newbiggin died. One morning when the routine was disrupted and the canaries might have had to wait for their seed. Another one coming in eight days' time. Although I said nothing the thought must have come to him, because he put the pole down and turned away, head down.

Somehow we got ourselves back to the kitchen, under Janet's questioning eyes, then out to the street and back up the hill, walking fast. I'd have run if I could to get away from that feeling that the old man was trying to console me for not being able to help him.

'What did you talk about?'

'Canaries. And he said Davie was kind.'

Another half mile in silence, heels jabbing down on the road. Unfair to Rose, I knew that, but went on being unfair.

'What about the brother?'

'He thinks Davie's guilty.'

'Did he say so?'

'No, of course not.'

We hammered on up the road. *Help. I'm sorry. Help. I'm sorry.* Then there were the other words that got into the rhythm and softened it. *That was just his problem, he was too kind.*

TWELVE

THE THREE OF US TRAVELLED to the Newbiggins' At Home next day in some style, gloved and hatted, bowling downhill in a little horse taxi behind a fat-rumped grey. Pauline, as expected, had guessed what we were doing.

'Are you going to tell them you're interested in the murder?'

'Oh, as soon as you introduce us. I thought something on the lines of "Fascinating about your uncle's murder, wasn't it? Do tell me more."'

'Nell!'

Sitting opposite me, Rose murmured, 'Don't worry, she doesn't mean it.'

'You never know, with her.'

'He can't be particularly grief-stricken about it, or he wouldn't be entertaining all and sundry as soon as he moves in.'

'That's probably his wife. She has ambitions.'

'Social ones, I take it. How lucky to catch the three of us at first cast of her net.'

'Stuart's not pleased. He says I'm to keep you under control.'

Pauline, on the other hand, was obviously far from reluctant to aid and abet me. This difference in their attitudes puzzled me, but I put it aside for more immediate business.

'Do you think Laura Newbiggin or the old aunt will be there?'

'Certainly not Laura.' (Why not?) 'And it's a long way for Mrs Bolter to come from Southport.'

'I don't suppose you met her, did you?'

'No, but Sarah knew one of the maids up at the hall and she gave notice because of her. Said she was a holy terror.'

'She certainly hates Davie.'

'Hardly surprising, I suppose. Have you found anything even remotely hopeful?'

'I wish I had. The only firm conclusion is what everybody knew from the start – that whoever shot Osbert Newbiggin had to know him and the household very well. He had to know about the recording of his voice, the gramophone in his study, the gun in the desk drawer, the telephone at the lodge. He even had to know that the odd-job man was out for the evening.'

'He could have kept watch, I suppose.'

'Yes, although if it was Davie, there'd be no point. He'd been invited to the hall at six o'clock on that one particular evening. Which is odd, come to think of it. That whole elaborate alibi plan depended on being able to get into the lodge and use the telephone there. How could he have known in advance that the lodge was going to be empty on the evening Newbiggin asked him to come up to the hall?'

'Perhaps the man went out at the same time every evening.'

'Possible. I must find out.'

That aspect of the thing hadn't struck me before, but it was all part of the puzzling mixture of calculation and opportunism in the killing. Newbiggin had taken the initiative in sending the note to Davie's house and if Davie were guilty he'd had a matter of twelve hours or less to come up with an elaborate plan. But perhaps that was a point against him too, explaining the inconsistencies in it.

We went along the High Street with little boys running after us and up the steep drive between the rhododendrons. The front of the house was a mass of motors and pony carts. At the top of a flight of steps the front door stood open. Inside were a nervy pale-haired man in his late thirties, already going bald, and a slightly younger woman, far too well-dressed in shades of grey and lavender. The woman fell on Pauline in a restrained rapture that showed she was, socially speaking, the kind of fish for which they were trawling. Embarrassed, Pauline introduced us as visiting sister-in-law and friend, with a wary eye on me. I think it was in her mind that I'd back them against the wall and start inquiries. All in good time. I was thirsty and wanted my tea first.

'You must find it very quiet here after London.'

The wife, Evangeline or somesuch, to me. She had small eyes and very full red lips, a combination that reminded me of a marine creature waiting for the current to waft something digestible towards its tentacles. I decided then and there that she had murdered her husband's uncle for the sake of his big house. With a gaggle of other guests we were wafted on towards a drawing room that was swagged and swathed like something from a harem, and forced to engage in the sort of inane conversations in which everybody tries to decide what everyone else is doing there. Of course the answer was the one thing to which nobody would admit. The arrival of a new couple in the biggest house in town would have created a minor stir, but the real interest was that for most of the guests it was the first time they'd been at the Hall since 'what happened'. Nobody mentioned murder, or death. The name of Osbert Newbiggin was seldom spoken and came in hushed tones, invariably preceded by 'poor' – an odd way to respect the memory of one of the wealthiest men in the area. We had: 'Rodney looks tired. I haven't seen him since what happened' or 'They've had the whole place redecorated since what happened' and even 'I'm surprised they're entertaining already, less than a year after what happened'. This last, from a woman with a penetrating voice, was instantly shushed by her partner but I had the impression that at least some of the other guests agreed.

'Well, life goes on,' somebody said, and they all sighed heavily and said yes, life went on, as if that were a pity.

Our host and hostess appeared from welcoming late-comers at the front door, followed by maids with trolleys of tea and scones, and the scrimmage for food began. Rose stayed by the window, apparently deep in conversation with a vicar, of all people. I collected a cup of tea and joined the group round Rodney. He had a washed-out look, as if the two generations of energy that had gone to piling up the Newbiggin money were running out in him. We all had to manoeuvre round an object conspicuously and inconveniently placed in the centre of the carpet. It was a cabinet in shiny Circassian walnut, with small doors at the front and a handle sticking out from one side. Evangeline seemed inordinately proud of it and when one of the maids was about to stand a tea-tray on it she hissed, 'Not on the gramophone', like a priestess defending an altar. The omens looked bad and, sure enough, once the scone plates were empty and the tea-trolleys withdrawn by the maids, Evangeline coughed delicately for our attention and informed us that we might like to hear a little music. Rodney, as a subordinate priest, lifted the lid of the cabinet, placed a twelve-inch record with a pink label on the turntable and wound the handle with the grave air of a man doing a complicated ritual. Everybody else assumed reverent expressions and began jockeying for the most comfortable seats.

For the next half-hour or so there was nothing to be done but sit and suffer it. We had Madame Tetrazzini trilling above the hissing and sissing of the needle, like a princess at the back of a cave with the sea monster snuffling outside it. We had Señor Caruso searching bravely for The Lost Chord in a forest of alien English vowel sounds. We had McCormack's *Kathleen Mavourneen*, Clara Butt longing for her Ain Folk in accents suggesting that they might be found somewhere south of Hyde Park, a tenor whose name I forget summoning Jerusalem, Jerusalem, and everybody looking devout over their empty teacups.

131

In the interludes between the discs we were treated to quite heated *sotto voce* discussions between Rodney and Evangeline on whether it was time to change the needle or whether a particular record should be played at 80 or 81 revolutions a minute, as if that would have made any difference. I sat there wondering how anybody could hope that it had anything to do with music, thinking that even the least competent live singer with an out-of-tune piano would be preferable to these preserved, dessicated sounds. Worse from my point of view, none of it had featured *The Messiah* or any of Osbert Newbiggin's own recording efforts with his local choir.

While the Imperial Russian Balalaika Orchestra was plinking and plonking away I looked around for possible allies. Three broad-shouldered men ranging from middle-aged to elderly were crammed tightly on a chintz settee. They were wearing identical dark suits of good quality cloth, with broad gold watch-chains looped across their waistcoats. Their expressions were properly respectful and yet I thought I detected a shade of disappointment on their faces. I'd seen them before, in the bass section of the choral society on Sunday night. As the last record was removed from the turntable and the maids came in to wheel away the gramophone cabinet the three of them closed in around Rodney Newbiggin. I moved in to listen.

'We were hoping to hear one of your uncle.'

'Or one of all the choir.'

'Foreign stuff is all very well, but you can't tell me it's got the same power to it.'

Rodney, apologetic and abandoned by Evangeline now he'd done his duty by the machine, said they'd thought it might not be quite respectful. The conspiracy of basses seemed a little dashed by this, so it seemed time to add my two-pennyworth. I said, stretching things a little, that I'd heard his uncle had a fine voice. The basses nodded and agreed.

'I gather he left quite a lot of recordings.'

The basses assured me that he had.

'I'd like to hear him again,' one of them said.

Before our combined forces, Rodney began to waver. 'They're most of them in his study. I think they've put the gramophone away, or we . . .'

'He had his own machine in the study. He'd have liked to think of us hearing him.'

The other two murmured their support of him in a deep bass rumble.

'I'd certainly be very interested,' I said.

Rodney looked for guidance to Evangeline but found her preoccupied with superintending a second distribution of tea and talking interior decoration. '. . . and all this terrible Victorian burgundy colour. So of course I told them to strip it all off and had it done in eau-de-Nil, with a line of bright grey for relief . . .'

He gave in. The four of us followed him along a carpeted corridor and through a door on the left.

His wife's mania for redecoration hadn't reached that room, and it looked very much as it had been in Newbiggin's portrait. Although it was carefully dusted it didn't look as if it were much used. Perhaps because of what happened – the murder, for goodness sake, I was becoming as mealy-mouthed as the rest of them – or perhaps Rodney found his uncle's personality too overpowering there. The bust of Handel was still in its place with an open horn gramophone on a small table beside it. Across the room was a broad leather-topped desk with a blotter and a container of pens. The fourteen-year-old Davie Kendal would probably have stood in front of that desk, cap in hand, when he made his first visit to the hall. There were bookcases on the left, mostly filled with the kind of books that are seen rather than read. To the right was a large alcove with white padded screens stacked at the back and cupboards from floor to ceiling along both sides. Apart from the screens it contained only a thing on a table. It looked like another gramophone except that the horn of it was a huge uptilted cone, its throat pointing towards us like something that wanted feeding.

'The recording machine,' one of the basses whispered.

Now that we were in the room there was a tension, as if we'd come to summon up spirits. The dim light didn't help. The blinds were half-way down, and the exposed parts of the windows shaded by bronze chrysanthemums in the flower-bed outside.

Rodney said, looking at the cupboards in the alcove, 'That's where he kept his record collection.'

I sensed his reluctance to step inside it. It had been there that his uncle lay dying and probably nobody had set foot in it since the first clearing up. I thought if you moved aside the screens at the back there might be bloodstains there on the wall. You could tell from their silence that my allies were already thinking better of it.

'What would you like to hear?'

'Oh, something from *The Messiah*, I think.'

What I'd most like to hear would be a record with Osbert's speaking voice on it, but I could hardly ask for that after making such a point about his singing.

Rodney took a few steps forward and opened one of the cupboard doors. 'Of course, quite a few of his records got broken.'

The records were stacked like dinner plates on a drying rack. There were some gaps but not many. Rodney's hand hovered over a section labelled *Messiah: bass arias* and came out holding a black shellac disc. There was total silence as he moved back to the gramophone in the centre of the room, wound the spring motor and carefully lowered the needle. After a few seconds of hissing and scratching a voice filled the dim room like the back of a whale coming out of the sea. A deep voice, more echoing than the professional recordings we'd been hearing next door in the drawing room, but quite distinct. Not speech as I'd hoped, but introductory recitative:

'Behold, I tell you a mystery; we shall not all sleep, but
we shall all be changed, in a moment, in the twinkling
of an eye, at the last trumpet.'

I was watching Rodney's expression and saw it shift from
nervous reverence to horror when he realised what he'd
chosen. The three basses saw it coming too, but to have
stopped it at that point would have been worse. The black
disc went on revolving at its mad speed, hissing like a nest
of serpents, and Osbert Newbiggin's voice launched into
the aria.

'The trumpet shall sound . . .'

Tum-tum TUM, tum tum-tum TUM went a distant piano,
taking the part of the trumpet.

'And the dead shall be raised . . .'

I could feel the collective shiver running through all of us.
The voice of the dead man booming out so confidently
within a few feet of where he'd lain dying, and in that
aria of all things, seemed like the darkest of black magic.
Without meaning to, my eyes went to the alcove and
if at that moment the big, confident figure of Osbert
Newbiggin had walked out of the shadows, I'd have hardly
been more surprised. Rodney had gone as pale as paper
and was staring at the gramophone horn as if it were giving
out the sound of its own volition. The three basses were
frozen into silence. After that first shiver none of us moved
or said anything until the aria came to its end and there was
only clicking and hissing again. Rodney moved over to lift
up the needle, making a longer business of it than seemed
necessary and keeping his face turned away from us.
    One of the basses cleared his throat. 'Ay, he had a
fine voice.'

In the shock of it, I'd hardly been aware of the quality. All right, I thought. Nothing exceptional. I think the rest of them were more than ready to move back next door to the teacups, but stubbornly I wanted to stay in the study. If that recording had been made before their quarrel, Osbert Newbiggin and Davie Kendal would have been together in the same room at the time. The great horn that had sucked in Newbiggin's voice must have received, infinitesimally faintly, the sound of Davie's breathing as well. Perhaps that too had been given back to the air of the study at some level that couldn't be heard, so that it was haunted by two men, one dead and the other all but dead.

I asked, on impulse, if he'd recorded anything secular.

One of the friends said, 'He did "Pale Hands" too. What about "Pale Hands"?'

I guessed that Rodney wanted to get the performance over, but he went obediently to the alcove, came back with another disc and repeated the process of getting it ready to play. The piano again, cool and distant.

'Pale hands I loved beside the Shalimar . . .'

There are few musical experiences more unpleasant than a bass being sentimental. It made me feel as if something were crawling over me because I felt and saw, as if he were standing beside me, not the square, confident mill owner but the middle-aged man who, incredibly, had wept when one of his employees told him to keep his hands off her. Up to that point I wasn't sure how much I believed the story. When I heard that ill-advised vibrato, I was sure. Although his friends presumably hadn't heard about it, the same unease seemed to be touching them. They were fidgeting as the disc spun the song to its swooning climax:

'Pale hands, pink-tipped, like Lotus buds that float
On those cool waters where we used to dwell,
I would have rather felt you round my throat
Crushing out life, than waving me farewell.'

The man who'd suggested the song had obviously forgotten what was in the second verse and was getting some reproachful glances. When the music ended and Rodney picked up the needle there was a different kind of silence, more embarrassed than reverent.

'He was better at *The Messiah*,' the oldest friend said. They thanked Rodney politely and filed out, as if from a chapel. I waited and stood behind him as he replaced the discs in the alcove.

'Was Laura the pianist?'

His shoulders went tense. 'Yes.'

'Is she here today?'

'No.'

And yet she was both a member of the choral society and a distant relative. He was in no hurry to turn round. The huge cone of the recording machine was at his elbow.

'Will you be doing any recordings?'

'No. I've no interest in that side of things. I inherited his shareholding in the Gramophone Company, but recording's an expensive business, best left to the professionals, in my opinion. Uncle Osbert thought otherwise, but then he was a remarkable man in many ways.'

An acknowledgement of his own lack of remarkable qualities.

'Davie Kendal was helping him with his recordings?'

'Yes.'

'Do you think that's what they quarrelled about?'

'I've really no idea.' He straightened up and closed the door of the record cupboard. He was in a dilemma. I was being intolerably inquisitive and he would be within his rights if he told me to mind my own business. His uncle would probably have done exactly that, but Rodney was third-generation mill owner and tamed by interior decoration. On the one hand, he wanted to hustle me out. On the other, he'd grasped that his wife would like to cultivate the acquaintance of the rising young surgeon next door and his elegant wife. As a member of their household, I enjoyed some protection.

137

'But weren't you working with your uncle?'

'Eva and I were in Germany all that summer. He wanted me to get some practical experience of new machinery he was thinking of installing for the mills.'

'And when you left, relations between him and Davie Kendal seemed normal?'

'Yes.'

'When did you know they'd quarrelled?'

'After I heard he'd been murdered.'

'Who told you then?'

He frowned, hesitated. 'I suppose the police did.'

'Not Mrs Bolter or Laura?'

'No. I don't want to be rude, but may I ask why you want to know?'

'I'm wondering if there's any remote possibility that your uncle was killed by somebody other than Davie Kendal.'

'The police didn't think so. Nor did the judge and jury.'

'And you?'

'I agree with them. Now, I'm sure you must be ready for another cup of tea. My wife . . .'

I pretended not to hear him. I was behaving intolerably and he couldn't do anything about it without annoying his wife. It was a form of socialised bullying and I should have felt ashamed of myself. Instead I thought of a thin old hand cradling a canary.

'There are a few loose ends though, aren't there?'

Nobody of normal curiosity could have ignored that bait. He didn't.

'What?'

'For a start, there were four people in the house and nobody heard the shot.'

'He muffled it with a cushion.'

'The pair to that one, I suppose.'

There were two leather armchairs in the study. One of them had a plump cushion on it in faded gold brocade. The other conspicuously didn't.

'I . . . I suppose so. I'd never really thought about it.' He looked at the surviving cushion as if he expected it to grow claws and a tail.

'From that portrait your uncle looked quite a big man, strong.'

'Yes.'

'So look what the murderer has to do.' I made a dive for the cushion and grabbed it with my left hand. It was surprisingly heavy, stuffed full of feathers, and I had to scrabble to get a grip on the brocade. Rodney started to protest then cut it off in mid-phrase, staring at me with eyes and mouth wide open.

'He makes a grab for a cushion with one hand and holds the gun in the other.' I raised my right hand. For a second there was sheer terror in his eyes, as if I really had produced a gun. If he'd yelled for help I couldn't have blamed him. 'I take it that there were blood splashes on that wall behind the screens?'

'Y . . . yes. So . . . I gather.'

'So the murderer, holding a cushion in one hand and a gun in the other, has to force a large strong man into the alcove, hold his head against the wall with the cushion, then shoot through it. What's the large strong man doing in the meantime?'

I advanced on him, making him take a step backwards towards the alcove, pushing the cushion towards his face. He wasn't large or strong, but his hand came up to keep me away.

'Exactly. He'd struggle. And the evidence is that he did just that, the overturned chairs and so on. But why wasn't he more effective and why didn't he shout?'

I took a step back in one direction, he in the other. He was looking quite shaken.

'I'm sorry, but I don't see how this casts any doubt on Davie Kendal being guilty.'

'No, but surely it casts doubt on the way he was killed. If so, mightn't there be doubt about the rest of it as well?'

He looked like a man who was giving it real thought, but

before he could answer there was his wife's voice from the other side of the door.

'Rodney, are you in there?'

She opened the door without waiting for an answer and went stiff with dislike when she saw me. Her husband was still breathing heavily and I was a few yards away grasping one of their chair cushions. It must have looked as if we'd been having a one-sided pillow fight.

'What are you doing, Rodney? The Pendle-Chichesters have been looking for you to say their goodbyes.'

He moved in a dazed way towards the door. I replaced the cushion and smiled at her. She didn't return the smile, waited for me to go past her then pointedly closed the door behind me. As she caught up with him along the corridor I heard her hissing something about '. . . knew it would happen . . . vulgar curiosity'. I was tempted to say something Johnsonian on the lines of 'Madam, I am often curious but seldom vulgar' and resisted it.

I found Rose and Pauline in the drawing room, eager to go, so we followed the example of the departing Pendle-Chichesters and said our goodbyes.

When we were walking down the drive Pauline said, 'What in the world have you done to Mrs Newbiggin?'

'Oh, you saw the look she gave me?'

'Saw it? It scorched me and I wasn't the one it was meant for. I'm surprised your hair isn't in flames.'

'Very inhospitable of her. All I did was borrow her husband for a reconstruction of the murder.'

Since that little tussle in the study I'd felt, goodness knows why, a rush of light-heartedness. There was something waiting after all, I didn't know what, but something.

Pauline laughed. 'For a moment I thought you were serious.'

'I am serious. By the way, was Mrs Bolter there?'

'No. I gather her arthritis is troubling her.'

'You say she moved to Southport. I must find out where exactly.'

'Lord Street, next to the hat shop.'

'Now how on earth did you do that?'

'I was trapped by some old biddy who'd been a friend of hers. What do you want to ask her?'

'Why she hates Davie Kendal so much.'

'I'd have thought that was obvious.'

We walked through the town, stopped at intervals by people who wanted to talk to Pauline, and back up the hill. When we'd seen her to her door, Rose and I walked across to our cottage. It was near dusk, with the occasional bat looping round us.

'What about the other one? Are you going to see her as well?'

'Laura. I must. Tomorrow, before I go to Southport.'

I wasn't looking forward to it. I could deal with reputed holy terrors like Mrs Bolter quite happily, but there was something about the thin, pale girl at the piano that bothered me.

'I'm going to Manchester tomorrow with Janet. They're letting her and her father in to see him. Perhaps . . .' She hesitated and I could see she was worried about how I'd react. 'There's a chance that I might see him too. Janet says she can tell them I'm a cousin from London and they might . . . since it's so close.'

'Rose, it won't do any good.' I hated the way she was being drawn into Janet's misery.

'If I could get him to say something that would help . . .'

'How? You know there'll be warders listening to every breath you and he take. If you're supposed to be his cousin, you can hardly cross-question him about the murder.'

'No, I suppose not. But I can't stand not doing anything. What would you ask him if you could?'

'What he and Osbert Newbiggin were really talking about. But if he hasn't told the truth about it all this time, he's not suddenly going to break down and tell you tomorrow.'

Another few strides, then she said, 'Did you find out anything this afternoon? Anything hopeful?'

'No. Well, yes . . . but it's more of a feeling than a hope. Please, when you see Janet tomorrow, don't say anything to her.'

Nothing to send yet to warm her.

THIRTEEN

ROSE AND I WERE BOTH out early in the morning, she to meet Janet at the station, I to catch my brother on his own. The bite of autumn was in the air, with the sky over the moor a pale, tight-stretched blue and a heavy layer of dew glazing the dried grass, making it slippery. I found Stuart in the outhouse where they stored the hen coops and the unused governess cart, wearing a respectable suit for ward rounds and pumping up his front bicycle tyre.

'I gather you've ruined our social prospects with the new neighbours.'

'Are you sorry?'

'First useful thing you've done since you came here. Pauline says you're going to visit the holy terror at Southport.'

He was in a cheerful mood. I hated to spoil it.

'I'm going to see Laura as well.'

He left the pump hanging from the wheel and stood up. 'Don't you start bothering that poor girl too. She can't help.'

'Who else has been bothering her, and why are you so sure she can't?'

'The prosecution didn't even call her as a witness. She didn't see anything the old lady didn't see.'

'Yes. Don't you think that's odd?'

'Why?'

'An old woman who must be seventy or so and a girl in her early twenties. But it's the old woman who sees the face at the window. It's the old woman who goes into the study

143

and finds Osbert Newbiggin dying. Wouldn't you expect the younger woman to notice more and do more?'

'It depends on character. From what I hear of old Mrs Bolter, she's as tough as an army mule.'

'And Laura?'

'She's not physically strong. In fact she's not a well woman.'

'She's not one of your patients?'

'No, she goes to one of the GPs in the town, Dr Clayton.'

'And yet you're taking an interest in her, even though Pauline doesn't like it much.'

He glared. 'Has Pauline been talking about it to you?'

'Not a word, but I can pick up signals. I'm sure you can too. Pauline's a generous woman and she'd usually do anything to help someone in trouble, but she freezes every time the name comes up in conversation.'

He bent down and started pumping at the tyre again, ferociously. 'It's like any other small town. There are some people who have nothing better to do than gossip.'

'And they've been gossiping about you and Laura. Stupid gossip, of course, but I assume there was some kind of starting point.'

'If I tell you, will you promise not to go and bother her?'

'I can't promise.'

'I wish to God you'd never started this. Damn Bill Musgrave and his wounded pride.'

'That's unfair, it isn't just wounded pride.'

'I've known him for three years. You've only met him once.'

'Twice. In fact he took me to a concert. If you put any more air into that tyre you'll have a flying bicycle.'

He dropped the valve cap and cursed it, meaning me. 'I'll miss that train.'

'Just tell me what you were going to tell me about Laura or I'll run after you all the way down the hill.'

'Very well, here's as much as I'm going to tell you, and I

144

won't have you cross-examining me about it. One evening last December, about a week before Christmas, I came home from work and found Laura Newbiggin collapsed on the station platform. I got the ticket collector to help me and we managed to get her to Dr Clayton. We had to wheel her sitting on one of the station trolleys because we couldn't get a cab. Dr Clayton's a young man, sympathetic. He did what he could for her and afterwards I got a cab at last and took her back to her lodgings. Three times since then I've looked in to see how she is. End of story.'

'What was wrong with her?'

'Haemorrhaging and exhaustion.'

'Tuberculosis?'

'Not as far as I know. She's not my patient, and in any case if she were I couldn't tell you about her.'

'December. That was a month after Newbiggin was murdered?'

'Yes.'

'While Davie Kendal was still on the run.'

'I suppose so. Now if you'd kindly let me get to work . . .' He nudged at my shins with the bicycle wheel.

'And she was already in her own lodgings then?'

'She'd just moved in to them. The place was as bare as an iceberg and twice as cold.'

The small legacy from her cousin wouldn't have been paid so soon after his death. Stuart wouldn't have left her without bringing in coal and food, even if he'd had to drag the coal merchant and grocer from their own firesides to get them. No wonder the town had gossiped. I stood aside and let him wheel the bicycle out onto the cracked stones.

'So will you promise?'

'Not to see her? I haven't promised. But I will be careful.'

He looked at me as if there were other things he'd like to say, then jumped on the bicycle and pedalled away fast down his uneven drive, medical bag on the back. I was sorry I had to keep annoying him.

*　　*　　*

145

I followed on foot down to the town and walked to the area near the station where Laura Newbiggin had her lodgings. A card in the window of a haberdashery shop offered voice and piano lessons by a qualified teacher at reasonable rates. There was no name on the card, just a street and number, and the neat italic writing had faded to a brownish colour on a yellowed background. It was a depressed part of town and didn't look as if there'd be much demand for music lessons or spare money to pay for them.

I followed the directions of the woman in the shop and found myself in a street of smoke-grimed terraced houses with gaps in the cobbles. The very few white scrubbed steps and polished door-knockers were no more than flags of protest against their grey and tarnished neighbours. Sounds of painstaking scales drifted faintly into the street, competing with the noise of trains and the more distant thrumming of the cotton mills. I followed them to a house as dingy as the rest with a faded red front door and cracks in the upstairs windows covered with brown paper and glue. Not wanting to intrude on a lesson I strolled up and down outside and heard the scales give way to 'Drink to Me Only' played like a teetotallers' march, repeated several times over without any obvious sign of improvement.

Five minutes or so later a girl with a music case came out wearing a knitted woollen cap and wiping her nose on the back of her glove. As there was no sign or sound of another pupil, I knocked on the door and waited.

It was a long wait. When the door opened at last she just stood there staring at me. Her eyes were large but quite empty and there was a bleary look about them. Her dark hair was scraped back so severely that it dragged at the pale skin of her forehead and the artery throbbing at her temple looked like a creature struggling for release. She was wearing a skirt of dark brown serge, a yellowish wool blouse buttoned tight to the neck, and a brown corduroy jacket. Apart from her face, the only parts of her body visible were her long hands and wrists as thin as sticks.

146

She said nothing at all. The possibility that I might be a new pupil in search of piano lessons clearly hadn't crossed her mind. She looked as if nothing had crossed her mind for a long time, like a patch of wind-blown snow without even hare tracks as a sign of life.

I'd made no plans because I wanted to see her first. Now that I was seeing her I could make no plans either because there was not the faintest sign of response or curiosity. It might have been tempting to say my brother had sent me to see if she were all right, but I keep deliberate lies for people I know deserve them, and I had no idea yet what Laura deserved.

'My name's Nell Bray. May I come in?'

Still without saying anything she turned and led the way through a doorway on the left. I followed, closing the front door behind me. The narrow corridor had a floor of bare planks. The faded wallpaper was rubbed in places to the texture of suede from decades of people brushing past it. Her room was not much better. An upright piano stood against one wall. Even though her pupil had only just left she'd already closed the lid on it. There was a piano stool with a brown leatherette top, torn at one corner, a small square table with a wooden framed calendar on it, one upright chair next to the piano stool, another against the wall. The net curtain over the window facing on the street was clean but beginning to tear because it wasn't quite wide enough and had been stretched too tight. The floor was covered with brown linoleum. The only thing on the bare off-white walls was a black framed certificate proving that Miss Laura Newbiggin was qualified to teach pianoforte. Nothing else at all.

Apart from prison cells, I'd never seen anything so bleak. I'd stepped out of a bright September day into December, as cold as the day when my brother had found her on the station platform and brought her back here. There was another thing that brought prison cells to mind – the terrible neatness. A speck of dust, the smear of a finger on the furniture, would have come as a relief, but there

147

wasn't one. I could see the top of the frame round the certificate and even that was dustless. A half-open doorway revealed a narrow bed with a grey blanket strained over it to hospital tightness, not even a rag-rug beside it to soften the icy surface of the polished linoleum.

Laura walked over to the bedroom door, closed it, then sat down on the upright chair by the piano stool. I sat down on the other chair.

'I heard you playing at the rehearsal on Sunday. You're very good.'

A 'thank you' fluttered into the air and died of cold. It must have come from her, but I hadn't seen a muscle of her face move.

'I've heard you too on the gramophone.'

No response at all to that.

'I'm sorry to intrude on you. I know this is very hard for you, but do you think I might ask you a few questions about what happened?'

'What?' Her pale lips had moved very slightly. They were dry and cracked and perhaps speaking with them was painful.

'You were there that night? Your aunt called you.'

'His aunt.'

'I'm sorry, his aunt, not yours. Mrs Bolter. She called out and you went to see what was happening.'

'Yes.'

'Where was Mr Newbiggin when you saw him?'

'On . . . on the floor.'

'What did you do?'

'I . . . I ran out.'

'Why?'

The obvious answer was 'to get help', but she didn't give it, just sat there staring at the window.

'It was November. Cold and dark.'

'Yes.'

'Nobody thought of using the telephone?'

'No.'

It still puzzled me, that unnecessary rush down the dark

drive. 'That evening, had you heard anything that might be a shot?'

'No.'

'A door slamming?'

'No.'

'When Mrs Bolter called and you went into the room, you saw him on the floor. Is there anything else you remember?'

'Discs. They were broken.'

'Yes. Did you see a gun?'

She licked her cracked lips with a pale tongue. 'I don't know. I don't know what I saw. It was all . . . his blood on everything.'

'Did you go right inside the room?'

'No. I just looked, and then she told me to go and get help.' Her hands lay lifelessly on her lap, side by side.

After a long silence I tried another tack. 'You and your cousin were both interested in music?'

'Yes.'

'Did you enjoy making the recordings with him?'

No reply. If the word 'enjoy' had ever meant anything to her, it certainly didn't now.

'Can you remember about a month before he was killed, there was somebody looking into your dining room one night. Who was it?'

'I didn't see.'

'Mrs Bolter must have said something. Didn't you look up?'

'I didn't see.'

Some time, in the quite recent past, this woman had been capable of singing 'as if it had just come into her head on a May morning'. I had my brother's word for that, or I shouldn't have believed it possible.

'What did you think of Mr Newbiggin?'

No answer, only one hand shifted and clamped itself over the other. We sat without speaking for a while. She gave no sign of impatience or of wanting me to go, although there was certainly no pleasure for her in my company. I thought, 'As soon as I've gone, she'll dust the chair I'm sitting on.' Even the duster would be thin, many times washed. There wasn't much to look at in the room, so that the single thing that was out of place stood out like a lighthouse. The calendar. It was the perpetual kind, wooden frame with slots on the front and little wheels at the back that you revolved each day to the right date. The month was September, the climate in the room was December but the calendar said 4 April. And yet it was as clean as everything else in the room. The table surface around it was clean too, so she must have picked it up every day to dust under it. Most people, if they pick up a calendar, will automatically move the date on without thinking about it. Laura was tidy to the point of mania, but she hadn't changed the calendar for five months.

I stood up. I thanked her. She followed me into the corridor and watched as I opened the front door. As I went down the path I heard it close behind me, not slammed. When she'd stood up to let me out she'd given a long sigh, not sad, not exasperated, no particular sound to it at all. But it had a smell. The acetone whiff – ironically close to the smell of pear-drops – of the breath of somebody who's starving herself to death. It had been faint, like everything else about her, but it stayed in my nostrils all the way to the station and didn't quite go until I was in the train for Liverpool where it was blotted out by the sooty smell of the carriage upholstery. I had time then, too, to work out dates from my memory of the court transcript and confirm what I'd suspected when I noticed her calendar. The fourth of April was the day when Davie Kendal had been condemned to death.

FOURTEEN

THERE ARE AT LEAST THREE hat shops in Lord Street, Southport. It's a place where the more prosperous people go to spend the money they make in Liverpool and Manchester or where they retire. The winds blowing in from the Irish Sea keep the smoke of the manufacturing towns away. On clear days at high tides you can even see the sea, a thin line out over the mud-flats behind the bandstand. Mrs Bolter had taken up residence in a house between the third hat shop where I enquired and a café, with white-aproned waitresses serving tables of sensible tweeds and hats plumed with pheasant feathers. The brass doorknocker and glossy black paint gleamed on her front door, not tarnished yet by the salt air. I knocked and the door was opened by a skinny maid with a nervous tic of the mouth and scared eyes.

'Is she expecting you?'

'No. I'm an acquaintance of Rodney Newbiggin.'

I gave my name and she closed the door to a crack and disappeared. I was depending on the hope that the holy terror would be bored in her seaside retirement and perhaps that was the case, because the maid came back and, in a nervous whisper, invited me to come inside.

Mrs Bolter was sitting by her parlour window in a high-backed armchair angled so that she could look at what was going on in the room, or out at the fashionable promenaders in Lord Street if she chose. She was a large woman, big boned rather than fat, dressed in a shapeless dress of loose green velvet with cream lace at the neck and cuffs. Her grey hair was piled up elaborately, almost frivolously, and seemed to have as little to do with the craggy face beneath it as icing on a pork pie. Her thick grey eyebrows jutted out a good inch from her forehead over cold, pale eyes. The skin under her jaw was pouched, but her chin looked as if it had spent most of its life winning arguments.

'Did Rodney send you?'

'No. I went to his At Home yesterday with my sister-in-law, Mrs Bray.'

'So they're letting all the neighbours in to gawp, are they? Her idea, was it? I suppose she's getting the place up like the pier at Blackpool.' Her eyes glinted at me, expecting answers.

'They've done some redecoration.'

'She'll finish up bankrupting him. I told him so, but they don't listen to me. I suppose you want tea.'

There was a bell on the arm of her chair with a brass elephant on the top of it. Her hand was so bent with arthritis that she took several attempts to get a grip on it but once she had it she rang it vigorously. The scared maid reappeared and was given an order for tea '... and you can bring my medicine too'. The room was pleasant enough, with bright floral wallpaper and new green curtains and carpet, but dominated by photographs of what I took to be the family. Most of them were from a generation ago, but there was a newer one of Osbert Newbiggin in evening dress with drapes behind him.

'So you thought you'd come for a look at the old woman as well.'

'I wanted to ask you about your nephew's murder.'

No point in going round the houses with this one, which suited me. She gulped and stared.

'Are you from the newspapers?'

'No. I've met Davie Kendal's sister. She's convinced her brother didn't kill him.'

'Then she's either a fool or a liar. I don't know who or

what you are, but I'd have thought you had better things to do with your time.'

'You know he's going to be hanged in six days?'

'Good thing too. I don't know why they keep them alive so long these days.'

'You've never had any doubt?'

'Doubt? He insulted poor Osbert who took him up out of the gutter, then he shot him with his own gun.'

'They never found the gun, did they?'

'What difference does that make?'

'Laura told the police she thought she saw it on the floor.'

Up until that point I think she was thoroughly enjoying the exercise of being rude to me, but as soon as I said the name the spark of enjoyment faded from her eyes, leaving them even colder than before.

'You haven't been talking to that little slut, have you?'

'Slut? Because she was in love with Davie Kendal?'

'In love? Is that what she told you? In love.' Both times, the phrase came out as a sneer.

'She didn't tell me anything, but that's what the quarrel was about, wasn't it? Nothing to do with anything that happened at the mill. Your nephew quarrelled with Davie because he wanted to marry Laura Newbiggin.'

'Doesn't make any difference what they quarrelled over. He still killed him.'

'Laura and Davie probably met when they were making those recordings. She was playing the piano and he was helping with the machinery. Things went on from there, and the summer before last Davie went to your nephew and told him he wanted to marry Laura. Osbert didn't like it. Perhaps he felt he'd as good as adopted Laura . . .'

'There was never any question of that.'

'Anyway, there she was, living up at the big house with you. Davie was only an employee, after all. I suppose Osbert thought he wasn't good enough for Laura.'

'Anybody would be too good for her.'

'That doesn't seem to be the way Osbert saw it. They

quarrelled about it and either he sacked Davie or Davie gave in his notice.'

The maid came in with the tea, a bottle of tonic wine and a glass. Her hands were shaking so much that the cups and glass rattled against each other. She put the tray down on a small table beside Mrs Bolter's chair and poured a glass of the wine with the cold grey eyes intent on her every move. Then she waited, quivering, for the nod that allowed her to escape. The old woman ignored the tea and gulped the purplish, viscous wine. She drank it from a cut-glass tumbler instead of a wine glass. It had the double advantage that it held more and was easier to grip.

'I'm sure that was why Davie was at the hall that night you saw him from the dining room. The jury thought he was prowling because he intended harm to Osbert. I think he just wanted to see Laura.'

'That girl lied to the police. She knew very well who it was that night.'

'You must have lied to the police, too. They thought all along it was something to do with the mill. Why was that?'

She took a long drink of the wine, looking at me over the glass.

'Was it because you thought it was some sort of blot on the family that Davie Kendal wanted to marry Laura? Why shouldn't he, after all?'

She put the glass down carefully on the tray, deliberately not offering to pour tea for me.

'And Davie didn't tell his family about any of this. He probably thought his brother wouldn't approve either.'

'What's it to do with you?'

'If there's anything else that hasn't come out . . .'

'What else would there be? He shot Osbert and that's that.'

'I gather you were the one who found him?'

'Yes.'

'It must have been a dreadful shock. No wonder you panicked at first.'

154

'Panicked!'

It was the first off-guard reaction I'd got from her. She stared at me, genuinely astonished.

'Yes, quite understandable. You knew you needed a doctor for him so you sent cook to ring the bell and Laura down to the town and all the time you forgot that the best way of getting help was there in the room with you. The telephone on his desk.'

'I don't hold with telephones.'

'Couldn't Laura have used it?'

'It wouldn't have made any difference. The doctor said there'd have been no hope for him.'

For the first time, I thought there was a touch of regret in her voice. She took another long gulp of the wine.

'Now, have you quite finished?'

'One more thing, you told the police you didn't hear the shot that killed him. Are you still sure of that?'

'Quite sure.'

Her eyes looked at me, unblinking. Their folded-back lids were pink and a little gummy, the lashes sparse. Knowing I was going to get nothing more useful, not even the cup of tea, I thanked her for giving me her time and picked up my gloves.

'You'll be seeing her again, that man's sister.'

'Janet Kendal, yes.'

'You can give her a message from me.'

'What?'

'Tell them, if the hangman's otherwise engaged and keeps him waiting, let me know and I'll come and do the job myself.'

She held up her hooked hands at me, laughed and rang the bell. When the maid opened the door to let me out I felt like advising her to make a run for it, go anywhere, because nothing could be worse than having to live like that. I've sometimes wondered why I didn't.

It was dark by the time I got back to the cottage, but the fire and lamp were unlit and there was no sign of Rose. She got back about half an hour later, and walked in and just stood there without the energy to talk or even sit down.

'Bad?'

'Oh Nell . . . For goodness sake, can't we *do* something?'

I helped her off with her coat, sat her down by the fire, brewed tea. After that she started talking and couldn't stop. She'd gone to Strangeways prison with Janet and her father. The cousin story had worked, to the extent that it got her access to Davie.

'It was only two visitors at a time, so Janet and I went in and Mr Kendal waited in another room. As soon as we went in, Janet said Cousin Rose had come from London to see him.'

'Was he surprised?'

She hesitated. 'I don't think the word means anything with him any more. No, he didn't seem surprised, but I don't think he'd have been surprised if a giraffe had walked in. You know, as if nothing made any sense so I didn't matter one way or the other.'

'What did he look like?'

'Pale, round face, hair cut short, very clean-shaven. You know, the warders shave him every morning because . . .'

'Because they think if he has a razor in his hand he might cut his throat with it. The warders were there, of course.'

'Yes, two of them. And they were listening all the time, just as you said they'd be.'

'What did you talk about?'

'Janet told him their father was waiting outside, and he just nodded. She said Jimmy sent his love and would be coming to see him. Then she asked if he was sleeping and he said yes, not too badly, thank you. He really said thank you. Do you know, Nell, I think that was one of the worst things about it.'

'Why?'

'The politeness. You know what people are like when they're visiting and they have to talk to each other even though they've got nothing to say and just want to get away and get on with what they were doing. It was like that with him. And even the warders were polite, to him as well as to us. It was almost as if . . .' She stopped again, then started in a rush. '. . . almost as if they were scared of him. That sounds ridiculous, it should be the other way round, but it wasn't. I don't mean scared of him, but scared of what was going to happen to him.'

'Did you say anything to him?'

'Only near the end. We just had a quarter of an hour with him. Janet asked him, didn't he have anything to say to his cousin Rose, and he thanked me for coming. I guessed she must have been expecting more than that, so I thought I'd try what you wanted to know. I started saying something like "When you saw Mr Newbiggin . . ." And I could feel them going tense, Janet and the warders, all except him. He looked at me very steadily and said, "I didn't kill him. Whatever you hear about me, tell all of them I didn't kill Mr Newbiggin." Then the warder said it was time to go and Janet got up all of a sudden and put her arms round him and he leaned against her for a moment. I don't know whether they were allowed to, but the warders didn't try to stop them and then we had to go. He had his head down when we went, not looking at us.'

'"Whatever you hear about me." I wonder what else he thinks anybody might hear.'

'I don't know. But it's not any use, is it? It doesn't tell us anything.'

'Did Janet say anything afterwards?'

'Not much. I think she was glad I'd heard him say what he said. Their father went in and we waited in this little room until he came back. He was trying to be brave inside Strangeways for Davie's sake, but as soon as we were round the corner from the gates his legs wouldn't hold him any more. He'd have just collapsed there on the pavement if Janet and I hadn't held him up.'

She'd gone home with them and stayed most of the evening trying to do what she could.

'Which was nothing, Nell. What can you say or do,

157

except that you'll get him out, keep him alive, and that's the one thing you can't do?'

She went quiet again, staring at the fire, then, 'If he were dying of something in a hospital it would be different. It's knowing that he's all right now, living and breathing and being fed and looked after, but six days from now he'll be taken out and have his neck broken by other human beings in cold blood. I think if it were my brother I'd go mad, waiting outside the gates, knowing he was just on the other side of the wall and they were doing it to him and I couldn't help him any more than if I were on the other side of the world. I'd break a hole in the walls with a pickaxe, use dynamite, anything. Can you imagine her, just waiting?'

'Is that what she's going to do?'

'I said I'd wait with her.'

We had no appetite for dinner, or for anything else. I fed the cats, kept brewing tea and putting logs on the fire. The light was dim because the wick of the lamp needed trimming, but we didn't even have the heart for that. After a while Rose asked if I'd found out anything useful during the day.

'Quite a lot, but I'm afraid it's not useful.'

I told her about the visits to Laura and Mrs Bolter, leaving out only Mrs Bolter's message about the hangman.

'Laura didn't tell you herself that she loved him?'

'No. It was only the calendar that made me realise. Most of her mind must have frozen that day the verdict was given. She can't bear to wind the calendar on because it brings it one day closer.'

'If she loves Davie, why doesn't she get out there and try to do something, like Janet?'

'Different character. And perhaps she thought it would only make things worse.'

'How could they be worse?'

'It might have made his chances even slimmer at the trial. One of the points for the defence was that nobody could find a real motive. The best the prosecution could

158

do was some undefined quarrel at work. If they'd known he loved Laura and Newbiggin wouldn't let him marry her, that would have strengthened the case against him.'

'They could have eloped together without Davie having to kill him.'

'Yes, but they didn't. Perhaps Laura was just too nervous. It can't have been easy as a poor relation living with Mrs Bolter.'

'She sounds a hateful woman. You don't suppose she could have shot Newbiggin herself?'

'I'd like to think so, but no. With any other woman I'd say she was fond of him. It hardly applies in her case as I can't imagine that old monster being fond of anybody, but he was important to her as head of the family. She had no opportunity either. The evidence at the trial was that she and Laura were together all evening, until she looked into the study on her way up to bed.'

'If Laura's as spiritless as you say, the old monster could have scared her.'

'Scared her so much that even when she's away from her she won't speak up to save Davie's life? No. Anyway, Mrs Bolter couldn't have shot him, even if she'd wanted to.'

'Why not?'

'Her hands are so arthritic she'd find it difficult to pick up a gun, let alone fire it. And remember it's not just the gun. She'd have to hold a heavy cushion to his head with her other hand. Not possible.'

'So what are you saying, Nell? That you think he did it after all?'

It took a long time to answer that. It was a question I'd been avoiding even in my own mind.

'I honestly don't know. But I'm afraid what I've found out today about him and Laura makes the case against him look even stronger.'

Rose's fury at that was mostly directed against Laura. Why had the girl been so spiritless that she just sat there in the big house, waiting for the man she loved to do something? Why, once the murder had happened,

159

couldn't she at least try to help – lie to the police, say she'd seen her uncle alive after Davie left the house? If she'd been determined and convincing enough, it might have swayed the jury. 'And at the very least, once the worst has happened and the man's condemned to death, why can't she come out in public then and let everybody know she loves him? It can't make matters worse now and if nothing else they might let her go and see him. Instead she just sits there starving herself and not turning the calendar. I could shake the woman, I really could.'

If anything else had provoked it, I'd have been glad to see the old combative Rose back again, with all the taming influence of school teaching in Wimbledon swept away. As it was, it only made things worse.

'That might not be fair to Laura. She's probably had a worse time than we know.'

I told her about the conversation with my brother. 'Of course, he's playing professional confidentiality even though she isn't his patient. But look at the facts. It's about a month after the murder and Davie has disappeared. Laura goes away somewhere by train, probably to Manchester. Later she's discovered ill and bleeding on the station platform and has to be taken to a doctor who's young and sympathetic. Now, what does that suggest to you?'

She was so caught up in her indignation against Laura that it took her some time to get to it, but I watched her in the dim lamplight and saw her face change.

'She'd been to Old Mother Miller.'

'Um?'

'That's what they used to call her where I grew up. Ten bob on the table, then a glass of gin and knitting needle. If a girl was away from work for a day and came back looking pale, they'd say she'd been to see Old Mother Miller.' Her voice when she said it was East End, not what they'd have recognised in Rose's training college.

'Yes. I think Laura was expecting Davie's baby. That might have been what the meeting with Newbiggin was

160

about. At the very least, it would have made it urgent to get her away from there and marry her. Then Newbiggin was dead, Davie on the run and she was shut up in the Hall with an old woman who regarded her as a slut. So she moved out to lodgings and made her own arrangements. When Stuart found her on the platform she'd just got back from the Manchester equivalent of Old Mother Miller.'

If I was right, that experience had drained the last of Laura's energy, what little of it was left after the murder and Davie's disappearance. She'd gone on trudgingly teaching the piano to keep a roof over her head, dusting obsessively because dust flecks were the only things in life still under her control. Quite soon – probably the day they hanged Davie Kendal – she'd let the dust settle at last and everything would be over. Rose caught what I was thinking.

'Do you think she'll kill herself?'

'The way she's going on, she won't need to.'

Soon after that we went to bed. After I'd blown out my own candle I could see the light of Rose's still flickering in the gap between doorpost and door.

At breakfast there were dark rings round Rose's eyes. She drank the coffee I brewed, but didn't touch anything else.

'Eat, for heaven's sake. The bread's stale, but the butter's good and there's some of Pauline's plum jam.'

I had no great appetite myself, but didn't want to see Rose wasting away as well. She spread butter listlessly on a fragment of bread, looked at it.

'What are we going to do today?'

'Are you going down to see Janet?'

'I suppose so, only every time I go there she can't help looking at me as if I'm going to tell her some good news. And there isn't any.'

'No.'

There'd been a spark. There in Newbiggin's study there'd been a spark, only it hadn't lit anything and the memory of it had been almost wiped out by seeing Mrs Bolter and Laura.

161

We went outside to see what the day was like – cooler, with clouds scudding across the moor – and stood under the rowan tree drinking our coffee. Birds had already stripped away most of its berries and leaves were beginning to fall. The clumps of heather clinging to the quarry wall were turning gradually from purple to brown. Then we saw Pauline coming from the direction of the house waving a piece of paper.

'Telegram. Telegram for you, Nell.'

It read: 'POSSIBLE DEVELOPMENT STOP CAN YOU MEET ME STATION TWO THIRTY STOP SAY NOTHING TO SISTER STOP'. It was signed Bill Musgrave.

FIFTEEN

THE DOG CAME OUT OF THE train before it was at a standstill, followed only slightly less precipitately by Bill Musgrave. He was dressed for an afternoon in the country, old tweed jacket, walking breeches, flat cap.

'Rolling Toby's turned up.'

'What does he say?'

'I haven't seen him yet. I thought you might care to come along with us. You're wearing your walking boots, I see. Very prescient.'

After such a famine of good news even the sight of him striding along the station platform with the dog at his heels made me feel better. I was struck again by his inability to hide his feelings and his impulsiveness. He himself had described Rolling Toby as the least reliable alibi witness in the whole of Lancashire, yet he was reacting as if to the first swallow of spring.

'How did you know he was back?'

'From the clerk to Davie Kendal's solicitor, a very promising young man called Andrew Witherspoon. He's become very involved with this case. Too much so, his employer thinks, but it is his first murder, after all.'

'Has Witherspoon spoken to him?'

'Not yet. I asked him to wait for me.'

'And what we're hoping is that he'll say Davie was with him at the time when that telephone call to Newbiggin's friend was made.'

'Yes. It would help considerably if we could prove that Davie was nowhere near a telephone around eight o'clock.'

'Meaning that somebody else would have had to play that recording of Newbiggin's voice?'

We were out of the station by now, striding along the street. He walked as he talked, fast and decisively. What with that and the immense dog, we were attracting some glances.

'You know, I've been thinking about that. The prosecution assume that the whole point of that attempt was to make it seem as if Newbiggin were still alive at about eight o'clock.'

'Which he was, of course. He didn't actually die until after the aunt and doctor got to him.'

'Yes, but I take it there's no doubt at all that he was as good as dead from the time that shot hit him?'

'Certainly. There's no medical dispute at all about that. He'd have been unconscious almost instantly, certainly in no state to make telephone calls.'

'And the prosecution's assumption was that the shot was fired at some time between Davie Kendal's arrival at the hall just before six o'clock, and when he was seen at the Cross Keys around half-past seven?'

'Yes.'

'So it would be to nobody's advantage to make that telephone call apart from the person's who killed him – always assuming that he really was unconscious and dying at the time it was made.'

I glanced at him and saw him looking at me in a disappointed way, as if I wasn't as intelligent as he'd hoped.

'Of course. What other advantage might there be?'

'So it's that apparent attempt to establish he was alive and conscious at eight o'clock that made the prosecution believe that Newbiggin must have been shot before the call was made?'

'Yes. The logic's faulty, of course. Person X knows he's dead – or as good as – but wants it to be thought he's still alive. So if somebody is pretending he's still alive, that must be Person X. Still, juries aren't logical animals and

164

there's no getting away from the fact that the record was found in his family's ash-bin. But if I could have found just one half-way credible witness who was talking to Davie at the time that telephone call was made, that could have shaken the whole prosecution case.'

'But Rolling Toby migrated.'

'Yes. In March, when there's a bit of planting work to be done in the market gardens in Cheshire, he packs up his pony cart and moves off. Then he just revolves round from asparagus cutting to strawberry picking to apples or what have you. Then back he comes again and as good as hibernates for the winter. He's early this year, thank the gods.'

'But he's still only a faint hope, isn't he?'

'Oh, don't you start saying that as well. I'm tired of faint hopes. I want a nice, fat, young, squawling, bouncing hooligan of a hope for a change. Why must all hopes be faint?'

As we walked towards the town centre I decided I'd better tell him what I'd been doing, not that he could be expected to like it.

'I think I've found something else that was missing.'

He stopped in his tracks.

'The motive.'

The smile that was beginning to form was wiped away in an instant.

'When you say motive, do you mean a motive for . . . ?'

'Yes. For Davie Kendal.'

'Oh, for goodness sake take it away. I don't want it.'

He began to walk again, even faster. I kept pace with him.

'I suppose I'm going to have to ask you.'

So I told him about my visits to Laura and Mrs Bolter. When I got to the point about Laura's calendar he asked if we could stop walking. There was a Baptist chapel behind us in black and yellow glazed brick, with a low wall enclosing a courtyard with three dusty laurel bushes.

We sat on the wall and the dog sighed and spread himself out in the courtyard.

'And you deduced just from the calendar that she's in love with him?'

'Mostly from that.'

'Did you ask her directly?'

'No, it only hit me afterwards. I knew there was something there. But the aunt's attitude confirms it.'

'That woman's a malicious old monster. I nearly choked from having to be patient when I was cross-examining her. I'd have liked to wring her thick neck.'

'You'd have hurt your hands on it. But it makes sense, doesn't it? I wondered why Laura didn't recognise that face at the window, when the aunt did.'

'So she lied to protect him?'

'Yes. Not that it did any good.'

'What I can't understand, if you're right, is why Newbiggin and the aunt were so much against it. After all, Laura was only a poor cousin, not the daughter of the house, and Davie was quite respectable.'

'Yes, but Laura lived at the big house with them and Davie was only a worker, after all. She'd be a cut above him.'

He kicked the wall. 'Silly snobbery. But this is all speculation.'

'We could find out for sure.'

'How?'

'Asking Janet Kendal. I'm sure she knew about it. The family's been keeping it secret because they think it would make things even worse for him.'

'They're right. One of the very few points in our favour was the absence of motive. Now if you're right he had the oldest and most banal one in the book – and one the jury would have gulped down like a winkle in vinegar.'

'As bad as that?'

'Look at it. Factory mechanic with ideas above his station, very properly sent packing by girl's guardian – who's been very good to him in the past – so puts bullet into his head. Hanging's too good for him, wouldn't you say?' He was glaring at me as if that really were my view.

'You'll be seeing him again, I suppose?'

He looked away from me towards the grimy laurels. His voice went quieter. 'At least once, yes.'

'Why don't you ask him?'

'If he loved Laura?'

'Yes.'

'What good would that do? I suppose he thinks he's been clever all along, not telling me.'

'I don't suppose he feels very clever now. But if he's innocent, surely anything that comes out might help?'

He looked at me and said nothing.

'You came to me and said you thought he didn't do it. That was how I got dragged into this.'

'Oh? I thought it was purely because of the sister.'

A minor victory for him, but it didn't seem to bring him much comfort.

'Do you still think he's innocent?'

'I don't know, I don't know, I don't know.' He kicked the wall we were sitting on so hard that a chunk of moss and mortar flew out and rattled onto the pavement.

'Because of what I've just told you?'

He nodded. I felt waves of resentment flooding out of him.

'Look, I don't know what you've heard about me, but I'm not some kind of magic charm to get the result you want. If you ask me to find out things, then I try to find them out. It's no use blaming me if you don't like them.'

'I'm sorry. I know it's not reasonable, only . . .'

For some time neither of us said anything. A starling landed on the gatepost, shrieked at us and flew off again.

'Is there anything else I should know?' His voice was subdued, reasonable.

'I think it quite likely that Laura was expecting Davie's child.'

'Was?'

'She lost it, soon after the murder.'

'Are you sure of this?'

'Not completely.'

'What makes you think so?'

'I'd rather not tell you at present. If it's relevant later, I might.'

'It makes things worse, doesn't it?'

'I'm afraid so.'

'That could be what Newbiggin wanted to talk to him about, when he sent the note to his house. It must have been something urgent to make him do that.'

'Yes.'

'Do you think the old monster knew?'

'Very probably, yes. She told me Laura was a slut.'

'Damn her and damn them all.' He stood up, held out a hand as if I needed helping. I ignored it. 'I suppose we'd better go and keep that appointment with young Witherspoon.'

As we walked he said, 'If Rolling Toby's got anything, it will need to be good.' But the hope and excitement that had been there when he got off the train had faded.

The solicitor's office was in the High Street. Bill produced a lead from his pocket, clipped it into Roswal's collar and asked if I'd mind holding him outside.

'He's a good enough solicitor, but makes a fetish of being tidy. Roswal unsettles him.'

All the time Bill was inside the dog stood four-square to attention, not moving but as tense as an electric wire. He came out in a few minutes, followed by a large and self-conscious young man in a dark suit and very new bowler hat. After introductions, the three of us set off up the High Street, with the dog, released from the lead, trotting happily alongside. Young Witherspoon was justifiably pleased with his detective work.

'It will be a good time to find him. He was drunk the night before last, so he'll have had all yesterday to sleep it off.'

Like Bill, he seemed to have no doubt that the return of

168

the tinker was a good thing for their case. I asked if he'd spoken to him.

'No, I left that for Mr Musgrave. I didn't want to put things into his head.'

I said nothing, not wanting to depress Bill again, but it struck me that after ten months of drinking and travelling his account of the night of the murder wasn't likely to be very useful. We went about half-way up the hill towards my brother's house, but turned off to the right into a rutted uphill track leading to a farm. There was a man in the farmyard throwing down hay from a rick and Witherspoon called up to ask him if he'd seen Rolling Toby.

'Came in with his cart half an hour ago. You'll find him up there.'

We went through the farmyard into a narrower track with dry stone walls on either side. It was almost overgrown with docks and nettles, except for two cart tracks up the middle. A hare jumped out of the weeds onto a wall in front of us and Roswal was after it like a javelin flung by a champion, until a shout from Bill stopped him in his tracks. He sat quivering, looking reproachfully at us over his shoulder.

'Should have let the dog have her,' Witherspoon said. 'We could do with a lucky hare's foot.'

'So could the hare.'

After half a mile or so we came to a sort of gate across the path, more an arrangement of branches and old timbers than anything. Once through that we could see a wooden shack, the kind of thing a castaway might build from flotsam on a desert island.

'His house?'

'No, that's the pony's stable. The house is nowhere near as grand.'

The path widened into a rectangular enclosure. At the back of it was another dry stone wall, then nothing but purple-brown moorland. A shaggy bay head with bright eyes looked out of the stable shack. Next to it was a lean-to made of sun-bleached planks that would have been just about big enough as a kennel for Roswal. As we set foot in the yard a small terrier exploded, yapping, out of it, bouncing up and down on four stiff legs. When it saw the big dog it stopped but stood its ground, growling.

A deeper, more human growl, something on the lines of 'What's going on there?', but with no division between the words, came out of the kennel. It was followed by a head like Mr Punch's and two bright eyes under hair like teased-out rope. The head drew after it a horizontal overcoat, green with age. Slowly Rolling Toby stood up until he was about forty-five degrees from verticality.

'Whoryewafter then?'

Bill clipped the lead on Roswal, who'd been growling back at the terrier, and told him to be quiet. Rolling Toby looked at us, picked up the terrier and dropped it fairly gently over the half door into the stable with the pony.

Witherspoon said, 'This gentleman wants to talk to you about Davie Kendal.'

''Im as did the murder? Not 'anged yet, then?'

Unlike old Mrs Bolter, there was no ghoulishness or malice in the way he said it. He'd have enquired about the crops or the weather in much the same tone. His accent was hard to place. It wasn't local and might have had a basis of Irish some time back, but overlaid with many things since then. His voice came wheezing from the back of his throat like wind in a cave. He had two visible teeth, side by side at the front of his mouth like a rodent's. And yet the general effect wasn't dislikeable because of the quick, lively eyes looking out of his lined face. We talked standing in a group in the middle of his yard because there was nowhere to sit down.

I thought Bill handled it well. He introduced himself as Davie's lawyer and established that Rolling Toby had been in residence on his plot at the time of the murder. He remembered the night because, like everybody else, he'd heard the bell of the hall tolling.

'Where were you then?'

'Oop 'ere.'

'Did you go down into the town at all that evening?'

He shook his head.

'You're sure of that?'

''ad naw munny, did I?'

'Were you in the Cross Keys that evening?'

Another shake of the head.

'Did you know that Davie Kendal was asking for you at the bar there?'

'No.'

'Can you think why he might have been asking for you?'

I expected another no, but instead he screwed up his eyes and nodded his head. A light came into Bill Musgrave's eyes. It was like watching an angler at the moment when the fish bites.

'You can. Why?'

''E wanted the lend of me little cart.' He nodded towards the battered wooden trap, up-ended beside the pony stable with a tarpaulin hanging from the shafts.

Bill looked from the cart to Toby and back again. 'Davie Kendal asked for you at the bar because he wanted to borrow your cart? How do you know that?'

'Cos 'e come up 'ere atterwards to ask for it.'

'Up here? You mean where we are now?'

A nod.

'And you're quite certain it was the same night that you heard the bell going?'

'Yes. It were before the bell, though.'

'What time?'

I could have told him that was a doomed question. The likes of Rolling Toby don't keep track of hours or minutes.

'It were late. After I'd gone to me bed.'

'What time do you go to bed?'

'When it gets dark.'

'But this was November. It would be dark before five o'clock.'

'Yes.'

Bill glanced at me and raised his eyes to the sky. 'So it was after dark, you were in bed, but before the bell started ringing. And Davie Kendal came up here. What happened?'

'I were asleep and me dog started barking, so I knew someone were coming. I got out, and there were someone coming up the track.'

'In the dark? Did he have a lamp?'

'No. 'E keep striking matches. I could see 'em and smell 'em. So I shouts out to ask who's there and 'e says Davie Kendal.'

'Had you met him before?'

'I knows all of them. 'E come up rabbiting a few times with the other lads.'

'Did you recognise him?'

'Once 'e'd got in me yard and I lit me bit of lamp, I did.'

'You've no doubt it was him?'

'No. So I says what does 'e want and 'e says 'e wants the lend of me pony and cart.'

'He didn't say anything about wanting to buy a dog?'

'No, 'e didn't.'

'When did he want your cart?'

'Then and there.'

'What was his manner like?' Then, seeing he was getting no reaction to this, 'Was he calm, agitated, in a hurry?'

'In a bit of a 'ustle, and out of breath from coming up the path.'

'Did you lend him the cart?'

'Weren't no use to 'im or anyone. I 'ad the wheels off it 'cos of coming by a bit of iron to mend the rims.'

'How did he take that?'

'Wanted to know if I could get them on again. Long job, I said, even by daylight. Then 'e wanted to know was there anywhere else 'e could get a cart.'

'He definitely wanted one then, that night?'

'Oh, yes.'

'So what did you tell him?'

'Not much I could tell 'im. I said 'e might try Northcotts. Nobody else 'as much call for getting traps out at night, not round 'ere.'

Witherspoon whispered to Bill, 'Northcotts is the funeral parlour.'

'What happened then?'

'Well, 'e went.'

'Back down the track in the dark?'

''E 'ad me little lamp with 'im. Gave me ten bob for it.'

'Ten shillings for a second-hand lamp!'

''E wanted it. 'E said 'e was in a 'urry to get down.'

'So he bought your lamp. What happened then?'

'Went off, down to the town.'

Bill was looking thoroughly puzzled by now, but still hadn't given up hope of hooking his fish. 'About what time would that have been?'

'I told you, after it got dark.'

'And that was still before you heard the bell ringing?'

'Yes. I 'eard the clock, though.'

'What clock?'

Involuntarily, we all took a step towards him.

'Clock down there, of course.'

'The town clock?'

'Yes. Struck while 'e was standing there. I remember 'cos 'e jumped like it was later 'n 'e thought it was.'

'What time was that?'

Rolling Toby looked at Bill as if he had doubts about his sanity. 'I told you, when the clock struck.'

'Yes, but what time was that? How many times did it strike?'

By now the look Toby was giving him was definitely pitying. ''Ow would I know?'

'Was it eight? Nine? Ten?'

I think Bill was having to restrain himself from getting the old man by the shoulders and shaking him, but all Toby did was move his head wonderingly from side to side. I took a hand.

'Once Davie had gone, what did you do?'

'Looked in on the 'orse then went back to bed.' He pointed to his kennel.

'But you heard the bell ringing from the hall?'

'Yes.'

'Was it long after he left?'

''Ow would I know? I was asleep. Woke me up.'

I glanced at Bill and saw he'd taken the point. The hall alarm bell had rung at about half-past ten. It would probably have taken more than half an hour for Rolling Toby to look in on the horse then get back to sleep in time to be woken up again by it. Therefore we could rule out ten o'clock. We could also rule out anything before eight, because Davie had only started his enquiries in the pub at seven-thirty. So Davie had been up here talking to Rolling Toby at either eight or nine o'clock on the night of the murder. The crucial question was which and yet there seemed no way of getting an answer to it.

'Can you count to ten?'

Luckily, he didn't seem to find the question offensive. 'I can count to ten bob.'

If that was a hint, I disregarded it. 'I mean, if you heard the clock striking now, would you know if it was eight or nine?'

He shook his head. 'No, missus. There's only two bits of counting a man needs.'

'What are those?'

''Orses 'as got four legs and women 'as got two. Don't need to count no more than that, do you?'

Bill went on trying after that, but to no more effect. It was clear that Rolling Toby wasn't being deliberately difficult and would have helped us if he could. He just failed to see any sense in what we were asking. In the end we gave up, thanked him and made our way back down the narrow pathway, feet squelching on the flattened dock-leaves.

'The man must have been desperate to come up here on a November night,' Witherspoon said.

I agreed with him. 'And now that we've seen the path, I don't see how he could have got up here by eight. It took us about forty minutes to walk up from the town by daylight. We know he was still in the Cross Keys around half-past seven. Even if he'd run all the way, he could hardly have been talking to Rolling Toby by the time the clock was striking eight.'

'And he wasn't running, he was stumbling around in the dark striking matches. So if Toby's right about hearing that clock striking, it was nine, not eight.'

Giving Davie just enough time to make a telephone call between leaving the public house and walking up to Toby's hovel.

Witherspoon said, 'Not that he'd have been much use in any case. A grown man, not able to count . . .'

The young man was bitterly disappointed in his witness. I suppose in his imagination he'd seen Davie saved from the gallows and an incidental boost to his career. Bill was disappointed himself, but at least tried to save Witherspoon's pride.

'That's not your fault. You delivered him. It would have been a near miracle if he'd been any use.'

But I knew that when I met him off the train he'd half-believed in that miracle.

When we were back at the road Witherspoon said, 'Why did Kendal want a cart in such a hurry anyway?'

I noticed that he'd become 'Kendal', not 'Davie'. Neither of us answered the question but Bill thanked him, told him he'd done much more than could have been expected. He'd be writing to the solicitor to say so.

'You'd better be getting back to your office. I'll see Miss Bray to her brother's home.'

I was about to protest indignantly that I didn't need seeing back anywhere but understood in time that he wanted to talk to me. Witherspoon shook hands with Bill and went off down the hill, shoulders drooping. His parting words were, 'Sorry it wasn't any use.'

Bill waited before he was out of earshot before commenting, 'Worse than no use.'

I didn't ask him if he still believed Davie might be innocent. I knew what the answer would be.

SIXTEEN

'YOUR BROTHER'S RIGHT, MISS BRAY. I'm a monster of vanity after all.'

We were back at Old Ferris's cottage and Bill had angled himself across one of the not-very-comfortable chairs, with the dog at his feet. The cats had taken one look and fled upstairs.

'I suppose the thing that hurts me most is that young Kendal took me for an idiot, and he was right. When I think of those sleepless nights, then involving you, my mooncalf conviction that he was innocent . . .'

'He's still your client and they're still going to hang him.'

'I promise you, I've tried to save his life with all the ingenuity and care I could bring to it, and I'll go on trying until the last morning. But Rolling Toby's yard felt like the end of the road.'

'I wonder.'

'He was certainly no use as an alibi. Kendal could have slipped out of the bar soon after he was seen at around half-past seven, done that four- or five-minute walk up the drive to the lodge, made the telephone call and still be a mile out of town talking to Rolling Toby when the clock was striking nine.'

'You think now that's what he did?'

'Don't you?'

'But why did he want a cart so desperately?'

'Suppose he decides he wants to get rid of the gramo-phone altogether. It's far too dangerous to take it back up to the house and he knows it will attract attention if he carries it through the street. So he thinks of the old rogue and his pony cart, only the pony cart isn't rolling. So the best he can do is break the record with Newbiggin's voice and dump the pieces in the family ash-bin. Oh, what a fool the man is.'

'You or Davie Kendal?'

He glared at me, then managed to turn it to a lop-sided smile. There was no doubt that he'd been badly injured in the vanity. 'I was thinking of him, but I suppose it would apply to either.'

'You know, it strikes me that may be the one spark of hope.'

'Foolishness?'

'Yes. What was the one thing anybody could tell you about young Davie before all this started? What attracted Newbiggin's attention to him in the first place?'

'He was good at arithmetic.'

'He was clever. Clever enough to get professional qualifications and a good job. That was what he was known for.'

'All right, he's a clever little fool. But he's still a fool.'

'Look at the prosecution's idea of what happened on the night of the murder. He keeps the appointment at the hall, having already decided to kill Newbiggin. He knows where the man's gun is kept, takes it out of the desk drawer and shoots him. He's cool enough to use the cushion as a silencer and to go through with this idea of using Newbiggin's voice on the disc to make it seem as if he were still alive when Davie left him.'

'But it didn't work.'

'No, but it still shows he was thinking coolly and planning in advance. He remembers to take the gun away with him in case of fingerprints. He loads the gramophone onto a wheelbarrow, takes it down to the lodge and has a drink at the Cross Keys to make it clear that he's out of the hall by half-past seven. About half an hour later he goes back and plays Newbiggin's voice down the telephone exactly as planned.'

'Which doesn't deceive anyone for an instant.'

'Yes, he got that wrong. But you'd agree that up to that point he's acting very coolly?'

'Well, yes.' Reluctantly.

'Then he quite suddenly goes mad. Remember he has no way of knowing that the voice trick didn't convince Newbiggin's friend. Up to that point, everything seems to be going as he planned it. But just look at what he does next.'

'Goes looking for a cart to dispose of the gramophone.'

'Without making any arrangements in advance? Without even providing himself with a lamp, so that he has to pay over the odds for Rolling Toby's? And if he was disposing of the record, why throw it in his family's own ash-bin, for goodness sake? Every household in town has an ash-bin and I'm sure people don't usually lock their back gates.'

'So he panicked.'

'But why at that point? Why this contrast between a man who's thinking with icy coolness up until about eight o'clock, and behaves like a total lunatic afterwards?'

'He has an idea the disc trick hasn't worked, so he's decided to make a run for it.'

'By pony cart? He'd have been better off on his feet and anyway the trains run till late. And why, after he's failed to get the cart does he go back into the Cross Keys?'

'Because he wanted to be there looking as normal as anybody else when the body was found.'

'Oh, he's suddenly gone sane again by half-past ten, has he? Then he panics again and disappears, as he should have done hours ago by your theory.'

'Well, what's your theory?'

'I haven't got one. But I just can't accept this picture of Davie Kendal alternating between cool practical man and panicking idiot. There's a reason why he did all this, and until we know what the reason was, we haven't found out what really happened that evening.'

I'd been mentally stunned by the Rolling Toby affair but now my mind was beginning to come to life again.

I'd been speaking more forcefully than I intended and saw Bill looking at me with an odd expression.

'What have I done? Have you caught my sickness when I'm losing it?'

'About believing him innocent? I may be sickening for it.'

'Are you one of these people who like lost causes?'

'On the contrary, I like winning.'

'And winners?'

I didn't answer. He stretched out in the chair, tipping it back, and closed his eyes. There was silence for a while, then, 'Has it struck you that the answer to the riddle may be your Laura factor?'

'How?'

'Your intuition – based on something even I should blush to regard as proof – is that Laura loves him. You also infer that he loves Laura.'

'It would explain at least why he was prowling round the house.'

'Then let's accept the hypothesis. Let us further assume that after killing Newbiggin, Kendal does intend to flee but wants to take the lady with him. Only our Young Lochinvar has no steed, so he has to try to borrow Rolling Toby's disabled chariot.'

I considered it for a while. 'It still doesn't meet my objection about his lack of planning. Anyway, if there was any such plan, why couldn't Laura have just walked out of the back door to meet him? They didn't need a cart.'

'According to you, the woman's deathly weak.'

'She is now, but ten months ago she was capable of running down a long drive to get help. Are you suggesting Laura was an accomplice?'

He opened his eyes. 'What do you think?'

'Wasn't she under Mrs Bolter's eye all evening? If there'd been anything to cast suspicion on Laura, I'm sure the old woman would have let us know about it.'

'I wonder.'

It was getting dark, but he made no move to go. He was

still leaning back in the chair with his eyes closed when we heard voices outside.

Rose's voice first: '. . . lamp not lit. She might not be home yet.'

'I'll wait for her.'

The second voice, grim and determined, was Janet Kendal's.

Bill sat up and glared at me. 'Did you tell her?'

'That there might be developments? Of course not.'

'Just as well. If I could slip out the back way . . .'

'There isn't a back way.'

His eyes went to the steep stairs and I'm sure that, for a second or two, he was seriously weighing up his chances of hiding. In justice I had to admit that part of his embarrassment was professional. When a barrister meets his clients or their families it's usually with a protective screen of solicitors and clerks in between. Here he was as good as naked. But I guessed too that he was nervous of Janet Kendal. He'd already admitted to me that she thought he could have made a better job of her brother's defence and he was almost her last hope for saving his life. That was bad enough even while he believed in Davie's innocence. Now Rolling Toby had shaken that belief and he was close to giving up hope. Janet would sense that. She lived close enough to despair to know the smell of it. He was still on the edge of his chair when the latch lifted and Rose walked in, followed by Janet. There was a moment of surprise when Janet saw him.

'Oh, you're here too, are you?'

The tone wasn't friendly, but made it clear that Bill wasn't her main target this time. After that glance at him, she turned on me.

'I want a word with you, Miss Bray.'

From behind her, Rose tried to signal a storm warning to me, but it was hardly necessary. A ship rounding Cape Horn might have run into the same cold challenge that came to me from Janet's face and voice.

'You'd better sit down.'

181

Bill, once he'd got over his desire to flee, had stood up politely as she came in. She plonked herself down in his chair without taking her eyes from my face. I sat down opposite her, which meant Bill and Rose had to stand. Instinctively, they both took a step back into the shadows.

'What were you doing with Laura Newbiggin?'

So that was it. Channels of communication in the town were as efficient as in a village, particularly where the Newbiggin family were concerned. I'd never intended to keep my visit secret, but I'd wanted more time before tackling Janet about the issues it had raised. Now there was no choice but to steer straight into the gale.

'I wanted to talk to her about your brother.'

'What's that got to do with you?'

I let myself get angry. 'You asked me to help, so you'll have to put up with my methods. If you call in the plumber, do you tell him how to do the job?'

'If he's poking around where he's got no business, yes, I do.'

'Talking to Laura is part of the business. If you really wanted me to help, you should have told me about her in the first place.'

'There's nothing to tell.'

'Isn't there? Isn't it relevant that your brother and Laura Newbiggin were in love with each other?'

Janet stared at me and said nothing.

'Why did you leave me to find it out the roundabout way? Was it because you thought it would make things worse for him?'

'It had nothing to do with what happened.'

'Even if that's true, the jury wouldn't have thought so. It would have been the motive everybody was looking for.'

'You say that, then you want to know why I didn't tell you. Weren't things bad enough already without putting that around?'

From behind me, Bill cleared his throat and started to say something but he didn't have a chance.

'I thought you were trying to help us, but all you've done is go poking around making things worse. I suppose you'll go running to the police now, tell everybody it's all right to hang him, they can all feel quite happy and comfortable about it. You sit there and ask me why I didn't tell you. Would you have said if he were your brother? Would you see him where he is and close out the last little blink of light? Is that what you'd do?' No trace of tears in her voice or eyes. She sat there waiting for an answer.

'If I can help your brother at all, it's by finding out what really happened that night. I can't do that by just picking up little scraps of it from whoever wants to give them to me. I have to find out everything I can, regardless of whether it makes things look better or worse for your brother.'

There was a movement from Bill. I didn't look at him. The last thing I wanted now was to think about Rolling Toby and his depressing evidence.

'There's been a very big fact left out so far, mainly because you didn't choose to tell me or anybody else about it. Without that, how can I or anybody else find out what happened?'

She said nothing. Her face in the dim light hadn't changed.

'Of course, all this applies if you think your brother is innocent. If he isn't innocent, then you were quite right not to tell me.'

There it was again, the question I hadn't dared ask Bill. The silence drew out for so long that I could hear the wind moving gently in the rowan tree outside and the wavering cry of a tawny owl on its first hunt of the night. Quietly, Rose made preparations to light the lamp. When the glow of it spread round the room, casting our shadows on the wall, Janet still hadn't spoken. I glanced up at Bill. He hadn't moved since getting up from the chair and his eyes were on her face. He glanced at me, then away again. There was enough light now to see the regret in his eyes, and whatever my brother would have said, it wasn't just wounded pride. I made myself concentrate on Janet, trying to move from our embattled tone to a conversational level.

'Well, since you've chosen not to tell me about it, I'll tell you and you can stop me if I'm wrong. I think your brother met Laura Newbiggin while he was helping with the recordings. He was attracted to her and she to him, not surprisingly. Davie was a good-looking and intelligent man and she . . .' I tried to put out of my mind the memory of Laura as she was now and to see her as he might have seen her that summer. '. . . she was a well-educated and accomplished young woman.'

White hands on the piano keys and a singing voice like a May morning. Delicate and probably interestingly reserved to a young man used to his strong and forthright sister and the rumbustious girls at the mill. That would have been part of the attraction. Had he imagined her alongside him in that upward ladder of photographs recording a successful man's career?

'He was still working for Newbiggin then. He'd quarrelled with his brother and moved into lodgings, but he was still talking to you, bringing you his washing. I think he'd have confided in you.'

Perhaps she made some comment on the number of clean shirts he was demanding. Perhaps he developed a new fussiness about the state of his cuffs and collars. Her eyes didn't leave my face, but she still hadn't said anything.

'You probably weren't pleased about it yourself, but . . .'

'It was no business of mine.'

The words when they came at last were defiant. Bill let out a long breath but said nothing.

'It was, though. Your first thought was that it would make things even worse between Davie and Jimmy. You were still hoping you'd be able to smooth things over between them. Jimmy was angry already about his brother's closeness to Newbiggin, and you knew very well what he'd say if he found out about Davie courting the girl from the big house.'

'They weren't courting.'

I let that pass for the moment.

'So you let Davie talk to you about Laura, but you decided not to pass it on to the rest of the family. So things went on for a while – until Mr Newbiggin found out about it.'

I waited for her to speak again but she didn't. Her right hand was gripping and kneading a fold of her skirt.

'He didn't approve, of course. Davie might be a bright young man, but he was one of his employees after all, and Laura was practically his ward. He might even have had someone else in mind for her. That was the cause of the quarrel between Davie and Mr Newbiggin. Nothing to do with work – it was Laura.'

'Is this true, Miss Kendal?' Bill's voice, surprisingly gentle.

She ignored it and kept staring at me.

'So they quarrelled and he told Davie to stay away from Laura and Crowberry Hall. And Davie took his revenge in the nearest way he could.'

'No . . .'

'I was thinking about the sabotage to the machinery. He must have been savagely angry to do that to his own work. But if he loved Laura and . . .'

'No.'

Quieter this time, more a moan than a protest. She was trying hard to keep a grip on herself, both hands kneading at the skirt now.

'No, it wasn't like that. He was leading her a terrible life. She wanted to get away from him, from old Newbiggin. He was sorry for her, that's all it was. Davie was sorry for her, and look where that's got him.'

'Laura wanted to get away from Newbiggin, and Davie was sorry for her?'

She nodded.

'Janet, I'm afraid there was more to it than just feeling sorry for Laura. Did he tell you that she was expecting his baby?'

Janet's face was frozen for a moment while it sank in, then she was on her feet. I thought for a moment that she was going to try to hit me and perhaps she intended to, but she stopped herself at the last minute, so close that I could feel her breath warm on my face as she leaned over me.

'That's a lie. Did she tell you that? It's a dirty lie.'

I stood up too. Rose and Bill moved closer.

'No, Laura didn't tell me.'

'Then how ... well, that doesn't matter. Whoever told you, they were wrong. What happened to it?'

'She lost it.'

'Anyway, it wasn't Davie's.'

'You think he'd have told you?'

She thought about it, took a step back.

'Yes. Yes, I think he would. Anyway, it wasn't like that between them. I told you, he just felt sorry for her.'

I decided to accept that for the moment, although I didn't believe it.

'You said Laura wanted to get away from Newbiggin because he was leading her a terrible life. Do you mean he was cruel to her?' I'd have bet that any cruelty in that household came from the old woman.

Janet hesitated, looked around at the three of us and seemed to come to a decision. She sat down warily, on the edge of the seat.

'Not cruel, no. It was worse than that. The old bugger couldn't keep his hands off her.' She stopped, her eyes fixed on mine, as if that were all that needed saying.

'Davie told you this?'

'Yes.'

'Tell me in his own words, if you can remember them.'

She began reluctantly. I'm sure she'd never told anybody else and it was as if she'd shut up all of it so deep inside her that to draw it out was like hauling coal along a shaft. But once she'd started the story took hold of her and it seemed as though we were hearing the young man's voice, sitting there in the kitchen with the smell of steam and

186

starch around them, talking low and urgently as his sister ironed his shirts.

'They took her in after her parents died, him and the old woman. She was grateful at first. It started with the singing. She'd be playing the piano while the old bugger sang, or she'd sing and play and he'd turn over the music for her. Well, she noticed that he'd put a hand on her shoulder and she'd feel his breath down the back of her neck, but she thought you get that sometimes with people not meaning any harm so she didn't say anything. Then there was the breathing, so heavy it was sometimes, she said, it put her off the rhythm of what she was playing and he'd ask what the matter was, in a funny sort of voice. But she couldn't say anything, because he'd taken her in and paid for her lessons after all, and it wasn't as if he was really doing anything she could object to. She thought.'

The last two words were thrown out with sudden, brutal sarcasm. Whether it was Janet remembering the way her brother had spoken them, or her own comment on Laura, I didn't know.

'Then she noticed that when he was singing and she was playing, he'd move closer to the piano. Not in the Handel, she said, it was all right when he kept to the Handel, but at the end of a practice they'd do a ballad or two – you know, the lovey-dovey ones.'

'"Pale Hands" and so on?'

'That's right. And he'd move closer and closer to the piano until he was pressing against it, and she'd keep trying to move the piano stool sideways without stopping playing to get away from him.'

'And didn't say anything?'

'Well, one day she told Davie about this and he told me, asked me what I thought. I said if she didn't like it she should just come out and say so, polite but quite firm with him. Anyway, that's what he told her.'

Young Davie might have been an expert on machinery, but on other dangerous matters he'd depended on his big sister's advice. Until then, I'd thought of him only as the confident young man of the photograph. A mistake.

'And did she do it?'

'Yes. The next time it happened she stopped playing and said would he mind not coming so close because it was putting her off her music.'

'And I suppose he got angry.'

She shook her head. 'Worse than that. He said he loved her and she shouldn't be cruel to him. Then he started crying.'

I must have made a sudden movement because I saw the wariness coming back into her eyes. She thought I disbelieved her, but she couldn't know how well this story of Laura's matched the account of the girl from the mill.

'Yes, that's what she told Davie and that's what he told me. He was annoyed with me because he said I'd given them the wrong advice.'

'I don't see how. At least she'd let Newbiggin know what she felt about him.'

'I'm not so sure of that. From what the silly little fool told Davie, she just burst into tears too and said he shouldn't cry, that she was fond of him and grateful to him and so on, anything to stop him crying. So, of course, that only made things worse. He stopped crying and stroked her hair and started singing again, and so it went on, only worse, week after week.'

'This was early last summer?'

'That's right. So she was getting desperate and Davie was getting desperate. I told him if he'd got any sense, he'd keep out of it, go up to the hall if he had to for work, but keep away from them otherwise. I told him a girl who hadn't got the sense to look after herself wasn't worth bothering with anyway. But Davie didn't see it like that. As far as he was concerned, Laura needed help and that was an end of it. He was soft, that way.'

I thought of her father and what he'd wanted so urgently to make me see about his son: *That was just his problem, he was too kind.*

188

'So what did he do?'

'Didn't take my advice that time. What he did was to go to the old bugger in his study and announce that Laura was his sweetheart, so would he please keep his hands off her.'

'That took some nerve.'

'Well, it didn't do him any good because the old bugger told him to get out of his house and never come back and Davie gave in his notice on the spot.'

'What did Laura do?'

'I don't know and I don't care what Laura did. Stayed there and burst into tears every time the old man touched her, I suppose.'

'Why didn't she just go away?'

'I would and you would, but she didn't. Hadn't got the spirit for it.'

'She and Davie must have had some way of keeping in touch. I suppose that was what he was doing that night when they saw him looking in at them.'

She shrugged. 'I suppose so. But he'd stopped talking to me about it by then. He knew what I thought of it all.'

Bill had listened to this without a sound, although I'd been very much aware of him standing behind me.

'So as your brother might have seen it, he was trying to rescue Laura Newbiggin?'

'I don't know how he saw it.' Bill's first question had been gentle enough, but the reply was defensive to the point of hostility.

'And you agree that it's unlikely that he and Laura broke off communications after the quarrel between him and Newbiggin?'

'It's no good you trying to twist my words. I don't agree anything. I've said I don't know.'

'The day that Newbiggin was killed, he sent a note asking Davie to come and see him. In the light of what you've just said, do you think that was to discuss something to do with Laura?'

'How should I know? Anyway, what's that to do with

189

anything? You're very good at asking questions, but it never seems to go anywhere that helps us.'

That was true enough from her point of view, but unfair to Bill. He took it well, though.

'I can see that, but I wish you'd been more open with me from the start. We were trying to help your brother, the solicitor and I, and yet you kept all this from us.'

She was on her feet again, but this time there was no risk that she was going to hit anybody. She was even too angry for that.

'What would you have done with it if I'd told you? Told them, yes, that's why he did it? Now you've got your motive nice and tidy with everything else they're going to use to hang him, and I hope you're pleased with it. I hope you're pleased with yourself, too.'

Then the door banged behind her and she was gone into the darkness. Rose said something about having to see her home, grabbed her coat and followed, leaving Bill and me staring at each other.

'I'm sorry.'

I didn't know why I had to apologise to him for her anger, except that he looked as if he needed something.

'I'm sorry too, for getting you into this.'

He lowered himself into the chair opposite me, looking more tired than if he'd walked forty miles. For a long time he said nothing, then, 'She's right in a way. I think if I'd known this from the start I might have advised him to plead guilty and done what I could in mitigation. Not that that would have worked either.'

'I think you'd have been wrong.'

The significance of that didn't get to him at first. 'Of course I'd have been wrong. Everything I've done with this case has been wrong.'

He brooded for a long time before it occurred to him to ask what I'd meant.

'No use as mitigation, you mean? Yes, it's hardly miti-gation to say the deceased was a lecherous and dislikeable man.'

'No, I mean about pleading guilty.'

'What?' His eyes, his whole body, were suddenly alive. 'You mean, you think he's not? After all we've found out today?'

'I don't know. There's a lot to think about – and yet . . .'

'You're not going to tell me, are you?'

He was a man not used to patience. His whole body was tense with greed for some sign of hope.

'You'd better go,' I said. 'I'll be in touch when I need you.'

He looked at me for a long time then, as abruptly as on his first visit, got up and went. I knew without being told that he'd cut across the moor to avoid Rose and Janet on the road. Difficult in the dark, but then he needed something to distract him. I didn't, which was why I'd told him to go.

SEVENTEEN

'THE TROUBLE IS,' I SAID, 'we don't understand passivity.'

Rose glanced up from feeding scrambled egg to the cats. 'You make it sound like a foreign language.'

'If it were, I could learn it. I can't think of any way of getting her to talk to us.'

Rose had got back very late the night before after seeing Janet home. I stayed up even later, but by breakfast time had arrived at only one conclusion – that I had to talk to Laura Newbiggin again. It didn't make me happy.

'At least she talked to you, didn't she? It's not as if she threw you out.'

'I only wish she'd had the energy for it, then we might have got somewhere. I found out just one useful thing from that visit and that wasn't from anything that Laura told me. If I hadn't happened to notice the calendar, we still shouldn't know about her and Davie. It's obvious his family weren't going to tell us.'

'You really can't blame them.'

Up until then we hadn't discussed the talk with Janet, knowing that it was dangerous ground. In the quarrel between Janet and Bill Musgrave, Rose would naturally take Janet's side. I wasn't taking sides – no, of course I wasn't – but I knew she was being unfair to Bill.

'Yes, I can. It means they don't trust us.'

'In their place I shouldn't trust anybody.'

'All right, but you realise there's one immediate implication of what happened last night and it makes a nonsense of what we thought we knew about the evening of the murder. Laura lied to the police and to me. Or at the very least she left out something.'

'What?'

'She must have seen Davie that evening, or communicated with him at the very least.'

'How do we know?'

'Look at the situation. He's already quarrelled with Newbiggin about her. He's suddenly summoned up to the hall for an interview which we know must be about her – very probably the fact that he's made her pregnant. He comes to the hall and goes away without trying to see her and she doesn't even try to see him. Is that remotely likely?'

'You say she's timid.'

'To the point of paralysis now, but surely not so badly then. And remember, she's already lied about one thing. She said she didn't recognise the prowler looking into the dining room, when she must have known it was Davie.'

'Will it help if she did see him on the murder night?'

'Something's got to help. If Davie really is innocent, there has to be something that makes sense of what he was doing that evening. It's just a case of finding it.'

It was my turn to wash up. As I collected up the breakfast things and took them over to the stoneware sink I wondered if I were the only person still clinging even to the hypothesis of his innocence. Bill's belief in it had been gravely shaken, if not destroyed altogether. Janet would fight for him right up to the gallows and yet the way she'd made the family keep quiet about his love for Laura showed that she had her doubts too. Her petition was for mercy, after all, not necessarily justice. As I scraped at the egg saucepan I asked Rose if she'd come to see Laura with me.

'Of course, if I can do any good.'

'Heaven knows what will do any good. I warn you, it's an odd feeling, talking to her.'

'In what way odd?'

'It makes you wonder if you exist. You talk to her and

she looks at you and even talks to you, but you feel there's a great blank in her brain, and it's making you a blank as well. It's as if you're being turned into a ghost, or those dried-up insects you see in spiders' webs with all the juice sucked out of them.'

I turned round to see Rose looking at me with a worried expression on her face, and I couldn't blame her.

'You'll see what I mean.'

There were no scales or tunes coming from the house where Laura Newbiggin lodged as Rose and I walked along the street towards it, only train noises and the shouts of children, truants or too young for school, playing marbles in the gutter. It was an overcast day, though still not cold, and the terraces of houses, smoke-grimed, were dark grey under a lighter grey sky. If you looked up over the slate roofs the distant curve of moorland was just another shade of grey. Poverty, neglect, the closeness of the railway – all the usual things – had drained the colour out of the street. Laura, with only a small legacy and a few shillings a week from piano scales, had no choice but to live there. Sheer superstition on my part to confuse cause and effect and feel as if Laura's presence were actually responsible for the monochrome, the drain into which all the colours ran and were lost.

We knocked on the door and waited a long time, with no sound coming from inside and no movement of the curtains.

'She might be out.'

I was sure – I didn't know why – that Laura never went out and yet I was surprised when the door opened suddenly and there she was, looking scared and even thinner and paler than I remembered her. She was so nearly insubstantial that she'd walked along the echoing passageway to open the door without making a sound we could hear from outside it.

'Hello. This is Rose Mills. Do you mind if we come in and talk to you?'

My voice in my own ears sounded like an outsider who'd blundered in on a seance. If I'd tried to make contact with her through a gyrating wine glass or floating trumpet it would have seemed more appropriate to that drowned white face and wide eyes that were turned in our direction but gave no sign of seeing us. I wasn't even sure that she recognised me from our last meeting. All the same, she stood back to let us in, then led the way into the front parlour and teaching room. It was just like the last time, the piano lid firmly closed and not a sheet of music visible, not a speck of dust anywhere and the air quite lifeless. I saw Rose's eyes go to the calendar. It was showing the same date, the fourth of April.

'Would you like to sit down?'

It was the first thing she'd said since opening the door to us. You'd never have guessed, from the flatness of the voice, that she was a musician. I sat in the same upright chair as before. Rose sat on the music stool and Laura the other upright chair. I looked up at her, willing her to hear and understand, but by no means sure that my voice would make any more impact on her than the sounds from the children in the gutter outside.

'We know about Davie Kendal. We're trying to help him. Do you understand that?'

Nothing. Not even a change in her face when I said his name.

'If there's any chance of helping him at all, we need to know what happened on the night Mr Newbiggin was killed. I know how difficult it must be for you to talk about it. I wouldn't ask you again if there were any other way, but I believe there are some things that only you know about.'

Still no reaction. I glanced up at Rose and saw her staring at Laura, puzzled. I only hoped that Rose would understand what I was doing and not blame me for it.

'I'm going to tell you what we know about that night. I'd like you to tell me when I miss anything out or get something wrong. Will you do that?'

A nod of the head, slighter than the movement of a leaf in a light breeze. Progress, though.

'We know that Davie came to see Mr Newbiggin in his study at six o'clock. Did you know he was coming?'

Another nod.

'Did you know what they were going to talk about?'

Up until then, I hadn't even seen her blink. Now her eyelids came down and her cheeks screwed up as if she were trying to lock them into place.

'Did you see Davie afterwards?'

No answer. Her hands were locked together in her lap, knees pressed against each other, their sharpness jutting through the fabric of her thick brown skirt.

'It was important to you, wasn't it, what he and Mr Newbiggin were discussing? You must have wondered what had been said.'

Her shoulders folded inwards, compressing her thin chest. With every question she was visibly shrinking. At this rate, I'd end up interrogating a streak of brown serge and lustreless hair.

'In your place, I'd have wanted to see Davie after he came out. Or had he made some arrangement to see you later?'

Shoulders met ears. Her head shrank forward until the closed eyes were pointing down at her knees. I'd have expected it to be bad, but not this hopeless. I tried shock tactics.

'Were you and Davie planning to go away together?'

Nothing. I caught Rose's eye and shook my head. She frowned, not at me but at Laura, as if she were trying to remember something.

'I think he wanted you to go away with him. He knew how miserable you were, because of Mr Newbiggin. That evening, he'd decided to tell Mr Newbiggin that you and he were going to get married and go away together. He must have made some arrangement for letting you know what happened.'

We waited for a long time. A fight broke out among

196

the children in the street: shouts, jeers, a long drawn-out howl, then a woman's voice, angry and weary, telling them to give over. Inside the room, you could have heard a moth stretching its wings.

'All right, let's leave that for a moment. I want to ask you about what happened afterwards, when Mrs Bolter found him dying in the study.'

I'd been worried about making her remember that, but since she wasn't responding at all, apart from contracting to a thin line, it could hardly make things worse.

'The account you've both given the police is that Mrs Bolter went into the study to ask if he wanted anything and found him unconscious on the floor. When I was here last time you told me that she called out. Is that right?'

She gave a little forward rock that might have been a nod.

'Where were you when she called?'

'In . . . in the sitting room.'

Her head was still bent and her eyes closed, but she'd widened out just a fraction.

'Had both of you been in the sitting room all evening?'

A brief hesitation. 'Yes, except when she went down to the kitchen.'

'Why?'

'To see cook. She always did.'

'When?'

No reply.

'Before or after Davie arrived?'

'After. About eight o'clock.'

'How long was she away?'

'Not long.'

'Then she came back and you both stayed there in the sitting room until she went in to see Mr Newbiggin?'

'Yes.'

'When Mrs Bolter called out, can you remember exactly what she said?'

'She called . . . called his name out. Then she shouted

197

for cook.' Her eyes were open now and she was looking at me.

'For cook, not for you?'

'Yes.'

'But you went?'

She nodded.

'And you looked in and saw Mr Newbiggin on the floor.
Where was Mrs Bolter exactly?'

'Kneeling beside him.'

'Was the cook in the study with her?'

'No, she came just after me.'

'What happened then?'

'Mrs Bolter told me to run and get help, and cook to
go and ring the bell.'

'But there was a telephone in his study, on the desk.
Don't you remember that?'

For some reason, that made her eyelids squeeze up
again.

'Mrs Bolter seems a very strong-minded woman to me,
not the kind to panic. And yet she sent cook up to the
landing to ring the bell and you running all the way down
the drive, when there was a telephone a few yards away
from her. Didn't you wonder at the time?'

But by now she'd closed up completely. I couldn't
understand it. It seemed to me that the worst thing for
her to remember would be that glimpse into the study
with Newbiggin dying on the floor, among the blood and
feathers and fragments of broken records. And yet she'd
answered my questions about that almost calmly until I'd
suddenly made a wrong move again. I couldn't for the life
of me work out what it had been.

I'm sure she wanted us to go, but couldn't summon
up the energy to tell us so. We were just part of the
awful, inexplicable events that had happened to her and
she was as powerless against us as everything else. That
wasn't a good feeling, and yet she was the only person
who could possibly answer the question of what Davie
Kendal thought he'd been doing that evening. To leave

without wringing an answer out of her would be as good as abandoning the case altogether, but I was very close to doing it.

'Did Mrs Bolter know what Davie and Mr Newbiggin were talking about that evening?'

No answer.

'Had you spoken to Mrs Bolter about what was worrying you?'

Deliberately, that could cover several things: Davie, her pregnancy, the sentimental attentions of Mr Newbiggin. The old woman wouldn't be anybody's first choice as a confidante, but perhaps Laura had been desperate. But all the question produced was a drawing together of the shoulder-blades that left her even more compressed than before.

I think at that point I'd have abandoned it, left her and Davie and the rest of them as a hopeless case, but in that frozen room something suddenly came to life. Rose. She left her seat on the piano stool and knelt down beside the dark rod of misery that was Laura.

'Listen to me, listen. You're not the first girl in the world it's happened to and you won't be the last.'

It was a voice I hardly recognised. It came from a long way back, before Rose's involvement with the suffragette movement and certainly before a teacher's respectability and Wimbledon. The voice of the East End sweatshops, harsh but full of life and fight.

'I was a lot younger than you are, only thirteen and it was my first job. The overseer was a nasty little blob of lard called Biggs.'

The surprise of it at least brought some movement from Laura. She turned to Rose as if she'd only just registered her presence. Her eyes widened. Rose went on talking in that harsh voice that wouldn't be ignored.

'He said he'd keep an eye on me because I was new there, said I was doing well, offered me overtime. All the girls wanted overtime, because of the money. So he told me to stay one night, after the others had gone home and

199

I found out what he meant by overtime, there on the table where they cut the shirts out.'

Laura's eyes were wide, her mouth slightly open, so pale inside it was almost white.

'All right, I know now I should have fought him off, gone for him with the pinking shears where it would have done most good. But I was scared of him, God help me. And I didn't tell anyone. All I had was a sister. She'd have gone for him with her bare hands if she knew, but that wouldn't have done any good, only got her into trouble. So I never told her. And I've never told anyone to this day, not until now.'

When Rose got to the bit about the cutting table Laura started trembling, just a little at first, then like somebody coming out of an ice-cold river. Rose's new – or old – voice went on.

'You feel dirty. Goodness knows, it was dirty enough there in all the other ways, but this was a different kind. I remember I scrubbed away at myself with carbolic until my sister wanted to know if the cat had been eating the soap. Didn't do any good.'

She put an arm round Laura's quivering shoulders. Laura gave a little moan and relaxed against her.

'Then there are things that remind you, even ten years afterwards. He wore a particular type of hair oil – very proud of his hair, he was – and I only have to smell it again and it comes back to me. I was in an underground train just last month and a man in the same carriage happened to be wearing it. Not him or anything like him, only just from the smell of it I had to get out at the next stop, feeling as angry and as dirty as if it had all happened yesterday. There are always things that bring it back to you, like that.'

Laura's eyes moved. She was looking at the piano, with its closed lid.

'Is that it? Yes, I suppose it would be. Songs?'

Laura's nod became a head trembling that she couldn't stop. I thought of the horror of having to make her living from something she'd come to hate.

'He's dead now. It's all over.'

But it wasn't all over, as Rose knew perfectly well. Our eyes met and hers gave me a signal: 'Take over now.'

I said, as gently as I could, 'That was what he wanted to talk to Davie about, wasn't it? Davie knew.'

She nodded.

'And Davie had told him that unless he let you marry Davie and go away, other people would know about it?'

'Yes.'

'So you knew very well what they were arguing about that evening?'

Another nod.

I tried the question she hadn't answered before. 'Did Mrs Bolter know what was going on?'

I thought at first she was going to ignore it again, then the words came as slowly as drips from an icicle.

'She . . . said I was . . . making a fuss about nothing.'

'And she knew what Davie was coming to talk about?'

'Yes.'

'Did she say anything about that to you?'

'She said he was . . . a wicked ungrateful boy.'

'For wanting to take you away?'

'Yes.'

'What about Mr Newbiggin? What did he say to you?'

Again she hesitated for a long time, then, 'He asked me not to go. He asked me to stay with him.'

Rose's arm tightened round Laura. She looked at me, but I couldn't decide whether she was asking me to stop or go on. No choice.

'When did he ask you to stay?'

'In the afternoon.'

'The afternoon before Davie came to see him?'

'Yes.'

'Where?'

The trembling started again. 'In his st . . . st . . .'

'In his study. He sent for you and asked you not to go away with Davie?'

'Yes. He s . . . s . . .' She clenched her hands, closed her eyes and started talking very fast. 'He said Davie couldn't look after me. He'd look after me always and we'd stay together and sing together and he ... I was sitting on the piano stool and he was walking up and down, then he got down beside me, kneeling down and put his arm round my back and ...'

From Rose's look of black fury, if a resurrected Osbert Newbiggin had walked in at that point, a lack of pinking shears wouldn't have saved him.

'It's all right, you don't have to say it, does she, Nell?'

'No. I can guess what happened then.'

I could too. Laura looked at me out of horrified eyes and Rose frowned a message not to say any more.

'Not what you think, Rose.' I waited until Laura had her eyes open and was looking at me. 'He knelt down beside you, put his arm round you and burst into tears. Isn't that it?'

Laura started nodding again and couldn't stop. 'He ... he wanted me to p ... p ... ut my hands round his throat, like the girl in the s ... s ... song.'

I quoted, '"I would have rather felt you round my throat/ Crushing out life, than waving me farewell."'

Rose said, 'He asked you to *strangle* him?'

'What did you do?'

'I ... I think I was crying too. Then he jumped up because he heard the gardener with the wheelbarrow outside on the lawn ...'

'Wheelbarrow?'

'It squeaks. And he stood turned away from me, in that alcove where he keeps his records, and said I'd better go.'

'Did you tell Mrs Bolter about that?'

'No. I ... She'd have been angry with me.'

'So you all waited for Davie to come?'

'Yes.'

'And Davie came and told him you were going whether he liked it or not. And when it was all over and Mrs Bolter was in bed, Davie was going to bring a cart for your luggage and take you away?'

'Yes.'

'Did Davie talk to you after seeing Mr Newbiggin?'

'Not talk. He left a note for me.'

Rose's arm was still round her. She was looking at me in a puzzled way, as if just waking up to what was going on.

'Davie left a note for you that evening, after speaking to Mr Newbiggin?'

'Yes.'

'How did he get it to you?'

'We had a place. Under the sundial.'

'Was that what he was doing the other time, when Mrs Bolter saw him?'

She licked her lips. 'Yes.'

'So that last evening, you knew there'd be a note there.'

'Yes.'

'How did you get it?'

'When she went to see cook.'

'So when she was in the kitchen, you went out in the dark to see if he'd left a note under the sundial?'

She nodded. The trembling was slowing down a little now, though she was still leaning heavily against Rose.

'What did the note say?'

'It said . . . it said everything was all right. I should wait until Mrs Bolter had gone to bed then pack all my things and be ready at midnight.'

'"Everything is all right." Was that exactly what he said?'

'Yes.'

Rose looked at me. That could be interpreted either way. Everything was all right because there'd been an agreement – or Newbiggin was beyond harming her any more.

'I don't suppose you kept the note, did you?'

There was a very long silence, then a nod.

'Have you got it here?'

Another nod.

'Would you show it to us?'

She turned her head very slowly and looked at Rose.

'I think you should,' Rose said. 'It might help.'

Very slowly, with Rose helping her, she stood up and shuffled over to the door leading to the other room. A patient up for the first time after an operation might move like that. I held the door open, revealing a dingy cube of a room, walls and ceiling all yellowish white, smelling of damp distemper. She shuffled over to a chest of drawers, with the veneer peeling away from the pale wood underneath, slowly opened the top drawer and took out a leather writing case. Her fingers were shaking so much that she needed Rose's help to prise the press studs apart. When she at last managed to get out the sheet of paper, she gave it to Rose, who glanced at it and handed it to me.

Dear Rose,

It's all right, everything's being arranged. Wait until Mrs Bolter goes to bed then stay in your room and do your packing, everything you have. I'll come for you with a cart at midnight.

Affectionate respects

Davie Kendal

The notepaper was a surprise. It was stiff, good quality, with the embossed heading 'Crowberry Hall'. The writing was in blue-black ink, neat and unhurried. It looked very much as if Davie had written it at Newbiggin's own desk. If so, that added yet another layer to the curious alternation of the cold-blooded and the frantic that had marked his behaviour that evening. If the 'everything arranged' referred to the murder of Newbiggin – and the prosecution would certainly have taken that view if the note had come to their attention – then Davie had shot his man, prepared the alibi attempt with the gramophone and calmly written a note to Laura with Newbiggin dying on the floor a few yards away. But how did that go with the madness of insisting that she must take all her luggage with her, then floundering through the night in search of a cart for it? We had to believe that in the course of a few hours Davie had varied from being a cold calculator to a creature with brains scrambled by panic. It hadn't made much sense before. With the note, it made less.

I looked up to see Rose and Laura sitting side by side on the bed, both staring at me and the note.

'May I keep this for a while?'

Laura looked uncertain and, I think, would have refused if she'd had the strength but again Rose intervened.

'Just for a few days. We'll look after it.'

We went slowly through to the next room. We'd got what we needed from Laura now but it seemed heartless to walk away and leave her. Rose asked if she'd eaten and Laura murmured something about soup, though whether as a recollection from the distant past or a vague plan for the future, I couldn't guess. Rose was still trying when there was a knock on the door and the sound of children's voices outside.

'For a lesson,' Laura said, getting up.

In the narrow doorway, identical twin sisters with thin pigtails looked curiously at Rose and me on our way out.

'We'll be back,' said Rose to Laura. 'It doesn't go on being as bad as this. Promise.'

I suppose the piano lid was opened and the reluctant scales started, but if so we were too far along the street to hear them. Rose walked fast with hard, angry steps.

I said, 'I couldn't have done it. She'd never have trusted me like that.'

'Well, perhaps there's one language I speak and you don't.'

The harshness was still in her voice. She was angry with me for hearing, for putting her in a position where she'd had to remember. I didn't blame her. If I'd said what I wanted to say – that I'd never admired her or anybody else more, that I felt ashamed of myself for my own security – that would only have made her more angry. All I could do was keep quiet and match my steps to hers.

When we'd turned out of the street and were going back towards the town, she said, 'I lied to her, too. I promised it wouldn't go on being as bad. But it will for her. They'll hang him and she'll blame herself for something she couldn't do anything about.' A few more angry steps. 'Well, won't they?'

'I don't know.'

'Oh, yes, you do know. It hasn't done any good, has it? Worse than no good. If we take that letter to the police they'll say it proves he killed the old man so that he could run off with Laura.'

I didn't want to talk about what was forming in my mind, but she'd deserved whatever I could give her.

'If I'm wrong, yes, it was worse than no good. But there's a chance, just the ghost of a chance.'

I told her what I was going to do. The angry rhythm of her walking slowed as she listened. We came to a complete halt by the clock tower.

'Will he do it?'

'He'd better. I'm going to Manchester to talk to him. Only there's something I must do first. Could you get Janet away from the house so that I can talk to her father?'

'The poor man. Must you?'

'Yes, just the one question. But the way she feels about me at the moment she probably won't let me get near him.'

'All right. I'll see you when you get back from Manchester.'

I watched her walking up the steep street to the Kendals' house, gave her a quarter of an hour to get Janet away, then

206

followed by a more roundabout route in case I bumped into them. Old Mr Kendal was alone in the house. I got the answer to my question, went back down the hill and caught the next train for Manchester.

EIGHTEEN

THE MAN ACTUALLY HAD THE nerve to keep me waiting. When I climbed the dusty stairs to his chambers, his clerk informed me that he was in consultation.

'Well, get him out of it.'

The clerk blinked, considered and finally wrote a note with infuriating slowness, half an eye on me as if he expected me to take off and circle wasp-like round the light bulb. Still without turning his back on me he shuffled sideways into the inner office, closed the door and presumably delivered his note. I heard Bill's voice. 'I told you I'm not . . .' Then: 'Who?' Then: 'Ask her to wait for five minutes. Get her a coffee.'

The clerk shuffled back. 'Mr Musgrave will be with you in five minutes.'

But I was half-way down the second cup of coffee before the inner door opened and solicitor and client appeared, chivvied on by Bill. He asked the clerk to see them downstairs, apologised for keeping me waiting.

'That solicitor sends me some of my best clients. I try to cultivate him.'

'I'm here about your worst client.'

He showed me through to his office. The dog Roswal had his chin on the clients' chair. Bill nudged it off and invited me to sit down, perching on the corner of his desk to listen.

'Developments?'

I told him everything we'd found out from Laura, only leaving out the way Rose made her thaw enough to speak to us. He listened eagerly at first, but when I told him about the note his face clouded.

'Did you bring it with you?'

Judging by the silence, he read it two or three times over. Then he sighed, folded it back in its original creases and returned it to me.

'Don't you want to keep it for a while?'

'Officially, I never saw it.'

'Is it Davie Kendal's handwriting?'

'Yes. I've had several letters from him in prison.'

'So why don't you want it?'

Another sigh. He looked out of the window. A pigeon was balancing on the ledge, flattening its breast feathers against the glass.

'If this had come to my notice before the trial I'd have been guilty of withholding evidence unless I took it to the police. Now he's been convicted, the case is officially closed. Still, I'd rather not have seen it.'

'It's fresh evidence. Isn't that what you needed to make them reopen the case?'

'Yes, but what kind of fresh evidence? If they had any last doubts about hanging him, this would convince them.'

'Why?'

'Surely you can see that.' Disappointment was making him less than polite. I was glad about that. 'Look, he quarrels with Newbiggin, he shoots him, then with the man bleeding to death on the floor he calmly sits down at his desk and writes a note on the man's own headed notepaper, probably with his own pen and ink, as calmly as if he's sitting in his lodgings. There's not a tremor in the handwriting. And what sort of note? He's not only trying to get the man's cousin to run away with him – he wants her to make sure she brings all her goods and chattels with her.'

'Is that really how you think it happened?'

'I'm telling you how it would look to a jury. From our point of view, this note's worse than useless.'

'What about the rest of Laura's evidence?'

'Newbiggin's behaviour to her, you mean?' I sensed in him a reluctance to come to that. 'Very well, let's accept that his actions weren't necessarily what you'd wish to see from a man who should have been protecting her. But a little too much susceptibility in a middle-aged man towards a talented young woman . . .'

'Please, Mr Musgrave, don't insult us both by talking such complete and utter nonsense.'

He'd been staring at the pigeon. His eyes came back to me, startled.

'Or if you must talk nonsense, keep it for juries. Unless you've wilfully misunderstood me, you know very well that it isn't just a question of middle-aged susceptibility. He raped that poor girl. He almost certainly did it more than once, with that awful old woman in the same house choosing not to know what was going on. Or if she did know she thought it was just the sort of thing that men needed to do, and poor relations without any money or influence had to put up with it. She actually told her not to make a fuss.'

'Hearsay. This whole thing is hearsay. On your account, the young woman's in a strung-up and nervous state . . .'

'Of course she's in a strung-up and nervous state. If she hadn't been, I suppose you'd have said that proved it couldn't have happened either.'

From under the desk, the dog let out a warning growl.

'All right, Roswal, she's not going to hurt me.'

'I wouldn't depend on that.' But I dropped my voice and tried hard to sound calm. 'All right, it's hearsay from a girl who's nearly dead from fear and worry. But I've spoken to her and you haven't. And there's the question of the baby she was expecting. We assumed it must be Davie's. I think it was Newbiggin's. Think of Davie's note. Does a young man go that far with a girl and then send her his "affectionate respects"?'

'Vile phrase.'

'The language of a young man who's not quite such a man of the world as he thinks he is. A naive young man who wants to rescue a girl in distress.'

'Very well, let's for the sake of argument grant that Kendal's a knight in shining armour and Newbiggin was a lecherous middle-aged monster . . .'

'Which he was.'

'I say, if we grant all that, if we go even further and assume that we can get Laura to give a sworn statement of all she's said to you, do you really think that will help Kendal's case?'

I said nothing. The impetus that had taken me from Laura's lodgings to this point was beginning to run out. He sensed that.

'Look, I'm sorry. I'm grateful for what you're trying to do, please don't think otherwise, but as far as the law's concerned there are just two faint hopes. One – which is the path his sister's on – is to persuade the Home Secretary to exercise his prerogative of mercy. I wouldn't say it to her, but in my opinion that's got as much chance as . . . as . . .'

'As a snowball in hell. I agree. And the other?'

'The other is to produce some genuinely new evidence to get the case reopened. You've done your best to get it. The note you've shown me might be evidence, but it's not helpful. The Laura story isn't evidence at all yet, and even if it were it would simply reinforce his motive.'

'Well, I've done the best I can . . .'

He started to make comforting noises, to say yes, of course I had, that he was grateful and so on. I cut him off in mid-coo.

'. . . now it's your turn to do your best.'

He rocked back and I could see that I'd kicked him hard in the vanity.

'You're implying I haven't?'

'I'm sure you've done very well so far.'

'So far?'

'We're not talking about the trial now. It's this question of new evidence. You say that what I've found out isn't useful. In itself, I agree, but it's a pointer towards the kind of new evidence that really would reopen the case.'

211

'What kind of new evidence?'

'What would you say to the gun that shot him, possibly with the fingerprints of the last person who handled it?'

'You've got that? Why didn't you . . .?'

The dog's head came out from under the desk, glaring at me. Not an impartial dog.

'I haven't got it. I know where it is, I think.'

'You think!'

'I know where it must be logically. It's the only thing that makes sense. Sense of the way Davie Kendal behaved that night. Sense of why Mrs Bolter didn't use the telephone.'

'Tell me.'

So I told him, while he strode up and down the small office, occasionally stopping to look at me.

At the end he said, 'You realise there's not a shred of evidence for all this?'

The words were hostile, but the way he said them was almost pleading. He wanted to believe it.

'There is, though. It was there in the police evidence and you all missed it.'

'What?'

'Those pieces of gramophone record in the ash-bin at the Kendals' house. Janet told me when the police found them they were all burnt and twisted with bits of cinders sticking to them.'

'Of course they would be if they'd had hot ashes on top of them.'

'How?'

He stared. 'The usual way, I suppose. Somebody shovels up the ashes and takes them out to the bin.'

'Yes, but when?'

'In the morning, I suppose, or whenever the fire gets made up.'

'The fire in the range at the Kendals' house gets made up between four and five o'clock in the morning. The father does it before he goes out on his knocking-up round. The morning after the murder the police arrived at their home at four o'clock and started looking for the gun. That morning, the range didn't get made up until very much later, so the ashes didn't go out.'

'Is this conjecture, or do you know it for a fact?' He was suddenly as tense as a whippet in a field full of rabbits.

'I know it for a fact. I went and asked old Mr Kendal just before I came here. With his son missing and the police searching his house for a gun, he had other things on his mind than taking out the ashes. The last lot of ashes to go into that bin went out as usual the day before – at about half-past four in the morning. Mr Kendal took them out there in the dark before he went to work. So how did those pieces of gramophone record come to be burnt, with cinders sticking to them?'

'You infer that they were already in the bin the day before?'

'Yes. While Mr Newbiggin was still alive. At least fifteen hours before somebody made that telephone call to Newbiggin's friend.'

'But it was a gramophone recording of Newbiggin's voice. The friend's quite unshakeable on it.'

'And he's right. I'm sure there was more than one copy made of that recording.'

'But if the pieces in the Kendals' bin weren't from the recording used in the alibi attempt, what were they doing there?'

'Helping to incriminate Davie Kendal – very successfully.'

He started walking up and down angrily. 'Conjecture, conjecture, conjecture.'

'I've told you how you can make it more than that. Find the gun.'

'Even if you're right about where it is, it could still have been Davie who put it there.'

'He wouldn't need to. Davie could have taken it away with him. The person we're looking for had no choice.'

'It's still not proof.'

'It's new evidence, though. You can't deny that. Or have you fallen as much in love with the idea of Davie's guilt as you once were with his innocence?'

213

'What a weathercock you make me out to be.' He sat down heavily in his chair. 'In any case, we haven't got this evidence, have we? We can't just walk in and look for it.'

'That's your job. I've told you where it is . . .'

'You've told me where you think it is.'

'. . . so all you've got to do is get the police in there and find it. If you move fast they can probably do it this evening.'

'It isn't as easy as that. I told you, the case is closed. No new crime has been committed. You can't lead the police into a citizen's home on the off-chance that there's evidence lying around.'

'Well, what can you do?'

He thought about it. 'If there really were new evidence, or the serious prospect of getting some, I could write to the Home Secretary requesting a retrial or a reference back to the appeal court.'

'They're going to hang him in four days' time.'

'The other way might be to get his solicitor to go to the detective in charge of the case and persuade him to reopen it, but . . .'

'Well, go to the solicitor, go to the Home Secretary or to the Lord Chancellor in his bath if necessary, only get the police in there.'

'Nell . . . Miss Bray . . . I wonder if you know quite what you're asking me to do. I have to work within the system. The law isn't a particularly charitable world, and if the word gets round – as it will – that I've become involved in anything quite so melodramatic, then there will be people who'll question my judgement.'

'Not if it works. You'll be the man who saved a hopeless case.'

'If it works. I don't suppose you're a betting woman.'

'You might suppose wrongly.' (I'd financed an entire term at Oxford with a judicious investment on an outsider.)

'Then what odds would you put on this attempt?'

'I'd say it was a certainty.'

His eyebrows rose. 'A certainty that we'll find it?'

214

'No, that's evens. The certainty is that if you don't try it you'll regret it for the rest of your life.'

He looked down at the desk, fiddled with a paper-knife. I thought he was going to refuse and disappointment became black anger.

'If I'm wrong, yes, perhaps people will gossip about you. Perhaps there'll be no more neat little solicitors bringing you in nice fat clients, and Davie Kendal will hang in any case. Perhaps over the years, as you get pulpy and prosperous and can't walk a mile uphill without stopping for breath you'll manage to convince yourself that you were quite right to be cautious.'

'Is that a prophecy or a curse?'

'Whichever you like. Do you remember that evening when you intruded on my brother's hospitality to ask for my help?'

'Was I being cautious then? I feel as if I've raised the whirlwind.'

'You said you'd give up the law tomorrow and take to shovelling coal for a living if you thought it would help Davie Kendal. I take it you've had second thoughts on coal shovelling.'

His expression when he looked up showed I'd hit him a blow where he didn't expect it, probably an unsporting one.

'That's unfair. I was convinced he was innocent then.'

'And now?'

'After that evening with Rolling Toby I began to think I was wrong.'

'Yes, but now?'

He looked at me for a long time. 'After what you've told me? You know, I'm only just taking it in but . . . but, yes, do you know, I really think he might be after all.'

Evens.

'So you'll do it?'

'Yes. Yes, I will try to get the case reopened and I will try to get the police to look there. I may be making the biggest mistake of a short and inglorious career, but I'll try it.'

215

Relief, and the conscious nobility of his expression, made me laugh.

'You think that's funny, do you?'

'Ever since you dragged me into this, I've had to feel sorry for people: Janet, and her father, and Laura – even Rose. There's no more room on the list. I totally and utterly refuse to feel sorry for you, Bill Musgrave, so don't angle for it.'

He laughed too, a good open laugh that made the leaning pigeon edge away from the window. 'All right, when I'm selling bootlaces in the gutter, you can buy a pair from me and not feel sorry.'

'I thought it was going to be coal shovelling. You're becoming very inconsistent in your choice of careers.'

After that, we got down to business. He'd almost certainly need a sworn statement from Laura, and I warned him that wouldn't be easy, but it would have to wait until after the gun was found. Without that, there'd be no case worth fighting. When I thought of how much was riding on that it was all I could do to control my impatience. I wanted to see him on his way to Davie Kendal's solicitor without wasting another minute.

For half an hour or so he asked me questions, including some very shrewd ones I hadn't expected, and took notes. Now the decision was made he was every inch the efficient barrister and my spirits rose. At the end of it he scribbled a note to the solicitor and called in the clerk to take it over to the telegraph office.

'He should have been in at the start of this, but circumstances aren't normal.'

'What happens now?'

'The solicitor and I will consult. I'll send you a telegram as soon as we know . . .'

'How soon will that be?'

'Tomorrow, probably. He'll want time to consider. Meanwhile I'll write to the Home Secretary today, to open the possibility that . . .'

'It's the weekend. Nobody will do anything until Monday and they're hanging him on Tuesday morning.'

'Still time enough, if we're lucky.'

'Time enough! With his family waiting and the Home Secretary off shooting grouse somewhere.'

'This is a gallop by legal standards.'

'Well, it's not fast enough. Supposing somebody tries to move that gun in the meantime? Supposing it gets moved accidentally?'

'If you're right, there's very little risk of that.'

'Even a little risk is too much.'

'Nell, I'm trying to move heaven and earth for you as it is . . .'

'Not for me, for your client.'

'Legally, I can't move any faster.'

'I'll just have to try the other way then.'

I stood up and made for the door. He shouted after me, demanding to know where I was going.

'Home. You'll hear from me – or possibly about me.'

He followed me through the clerk's office and shouted after me down the stairs that I wasn't to do anything stupid. Fine behaviour for a barrister.

NINETEEN

PAULINE WAS DISBELIEVING WHEN I suggested that she should invite Rodney and Evangeline Newbiggin to tea next day.

'I know we owe them hospitality, but I'm really in no hurry to see the woman again. Besides, it's such short notice for her.'

'She'll leap at it. You can tell her you want to consult her about the drawing room curtains or somesuch.'

'I'd as soon consult King Herod on the care of infants.'

I'd called at the house as soon as I got back from Manchester and coincided with the boys' tea-time. She removed a knife from Duncan's reach, told John to stop making bread pellets and looked at me.

'Are you going to cross-question them? After all, they weren't even here when it happened.'

'I promise, I've no intention of questioning them. In fact, Rose and I won't be there.'

'Nell, is this fair? You expect me to invite the tedious woman to tea in a hurry and you won't even be here to help. What's happening?'

'What's she doing now?'

My brother came in, city-clad and cycle-clipped, cheeks red from his uphill ride, kissed his wife, rumpled the boys' hair. All I got was a look of deep suspicion.

'She wants me to invite that terrible decorating snob Evangeline and her husband to tea tomorrow and she won't say why.'

'I think it's time you started getting on better social terms with your neighbours.'

He made a rude noise, which John copied, bringing an instant threat of no cake from Pauline.

'If Pauline writes the invitation now I could take it down to the town and catch the evening post.'

He stared at me. I hadn't told him about either of the two visits to Laura, although he'd known I'd intended to see her, and I guessed that he wanted very much to know what had happened. With Pauline there, he couldn't ask.

'Nell, is this going to hurt anybody?'

'Only somebody who deserves it very much.'

He wasn't reassured, but in the end he nodded reluctantly. 'If Pauline can put up with them.'

I fetched paper, pen and envelope from the study and Pauline wrote a note at the table, then handed it to me for delivery. I freewheeled down the hill on Stuart's bicycle and put it into the post box near the clock tower. First phase accomplished, by far the easiest. Over supper in the cottage, Rose and I discussed the next part. The servants were the problem but I was counting on the fact that the period between clearing up the lunch and beginning dinner preparations was the slack time in most households, particularly on a Saturday with the mistress out to tea.

'They're almost certain not to lock the back door. If they do, I'll just have to find a window. Then as soon as you see me go inside, you run as fast as you can down the drive to the police station. You've got the story clear?'

Rose recited 'I was trying to call on Mrs Newbiggin – not knowing she was out, of course – when I saw somebody behaving suspiciously round the back of the house. After what had happened there I was frightened. I didn't try to challenge the person or raise the alarm. My first thought was to get to the police.'

'That's it. And you're scared, none too bright and – quite genuinely – breathless.'

'Is it male or female, this person I saw?'

'Probably male, I think, and quite large and active. We want them to send more than one policeman as a witness. Try for a sergeant, if you can.'

'Do I come back up there with the police?'

'If they'll let you. But once you've got them on the way, your job's done.'

'Apart from worrying.'

'We'll both be doing that.'

Pauline's answer was delivered by the gardening boy from the hall on Saturday morning. Rodney Newbiggin was regrettably otherwise engaged in Manchester but Evangeline was delighted to accept her kind invitation. By four o'clock in the afternoon Rose and I were tucked out of sight behind a boulder on the slope of bracken and heather between Crowberry Hall and the old quarry. We'd come the back way, by the bramble slide. If we looked round our boulder and down towards the house we could see the first curve of the drive before it disappeared downhill into the rhododendrons. Apart from the buzzing of insects it was a quiet afternoon, with a pale grey sky keeping a lid on the valley and the sleepy, used-up feel you get in the air at the very end of summer before the first frost.

When the car engine started it sounded as loud as a thunder-clap. There'd never been any fear that the socially ambitious Evangeline would change her mind about Pauline's invitation, but it was a relief to hear it all the same. A minute later a black motor car came into view on the bend going down the drive. From our position up the hill we could see the top of a dark cap in the driving seat, a purple hat in the back: Evangeline and chauffeur. When it had plunged out of sight we began walking downhill towards the back of the house. We didn't try to hide. If anybody had seen us at that point we'd simply say we were out walking and apologise for intruding on their grounds.

When the bracken gave way to a stretch of turf and the back wall of the garden we stopped for a good look. We knew the formal gardens already. Near the back of the house a balustraded wall marked off a utilitarian sunken courtyard with pigswill bins. From the gardens it would be invisible – although you might have caught a whiff from the bins on a hot day – but from where we were standing you could see that it led into the scullery and kitchen area. A sash window in that part of the house was standing half open and the sound of clattering saucepans came up to us. They weren't very energetically clattered. As we watched, a maid came out with a bucket, up-ended it into a swill bin, and went back inside without looking up.

'Right, that's lunch dealt with. They'll make themselves a cup of tea now – wouldn't you?'

Rose and I scrambled over the drystone wall into the garden. Once there, we were intruders with no chance of looking honestly lost, so we went at a run past the pool and gazebo, dodging round the Greek urns of the formal courtyard, to the main back door of the house. So far, not a sound from the kitchen area. From outside, the door was simply latched, but when I lifted up the latch and pushed gently it didn't give. Bolted from the inside. I shook my head at Rose and we went round the side of the house. This was risky because there was a gravel path to negotiate and the chance of running into the gardener tidying up beds for winter. But the chrysanthemums and sedums bloomed undisturbed and there was still no sign of anyone. I touched Rose's elbow and pointed to the third window along. It was propped open about a foot at the bottom, probably to let the room air. As near to an open invitation as anybody could want. We stepped onto the flower-bed, trying not to crush the plants too badly. It was almost too easy to slide an arm through the gap and remove the wooden wedge that was keeping the window secured on the inside. With one leg over the sill I waved off Rose and mouthed the word, 'Run.' One anxious glance, then she was away across the lawn towards the drive. At that speed, she'd be telling her story to the desk sergeant within minutes.

I took off my shoes, and went in stockinged feet on thick carpet. I was in the drawing room with the eau-de-Nil and grey paintwork, so pleased to be there that I could almost have hugged the armchairs, even if they were the colour of wet seals. I crossed to the door, opened it and looked out on the corridor. Empty. Into the corridor, through the second door on the left and I was back in the study of the late Osbert Newbiggin, alone and unobserved. I took a few deep breaths and walked across to the alcove. The huge horn of the recording machine was still there in the dim light, like a sea monster in its cave, but I resisted the impulse to touch it or even look at it too closely. Rose would be well down the drive, past the lodge cottage, following the track of Laura on her unnecessary run that night. Nothing to do but wait now.

I put on my shoes and sat at the chair behind the big mahogany desk. Perhaps nobody had sat at this desk since the evening Osbert Newbiggin died. November then. By six o'clock it would have been long dark outside, curtains drawn and probably a fire in the grate. Newbiggin at the desk, Davie Kendal standing on the mat in front of him, nervous probably, but with an ultimatum for the dragon. *Either Laura is set free to marry me, or the whole town knows what you've been doing with her.* I wondered how Davie would have put it. Too embarrassed, probably, to name the brutal reality of the thing even if he knew it – and I was by no means certain that Laura had told him the worst of it. But Newbiggin would have thought he knew to the last detail. He'd have known too that Davie meant what he said, that with his brother's help he could at least spread the story around the town enough to damage the reputation that Newbiggin treasured. No more respectful paragraphs in the newspapers. No more bass arias at concerts. No more applause, only the whispers half heard and the family men who didn't want him at their dinner tables any more, who'd make sure that their daughters were never in the same room with him. He had a loaded gun in his desk. He must have wanted very much to take it out and shoot Davie Kendal.

By now Rose should be running up the steps of the police

station, hat in hand, hair flying, gasping out her message. They'd listen. Rose had a gift of making people listen, even in less interesting circumstances. A fine teacher. Those fools of governors in Wimbledon. I stretched my legs under Newbiggin's desk, wondering what Bill Musgrave was doing. Still consulting with the solicitor perhaps or at best discussing whys and wherefores with some drowsy turtle of a judge. I tried the right-hand desk drawer, but it was locked. The left had headed notepaper in it, exactly the paper on which Davie had written his note.

'. . . do your packing, everything you have. I'll come for you with a cart at midnight. Affectionate respects . . .'

Newbiggin would have given him the paper and pen, watched while he wrote it, even dictated the terms. I could almost hear the voice: '. . . don't want a thing of hers left in the house, not a thing. No, I don't know where you're going to find a cart at this time of night. You want her, that's your concern now. And not a minute before midnight. I'm not having Mrs Bolter upset. You can leave this where you usually leave your love letters. I know what's been going on.'

But defeated, for all the bluster. And Davie had written his letter at the big desk, tucked it under the sundial and – probably shocked to find it had been so easy after all – gone off into the night to look for a cart because nobody had warned him that after you'd finished off your dragon you still had to deal with the princess's suitcases. And all this time the old woman and the girl were waiting with nothing to say to each other, pretending perhaps to read or sew. No, not sewing for the old woman, with those hooked hands. Just sitting like a tough lizard on a cold rock, waiting.

Waiting. Rose would have told them her story now. Surely they wouldn't dawdle. After the murder, even a cat coughing at Crowberry Hall should bring them. Then from outside I heard the sound of the car engine roaring up the steep drive. It came closer, gravel spluttered, then the engine died. Inside the house there were quick

223

footsteps in the corridor and a voice from the kitchen regions.

'It's not her back already, is it?'

The footsteps went on, past the study door, and must have turned into one of the rooms overlooking the front drive. There was a pause, then they came back past me at a run.

'No, it's not her. It's two policemen. They've got a girl with them.'

'Police! What's happened now?'

An authoritative knock on the front door. A whispered consultation just outside the study as to who should answer it. Another knock, more impatient. The cook hissed at the maid to get on with it. Then the sound of the front door opening and the girl's scared voice.

'What's happening? Is it something with Mr Newbiggin?'

She must have let them in because the next bit of the conversation took place not far from my door. A male voice, calming, a little patronising.

'This young lady thinks she saw a man climbing in through a window. Have you ladies noticed anything of the kind?'

A little scream from the maid. The cook asked what window and the police officer must have turned to Rose.

'Do you know what window it was, Miss?'

'One of the big downstairs ones on the right.'

That from Rose, composed but with just the right hint of nervous agitation for a nice young lady who'd witnessed a burglary. Perfect. It was good to think of her just a few yards away. Two policemen as well, just what we wanted.

'Are the lady and gentleman of the house at home?'

Both out, the cook told him.

'Would you have any objection if we searched the house as a precaution?'

Evidently not. I heard them go into one of the rooms at the front, emerge a few minutes later and try the one opposite. They seemed to be going round in a group, the two policemen, the cook, the maid and probably Rose.

They tried the dining room next because the cook said that was where most of the silver was kept. This took longer than the other rooms because presumably they had to count the jugs and pitchers and so on. By the time they came out, I was willing them to get on with it and thought of dropping a paper-weight to speed things up. No need.

'Do you know if Mr Newbiggin keeps any money in the house?'

'Not that I know of.'

'Does he have a study?'

The doorknob turned. I moved over to stand beside the alcove. It was the sergeant who came in first, followed by the constable, then the cook, the maid and Rose. His eyes opened wide. He stared at me, turned to the cook and maid.

'Do you know this woman?'

'Never set eyes on her in my life before.'

Which, from the cook, was quite true. The maid had handed me a cup of tea at the At Home but if she recognised me – which was unlikely – she said nothing. He turned to Rose.

'I thought you said it was a man you saw climbing in.'

'I thought so, but I might have been wrong. After all, she is quite tall.'

The sergeant looked me up and down. Charge upheld, I was quite tall.

'So what are you doing here, Miss?'

I stepped aside so that he had a clear view of the huge horn of the recording apparatus.

'I was planning to take that away, but as you see it looks very heavy. I shall need some help.'

That struck him dumb. I don't suppose his experience so far had included burglars who requested his help in carrying the swag away.

'Did . . . did you have the owner's authority to carry this away?'

'No, but since it contains evidence in a murder case I

225

think somebody should get authority as soon as possible. Meanwhile, sergeant, I think it may be safely confided to your care. If you could arrange for somebody to keep a watch on it until you sort out the legal technicalities . . .'

'This murder you're talking about . . .'

'The killing of Osbert Newbiggin. I daresay you were here at the time, sergeant.'

'Yes, I was.'

He deserved to be a sergeant. A less intelligent man would have had the handcuffs on me as soon as he walked in. This one knew something more interesting than simple burglary was going on.

'You were probably one of the officers who were searching the shrubbery for a gun.'

'Yes, I was.'

'You were wasting your energy. It was in there all the time.'

The huge horn and the sergeant gaped at each other.

'In there?'

'It will be covered with ten months of dust. I don't know how long fingerprints last, but if they last that long, the prints of the person who put it there will be on it. Nobody's touched it since.'

He tore his eyes away from the horn and looked at me.

'Are you one of these private detectives, Miss?'

'I suppose I'm a very public one.'

'Have you Mr Newbiggin's permission to be in this house?'

'No. I came in through a window as this young lady told you.'

'Are you aware that you have effected an illegal entry?'

'Certainly.'

He asked my name and address, which I gave him, along with the information that I was staying with my brother. The constable produced a notebook and wrote it all down. When I mentioned Stuart's name I noticed a subtle change in attitude. Whether he liked it or not, my brother had

226

become a known and respectable citizen – or had been until I arrived.

'Now, if we can get back to the main point, I suggest that we go down to the station, you charge me with illegal entry or whatever you like and I'll get in touch with my solicitor. Only for pity's sake leave the constable on guard here.'

The sergeant considered for a long time. Rose glanced at me, eyes full of anxiety, looked away. The maid and cook stood by the door, apprehensive of being at fault in some way but not wanting to miss a word. I was trying to will the man to behave as I wanted. If he panicked and carried me off without securing the machine, it could still go wrong. The fear underlying it that I might be wrong after all – that there might be nothing in there – had dwindled to nothing beside this. He walked over to it, bent over the horn and tried to look down inside it. Useless. Only a smooth throat sliding away to blackness and the smell of dust.

'Go and get your lamp from the car.'

The constable went away and returned after several minutes with a bull's-eye lantern, already lit. The sergeant told him to hold it while he looked down and then grabbed it from him and performed various neck exercises, without result. He got down on his knees and looked at the outside of the thing, where the horn joined on to the wooden case holding the recording machinery.

'It would unscrew, but we'd need to get the owner's . . .'

A voice in the hall, loud and petulant. 'Eva, somebody's left the front door open. And what's that motor car doing outside?'

'It's Mr Newbiggin.' The cook's voice, apprehension combined with happy anticipation of a row that wasn't her fault. 'We're in here, sir.'

Rodney came rushing into the study, overcoat on, hat in hand. He stopped dead when he saw the semicircle of us staring at him. The sergeant took control.

'Good evening, sir. This lady has effected an entry to your house. She claims the gun that was used to kill your uncle is in this piece of apparatus. Have you any knowledge of this?'

Hardly breaking things gently. Rodney collapsed into a leather armchair and dropped his hat on the carpet. 'A gun? In there?'

'So she says, sir.'

'It's . . . it's the surgeon's sister. Our neighbour. What does she know about it?'

'It appears she's some kind of detective, sir.'

I didn't try to explain. I was getting used to it.

'But they've already had the trial.'

'Yes, sir, but as you know we never found the murder weapon. There's no obligation on you at all to do anything at this stage, but I wonder whether as a favour you might allow us to dismantle this apparatus to check.'

Rodney nodded, still in a state of shock. 'If you think it necessary.'

'Would you have such a thing as a screwdriver, sir?'

Rodney used the telephone on the desk to summon the handyman. He arrived with his tool bag, wiping toast crumbs off his moustache, and he and the sergeant began work, kneeling in the alcove on either side of the machine. The cook and maid were sent about their business. Rodney, still in his overcoat, hovered and made unhelpful suggestions. Nobody told Rose to go, so she stayed.

'Bring it over into the light.'

Between them the sergeant and the handyman carried out the horn, now freed from its base. It tapered to a small pipe at the end.

'All right if we turn it over on the carpet, sir?'

The carpet in front of the desk. Rodney nodded and they up-ended the thing. If all the divas in the world poured their voices into the throat of the horn in harmony, they couldn't have sounded as sweet to me as the thud of something falling softly onto the carpet from the depths of it. Then the men lifted it away, like a huge mould that had given issue to a very small blancmange. Only this thing was small and black and metallic, surrounded with a ring

228

of fluffy dust and dead grey moths. There was something else too.

'What's that?' I knew, but I wanted them to see.

The sergeant knelt down beside it, but didn't touch. 'Looks like a man's handkerchief.'

'Bloodstained.'

Rusty-brown now, but unmistakeable. He got to his feet. 'Is there a key to this room, sir? Do you mind if we lock it?'

No, Rodney didn't mind. He looked too dazed to mind anything. Quite a lot later, as Rose and I and the two officers went down the front steps to the police car, we met Evangeline coming in from her tea-party. She looked like a woman who needed an explanation, but we didn't stop to give it.

TWENTY

AN HOUR LATER, DOWN A more modest set of steps, I found other people wanting explanations, my brother Stuart and one more. Stuart was no surprise. Since the police had no business with Rose – other than as a witness – she'd left soon after we arrived at the station and would have taken the news to him. They were standing under the blue police lamp. Stuart was still wearing cycle clips and his martyred elder brother look. The man beside him was an assemblage of tweed suit, trilby hat, pipe and deerhound.

'Bill Musgrave. What are you doing here?'

At least, unlike Stuart, he looked cheerful.

'Roswal and I were coming to bring you good news – or so we thought. Davie's solicitor and I had been making progress. We had hopes of getting the police to reopen the case with the prospect of fresh evidence.'

'I've found it.'

'So I gather from Miss Mills.'

Stuart broke in, 'She's gone and got herself into trouble again.'

'Well, what's a bit of breaking and entering between friends. Have the police actually charged you, Nell?'

'No. They've taken a statement and told me not to go away. Anyway, I don't think it rates as breaking in, the window was open. The point is, that gun's now in police hands and there was a bloodstained handkerchief. Did Rose tell you that?'

'Every detail.'

'And they're taking it to look for fingerprints?'

230

'Officially, they won't say so. Unofficially, they're sure to. I'll find out more tomorrow. Shall we walk?'

We walked along the street away from the police station, getting some curious glances as we came into the circles of light by the lampposts, probably on account of Roswal although I daresay I looked a mess. I'd left my hat somewhere, lost my comb and could feel my hair wandering all over the place.

Stuart recovered his bicycle, propped against the wall, and announced he was going straight home to give Pauline the good news that I wasn't locked up, although judging by his tone he classed that among the very small mercies. 'She's having terrible trouble with the boys. You'll give them nightmares.'

'Good for their young imaginations. Tell them I'll see them tomorrow.'

He rode off.

'Have you and Roswal had your walk, then?'

'Abandoned. Would you care to escort us both to the railway station?'

I was grateful to him for not making any fuss. There were very few men I knew who'd react without flapping and blame-casting. There was also the little matter that I'd accomplished within hours something that would have taken the law days. Of course, I couldn't expect him to admit that. We walked along the High Street, past the Cross Keys and the clock tower, and turned down the long road to the station. There was a cold wind blowing off the moors and yellowed ash leaves skittered along the pavement ahead of us.

'How long will it take them to get fingerprints?'

'Not long, if they can. We'll know on Monday.'

'If there are none of Davie's on the gun, and the ones there match up with the person we think they do, it will have to go straight to the Home Secretary, won't it? He'll know the sentence is unsafe.'

'It's still a big if.'

The wind went colder and the leaves whirled up, taking

away some of the warm feeling of relief and safety I'd felt since seeing the gun in its circle of dust.

'They can't be Davie's. You agreed with me. We know what happened.'

'The question is, will there be anybody's? Ten months is a long time, Nell. Essentially, fingerprints are grease traces and it's been lying there covered with dust. It might not be conclusive.'

'But where it was found proves something. Davie would have been mad to throw it in there when he could have taken it away and disposed of it anywhere he wanted.'

'But we've still got to prove it. Finding the gun there is useful. It's indisputably fresh evidence. But if the fingerprints aren't on it, it's no proof.'

We came to the station. He gave me Roswal's lead to hold while he searched in his pockets for his return ticket.

'I'd offer to escort you back to your cottage, but I know what you'd say to that.'

I'd been doing some hard thinking in the last few minutes.

'I'm not going back. I'm coming with you.'

His eyebrows shot up. 'I'm glad my company is so irresistible.'

'It's tolerable. The point is, I need to be at Southport first thing in the morning. I can stay at a hotel in Manchester and catch the first train.'

'Southport. That's where . . . No, I'm not going to ask.'

'After what happened today my nerves are in such a bad state that I feel the need for sea air.'

'Of course. Any doctor would recommend it.'

As he took the lead back from me his hand touched mine and he looked at me. 'Sea air. I wish . . .'

'Wish what?'

'That we were somewhere else. Warm sea air.'

'And palm trees and conch shells and malarial mosquitoes. Have you got a pencil and paper?'

We had ten minutes to wait for the Manchester train,

just long enough to scribble a note for Rose and find a couple of lads idling by a parcel truck to deliver it for a shilling apiece.

When we got to Manchester I wanted to go to one of the cheap hotels by the station, but he insisted on escorting me to the Queen's, booking me a room and taking me to a late supper in the dining room, with Roswal lying under the table as quiet as a sheep, apart from gulping down the morsels that Bill slid to him. We ate Beef Wellington, drank claret, talked about the Andes and the Alps and a few other things but didn't mention Newbiggins or Kendals. Afterwards I watched from the hotel doorway as he and the dog strolled back to his chambers.

When I tried to settle my bill the next morning they told me that Mr Musgrave had already paid it. He'd left a note too, very short: *Enjoy the sea air.*

When I got to Southport there was drizzle in the air and the tide was still out. One day I'd get there and catch it in, but it had never happened yet. The quiet of a Sunday morning lay over the shops and cafés of Lord Street, apart from the sound of distant church bells.

When I knocked at Mrs Bolter's door the thin maid looked more scared than ever. She was wearing a green cotton apron over her black dress and had a smear of boot polish on her cheek.

'She's not up yet.'

'I'll give her ten minutes. Tell her something's been found at Mr Newbiggin's house and she should know about it.'

The door closed. I stood there long enough for a lad to finish sweeping the pavement in front of the house opposite and carry out a stoic bay tree in a pot for its daily struggle against the salt breeze. As he brought out its partner, the door opened.

'You're to come in and wait.'

She said it in an appalled whisper. I followed her into the room where I'd had my first conversation with Mrs Bolter.

233

The blinds were down and the dimness had a musty smell of stale port and liniment. There were noises from upstairs of somebody moving about heavily. I sat in an upright armchair upholstered in shiny brown cloth next to an aspidistra. Its leaves gleamed and reflected the little light that filtered through the blinds. I thought that the maid would have to wash them daily in cold tea. Even wickedness had its routines, or perhaps wickedness needed them more than most. Heavy steps on the stairs, wheezing breath. Was the wheezing a little too heavy, demanding pity? She came in, shoulders hunched, head and eyes protruding.

'Well, what is it? I haven't had my breakfast.'

I waited while she settled in the chair opposite me. She had her back to the window so her face was almost in darkness, except that her eyes reflected the light as the plant leaves did.

'The police found a gun yesterday, in the horn of the recording machine.' I'd no intention of telling her how the police had been led there. 'There was a bloodstained handkerchief with it.'

'Did they have a search warrant?'

There was a change in her voice from the plaintive complaint about breakfast. Being a poor old woman wouldn't help her now.

'No.'

'Why did Rodney let them in?'

'He wasn't there.'

'They're not allowed to do that.'

'They asked his permission to take it away for tests. He gave it.'

'Tests?'

'Including fingerprint tests. If you handle something, a little grease from your fingers stays on it. Probably more if your fingers are sweating – wouldn't you think.'

Her eyes moved from side to side.

'They're unique, you know. They can compare it with others. A glass somebody's handled, say, or a piece of furniture.'

'Why did Rodney let them take it?'

'He wants to know who really killed his uncle. He doesn't want an innocent man to hang.'

She made a disgusted little noise, as if a fly had landed on her nose and she were trying to blow it off. 'He deserves it.'

'For loving Laura and wanting to rescue her? Was she such a valuable family property? Or was it for knowing what had happened to her and threatening to tell other people about it? Was that why he deserved hanging?'

'Such a fuss to make over a little slut.'

It came as a growl from her chest. I didn't even see her lips move.

'Whose fuss? Davie's fuss, do you mean, or somebody else's?'

The eyes flickered.

'Osbert's. An odd man, your nephew. On the one hand, the strong, practical mill owner, respected by everybody.'

'He was.'

'Oh, I know. The charities, the choral society, the black horses at the funeral. But there were some girls watching that funeral procession go past who knew the other side. A man who wanted something from them, a soft and sentimental man who cried when he didn't get it. Then Laura came.'

'I wish she'd died first.'

'She was all the girls in one – soft and shy and musical and all of it in his house, his to watch and listen to and touch all the time. You must have seen it happening.'

'He did everything for that girl.'

'Food and clothes and music lessons and a roof over her head. And ruining her life.'

'What about his life? What about gratitude?'

'Was that how you saw it – that she should put up with anything he wanted to do to her, out of gratitude? Yes, I suppose it was.'

Silence.

'I suppose it would have gone on, probably until the girl

went and drowned herself nice and quietly in the quarry one fine day. Only along came Davie Kendal. He probably didn't know the full story, probably still doesn't even now, but he knew enough to see she needed help.'

'Ungrateful and interfering.'

'You knew very well why he was coming there that last evening. He'd already told Osbert that either Laura came away with him or the whole town knew how she'd been treated. He was coming for an answer and you knew it. You'd have discussed it with Osbert. You were the only one he could trust.'

The flicker of a smile, instantly trapped between pursed lips. In spite of everything she was proud of that.

'You'd have told him "let him take the girl, she's not worth it". Didn't you?'

The slightest of nods.

'And he'd have to agree with you. The alternative was madness – but then he was very nearly mad by then. He told you, yes, she could go but then he pleaded with her not to, I know that. Even with you, I don't think he made the decision calmly.'

'Silly. Over a girl like that.'

The lips unpursed in a little twist of contempt and the words escaped. If Laura could cause all this then the world was a place badly arranged.

'And he threatened to kill himself. Laura must go, if there was no alternative, but he couldn't live without her. And you told him what you've just said to me. "Silly. Over a girl like that." Only you must have had some fear that he meant it, because you went into the study that night, and when you found him lying there with the gun beside him, you knew what had happened. You called for help, but by the time they got there, you knew you didn't want the world to know how silly he'd been. You were clever. You sent them running off at once, the cook up to the landing to ring the bell, the maid for bandages, Laura down the drive. If the police came with the gun still there beside him, they'd know he killed himself and at the inquest it would all come out and the world would know that Osbert Newbiggin had committed suicide over a slip of a girl.'

She was breathing heavily and her eyes were fixed on me, waiting for me to go on.

'You had to get rid of that gun and you had only a very short time before the maid came back with the bandages. The ideal thing would be to lock it back in the drawer where he'd kept it, but you didn't have time to do that, with your hands as they are.'

She looked down at the bent arthritic fingers.

'You could just manage to pick it up, then you had to dispose of it quickly. You saw the horn of the recording machine, and down it went, then the handkerchief he'd used to hold it, so that his fingerprints wouldn't be on it. The best you could do. Perhaps somebody might have found it one day – but by then Davie Kendal would have been hanged as a murderer and nobody would have known the significance of it.'

'What are they going to do now?'

'What do you expect them to do? You've lied to the police. You've concealed evidence of suicide and committed perjury. You've sat here waiting for an innocent man to be hanged. What do you expect them to do?'

I waited, but she said nothing. She seemed to be considering.

'I wonder if he'd discussed it with you, that terrible plot of his. It wasn't just a matter of killing himself, he wanted to kill Davie Kendal as well.'

'No.'

'Davie had won. The lad he'd taken from nowhere, given his chance in life, was going to take Laura away from him. Either Laura or his reputation, and he couldn't do anything about it.

'When Davie came to his study that evening, he must have been tempted to shoot him straight out, only what would that have done for him? Davie would have died a victim and Osbert as his murderer. That would be a triumph for Davie too, in its way. But since he'd decided to die anyway, he spent the last day of his life trying to make sure that Davie would suffer. You say he didn't discuss it with you.'

'No.' Her head was down and the voice only a mumble.

'You must have guessed afterwards, though. It was Osbert himself who wheeled the gramophone down to the lodge, Osbert who played his own voice over the telephone. The police thought that it was Davie trying to prove that Osbert was still alive then. It was quite the reverse – Osbert still alive, trying to prove that he was dead. He knew the police would leap to the conclusion that Davie had shot him about two hours before and was trying to confuse the times to give himself an alibi. And he'd got Davie out of the way by sending him on that wild-goose chase for a cart for Laura's luggage. He had an ingenious mind, I'll grant him that.'

'He was a good man.'

Another growl. I let that pass.

'He took the precaution of slipping that recording of his own voice in the Kendal's ash-bin when he went to deliver the note to Davie in the early hours of the morning, before his workers were up and about. He had another copy. Once he'd played it over the telephone from the lodge, he probably brought it back to the study and broke it with the other records when he was trying to make it look as if there'd been a struggle. The police wouldn't have been looking for that once they'd found the one he left at the Kendals'. Then he shot himself through the cushion, with his handkerchief wrapped round the gun. If the police had found a bloodstained handkerchief they'd have assumed it had happened in the struggle with Davie. But they didn't find it, because you'd thrown it into the recording horn. It will be your fingerprints they'll find on the gun, not Osbert's. They probably know that by now.'

After Bill's warning, I was by no means sure of that. It was a game of bluff but I had all the cards.

'What will they do?'

Her eyes were back on me now. The voice was weaker,

the hint of a quaver in it. I could hate myself for bullying her like this and when I clutched for a memory to help me, what came was an old hand, gently holding a canary.

'They'll probably come for you in a car, a sergeant and a constable, and they'll take you back to the police station at home to question you.'

Her body jerked as if I'd hit her. The Newbiggins had practically reigned over that town. The idea of eyes watching her as she walked up the steps to the police station, a uniformed policeman on either hand, was what broke her.

'If you're lucky, they'll let you out on bail before the trial. Then—'

'What do you mean, let me out?'

The glints of light had become ordinary round eyes, old eyes with chalky rims, swimming with tears. I thought of Janet's face in the firelight, Laura's pale hands.

'Out of a cell. Don't think they won't send a respectable old lady to prison if they have to. I know of one at least, and a good family didn't save her.'

She'd died in prison, of pneumonia. I didn't add that but then I didn't need to, because now slow, cloudy tears were running down her cheeks.

'What can I do?'

'To avoid being arrested and charged? I don't know, but here's what I'd try in your position. I'd get a message to Davie Kendal's solicitor saying I had information that might help his client. Then I'd make a statement to him exactly as it happened – Laura, and Osbert threatening to kill himself, and the gun and what you did with it.'

'Not Laura.'

'Then, if you're lucky – if you're very lucky – that may be enough to get the verdict against Davie quashed and the police might decide not to prosecute, on the grounds that you were too scared and confused to know what you were doing.'

(About as scared and confused as Medusa, I thought, but the police might be swayed by her grey hairs.)

'Not Laura. I'm not telling them about him and Laura.'

A sticking point. We could all wreck on this.

'I'm making no promises, but supposing they were satisfied with part of the story – that Davie wanted to marry her and Osbert as her guardian was reluctant? A normal family difficulty.'

'Normal family difficulty.' She clutched the phrase to her and clung to it, nodding and crooning over it. 'Oh yes, normal family difficulty.'

After a while she looked up and her eyes were bright and tearless again. 'You can send him to me. Send him to me quickly, before the police get here.'

'Who?'

'The man's solicitor, of course. Get him. Send him here.'

She was trying, painfully, to screw her head round towards the window. I realised that she was already expecting to hear the motor car stopping outside, hear the official tread of police boots to her newly painted front door. There was no telephone in the house, one of the few times in my life when I'd wanted one. I went into the street, without waiting for the maid to let me out, and in a few minutes had managed to commandeer one in the office of an enterprising fishmonger who'd come in on a Sunday to repair a shelf. Bill had no telephone but had come to an arrangement with the tea merchant on the ground floor at his chambers. I stood in a smell of wood shavings and fish and heard feet echoing down the stairs, then his voice asking what was happening.

'Is Davie's solicitor with you? Get him here now, and a clerk as witness. I'll be waiting for them at the railway station.'

I doubt if a solicitor had ever moved faster, but it seemed a long time. I met him and the clerk, briefed him on the fast walk to Lord Street and left them at the front door. Not my business now. I was back in Manchester in Bill's office when their call arrived: 'We have it. Returning at once.'

'We've done it, Nell. They can't hang him now.'

Something came over me, Southport air too strong perhaps. I turned away towards the window, trying to control my shaking.

'Miss Bray?'

He hadn't rushed to put his arm round my shoulders or make comforting noises. I respected him for that.

'Oh, Nell. Look, it's all over. Oh, poor Nell.'

And after all, respect isn't everything.

TWENTY-ONE

IT WAS TWO DAYS BEFORE we knew for certain that a reprieve had been granted, that Davie Kendal wouldn't hang. The usual slowness of the law becomes a crawl when it's a case of letting out an innocent man and even after the reprieve came through he was still a convicted murderer, still in prison. But by then everybody, even police and prosecution, knew that the conviction was unsafe and would be quashed, that Davie would be a free man, to pick up what was left to him of his life. When Janet walked up to the cottage to tell us about the reprieve I already knew because Bill had sent a telegram, but we let her give us the news as if we hadn't heard. Then she and Rose fell on each other's shoulders and cried, probably the first time she'd cried since it all began. She thanked me, and yet there was a constraint about her thanks. I understood. Too big a burden, and anyway why should she feel grateful to me or anyone for helping to right something that should never have happened at all?

She said her father wanted to see me, so next morning I went down to the little terraced house. It was full of neighbours and Jimmy's trade-union friends, dazed with relief, as festive as a wedding. Mr Kendal stood anxiously beside me in the parlour while I drank a cup of tea and crumbled a biscuit, but didn't say anything that mattered until we were alone together in the yard outside, staring at his treasury of canaries. As before, the deft old hand went in and came out clasped round a bird.

'My best cock bird. He won at Rochdale last year.'

The bird's round bright eyes looked up at me.

'I'd like you to have him.'

I thought of the cats and almost laughed, then saw the look in the man's eyes, much more anxious than the bird's.

'Thank you. But will you keep him and look after him for me?'

A nod and the bird went back on his perch, unaware of his change of ownership.

'It would have been yesterday morning.'

'Yes, I know. But it's over now.'

He nodded again, and we went back in to join the party. There'd be a bigger party one day when Davie came home again, but I'd be back in London by then. I was free to go because the police had given up any idea of prosecuting me for illegal entry to Crowberry Hall when Rodney said he-had no intention of pressing charges. Stuart Bray's sister was known to be a little eccentric and these things happened between neighbours. I knew very well where the line about eccentricity had come from and tackled Stuart about it. I'd got off lightly, he said. It had cost him a dinner invitation to the Newbiggins, plus having to put Rodney up for membership of his club to make sure there were no charges, so some humble thanks were due from me to my kind and protective big brother. Naturally, he didn't get them.

'And another thing, what am I supposed to tell Simon Frater? He's been on the telephone to me at the hospital, wanting to know how you are.'

'What did you tell him?'

'Very little. He's worried enough about you as it is. You really might have more consideration for his feelings, Nell.'

'His feelings! If it hadn't been for you two, I'd have had a nice peaceful time in London.' I relented. 'Give him my very best wishes, tell him I'll see him soon but I haven't had time to read the Plautus book.'

'That's all?'

'Yes.'

I couldn't face Laura again, but Rose went to see her to make sure she knew about the reprieve. She did, because the solicitor had already been to see her and take a statement. It must have been a painful business all round, but once they'd managed to get it into her head that she'd do good rather than harm to Davie by talking, she did it. Perhaps there was hope for her after all.

'But the piano lid's still closed,' Rose said.

'Ah well, there are other instruments.'

'Will she marry Davie, do you think?'

'Goodness knows. Perhaps the princess and the dragon killer don't always have to marry.'

'You sound more cheerful.'

'Probably the prospect of going home again. Did you put this dead mole in the cat basket?'

'The boys did, as a leaving present. It was dead when they found it.'

'Did I tell you I've been given a live canary? Oh, and Pauline's invited us over for supper tonight.'

'Will he be there?'

'Who did you have in mind?'

'You know very well.'

'Not unless he decides to gatecrash again.'

I knew he wouldn't. Bill and I had already said our goodbyes. He'd come to London soon, he said. Always glad to see him, I said. Rose and I gathered together the assemblage of plates, cutlery and saucepans that Pauline had loaned us, keeping only a jug and two cups for coffee in the morning. Just before it got dark the boys came over with the donkey, panniers slung across its back, to carry it all to the house. We followed them across the lawn and when we were a few steps away from it the cottage seemed to have turned back to a tumble of boulders. We slept there that night and nobody came to throw stones at the windows.

Next day Pauline and the boys came to see us off and settled us with the cats in a carriage with enough fruit, flowers and magazines to see us from Manchester to Marseilles, let alone London. Then the boys were dragged reluctantly away to keep a dental appointment and we were left in peace for the last few minutes before the train drew out. Rose seemed thoughtful.

'Sorry to be leaving?'

'Nell, there's something I should tell you. I'm not.'

'Not sorry?'

'Not leaving. Not permanently, that is. The fact is, I think I've got a teaching job.'

'Here? How?'

'Remember that clergyman at the awful tea-party?'

'The one you got trapped by?'

'I wasn't trapped. He was very nice for a clergyman and he's the governor of a school. One of their teachers is leaving at Christmas to get married and they're desperate to replace her. So provided my references are all right . . .'

'Of course they're all right. Simon will write you another beauty. You could stay with Stuart and Pauline. I'm sure . . .'

'Janet's seeing to that. The woman next to her has a front room spare. Nell, you don't mind, do you? It's all worked so well, and I like it here. I feel at home here.'

'So good riddance to Wimbledon governors?'

'Bloody good riddance to Wimbledon governors. You're pleased, Nell?'

'Pleased? I'm delighted.'

When she'd come to see me in Hampstead she'd been near defeat, we both were. This was the old Rose back again, and if transplanting was what it took to do it, then so be it.

'Anyway, Manchester and London aren't a world away from each other.'

(Who'd said that recently? I had, to somebody else.)

Rose picked up a handful of fallen petals from the seat and went to throw them out of the open window, just as the whistle blew.

'Nell, there's an enormous dog bounding up the platform. Do you think somebody's left it behind?' Then, 'Oh, it's . . .'

The train lurched and began to move. Bill, breathless, arms loaded with something, appeared on the platform side. The train gathered speed and he had to run to keep pace with our carriage. Roswal bounded beside him. I opened the window as wide as it would go and something large and soft came flying through. Neither Bill nor Roswal. They were still dashing beside us on the platform and Bill was laughing and waving now. Then there was no more platform and we left them there, the man still waving until the track curved and we couldn't see them any more. We wound up the window and examined the thing that had come through it.

'It looks like a travelling rug.'

'Yes, it's done a lot of travelling.'

His blanket from the Andes, souvenir of adventures, the brightest thing in his office. I smoothed the soft wool over the seat opposite and admired it.

'It's very nice,' Rose said, 'but I don't know why he bothered. It's not as if it's cold yet.'

Not quite as cold as it had been.

LET'S FACE THE MUSIC AND DIE

Sandra Scoppettone

'Lauren Laurano is one of the best detective characters in one of the best detective novels I've read' – *Val McDermid*

'Ms Scoppettone has created an original and daring private detective' – *New York Times*

Lauren Laurano's friend Elissa is in trouble. Her elderly aunt has been found brutally stabbed to death, and Elissa, with no alibi and in line to inherit a large sum of money, is the chief suspect. Undaunted, Lauren takes on the case, using her unique combination of street-savvy detecting and electronic know-how to find the real killer. Tapping into the Internet for clues, Lauren gets more than she bargained for. First on-line, then in person, she meets Alex, a young woman to whom she is powerfully attracted. And just as Lauren thinks she has her hands full, one of her dearest friends is hospitalized and Lauren begins receiving death threats herself.

Both stalking and being stalked, torn between her new lover and her longtime partner, Kip, Lauren is forced to use resources she never knew she had – just to stay alive . . .

Virago Crime
1 86049 318 1

Coming soon from Virago

DESIGNER CRIMES

Lia Matera

'Lia Matera just keeps getting better' – *Sara Paretsky*

Lia Matera is back with her biggest and best mystery yet –
as San Francisco attorney Laura Di Palma tackles two
cases that have her running for her life and from the law.
Joyce Kinsley, labour lawyer, is shot and dies before
Laura's eyes uttering the words 'designer crimes' – the
only clue to her killing. Meanwhile, Laura is defending a
high-school friend accused of grisly murder. Somehow
the cases seem inextricably linked, and Laura finds herself
fighting for her life to find the connection.

Virago Crime
1 86049 364 5

☐ Let's Face the Music and Die	Sandra Scoppettone	£6.99
☐ Everything You Have is Mine	Sandra Scoppettone	£6.99
☐ I'll be Leaving You Always	Sandra Scoppettone	£5.99
☐ My Sweet Untraceable You	Sandra Scoppettone	£5.99
☐ Designer Crimes	Lia Matera	£5.99
☐ Face Value	Lia Matera	£5.99

Virago now offers an exciting range of quality titles by both established and new authors. All of the books in this series are available from:

Little, Brown and Company (UK),
P.O. Box 11,
Falmouth,
Cornwall TR10 9EN.
Telephone No: 01326 372400
Fax No: 01326 317444
E-mail: books@barni.avel.co.uk

Payments can be made as follows: cheque, postal order (payable to Little, Brown and Company) or by credit cards, Visa/Access. Do not send cash or currency. UK customers and B.F.P.O. please allow £1.00 for postage and packing for the first book, plus 50p for the second book, plus 30p for each additional book up to a maximum charge of £3.00 (7 books plus).

Overseas customers including Ireland, please allow £2.00 for the first book plus £1.00 for the second book, plus 50p for each additional book.

NAME (Block Letters) ....

....

ADDRESS ....

....

....

☐ I enclose my remittance for ....

☐ I wish to pay by Access/Visa Card

Number ☐☐☐☐☐☐☐☐☐☐☐☐☐☐☐☐

Card Expiry Date ☐☐☐☐